To Ginny
My Sister in
Christ
C.R. Craig

THE RED DIRT ROAD

C. R. CRAIG

THE PERFORMANCE OF LIFE

THE RED DIRT ROAD

TATE PUBLISHING
AND ENTERPRISES, LLC

This novel is a work of fiction. Names, descriptions, entities, and incidents included in the story are products of the author's imagination. Any resemblance to actual persons, events, and entities is entirely coincidental.

The opinions expressed by the author are not necessarily those of Tate Publishing, LLC.

Published by Tate Publishing & Enterprises, LLC
127 E. Trade Center Terrace | Mustang, Oklahoma 73064 USA
1.888.361.9473 | www.tatepublishing.com

Tate Publishing is committed to excellence in the publishing industry. The company reflects the philosophy established by the founders, based on Psalm 68:11,
"The Lord gave the word and great was the company of those who published it."

Cover design by Joana Quilantang
Interior design by Honeylette Pino

Published in the United States of America

ISBN: 978-1-68142-203-9
Fiction / Family Life
15.03.31

CONTENTS

ACKNOWLEDGMENTS

For the greatest performances in life I thank God for the reality of love he has given me:

Trish Craig is the essential person needed in completion of becoming a man of God. The journey then and even now would be unbearable without you. Thirty Three years of marriage and I'm so loved by my closest friend; thank you Heavenly Father.
My Children, Cache the great, Carissa the determined, Callandra the sensitive and Clint the hunter. 3 John 1:4 I have no greater Joy than this, to hear of my children walking in the truth. {NASB}.
Carissa C. Orren, my personal photographer who makes me look marvelous. Thank you for driving so far for someone you love, I am so blessed.

INTRODUCTION

In the beginning, yes, this is the way it all starts, but I assure you that for each of us, there is a different starting pistol. Like most, just getting out to the starting block can take quite the effort, but nonetheless, it is well worth it. The word *beginning* in itself has such a romantic quality that the heart leaps with excitement with the slightest possibility of getting a fresh start. The mind focuses to charts unknown while the eyes can barely make out the first one hundred yards right in front of your nose.

As the moment nears, it has already passed. You look around to see where you are in this exciting moment and realize that the start is now well into effort, and with effort, there comes error, parts of life you never really saw coming, or so you tell yourself, attempting time and time again to convince the gray matter that *this* really is not your fault. How on heaven's green earth did so many errors occur in such a short time span? Seems like yesterday was just the beginning, the excitement so new and exhilarating, but now life has occurred and looks to derail you in such short manner as to cause great embarrassment to you and your love ones. This is just one life. I pray you enjoy the journey on *The Red Dirt Road.*

1

THE BEGINNING

The beginning for Jay was when he was ten years old. All recollections of an earlier life lay hidden deeply before the time of the very first deal. You see, his father had just received a promotion sparking celebrations—celebrations that went from weekends into weekdays. These moments of continuation led to a lapse in normal disciplinary actions that bedtimes became debatable, an option never before presenting itself to young Jay.

Once asking for a glass of water from one of the happy occupants of party town, young Jay received his first drink of vodka, which did not sit well with Redhead Momma who, even though partying, was ever on alert for the young ones that resided at party town. This was a tide changer for the smooth ebb and flow of party town's patrons.

Early morning and awake to the sounds of battle, nothing like the normal disturbances that allow one to roll back over in comfort, knowing it is nothing more than Redhead Momma and Dad once again debating for dominance. This was war, screeches cutting the air, impacts of arsenal yet to be identified, words that have been heard before but never with such a tone of destruction.

The journey from safety to line of sight seemed to take forever for young Jay, the sound of water running just outside the door or the bathroom. Young Jay slowly peered around the door molding to see the outline of his giant dad shadowed in bright light that pierced the surrounding darkness. Blood, he could see lots of blood. Looking upward, he saw a resemblance of his dad washing the beautiful bright-red color from his face, such a beautiful color, the color of blood.

Their eyes locked with silence that seemed eternal. His dad's head then dipped closer to the sink in an attempt to conceal the blood running from his forehead, the site of impact, the projectile still unknown, a question that begs to be answered.

"Son," said Giant Dad.

Fear locked young Jay's feet as well as heart. Panic had set in, then rapid breathing.

"Yes, sir," was all that he could summon.

"Go back to bed. Everything is all right."

Fear now fleeted as young Jay hit the top bunk in a single bound, heart racing, mind out of control. What, why, what he saw was real, the red so majestic a color. It was real, he saw it, and that moment will never ever leave!

Saturday morning finally came, and as usual, all signs of party town were nowhere to be found. Coffee filled the morning air as Giant Dad was whistling in the kitchen. "Hi, kids, want some pancakes for breakfast?" Whistling and pancakes was Giant Dad's special thing on the weekends, happy as happy can be. With a smile that can light up the darkest of hours, Giant Dad was a real morning person no matter what kind of night came before.

"Turn the cartoons down, kids. You don't want to wake Mom up too early." Redhead Mom was not a morning person. Just hearing the bedroom door opening started the lotto wheel turning. Which redhead mom would we have this day? Not that it really mattered seeing how Redhead Mom could change attitudes like the kids could change channels. There's about the same number of redhead moms as available channels, also a veritable variety. There's more to come on the topic of tropical storms or paradises as time goes on.

Pancakes were even better than the cartoons as this Saturday morning slowly dragged along, yet young Jay's mind was running on the previous battlefield, and the projectile-littered living room of possibilities. One by one, he scanned the possible impact bombs, but no luck, as it's hard for a ten-year-old to grasp so many possibilities. So much blood, it had to be large or directed from a fearless foe—Redhead Mom!

* * *

Mellow days that followed were always welcome. Young minds develop normally with brief moments of tension that firmly hold them in their places of importance. Young Jay felt the freedom of being allowed to push the mower himself this past Saturday, a day of reckoning, a young man on his way to adulthood. Yes, this feeling was worth getting used to.

Silence seemed to disrupt young Jay's concentration of inevitable manhood, a silence between those who held the balance of all power in the universe. A tension went along with this silence that even the young at mind could detect, especially a mind on the brink of adult revelation. His concerns would soon find merit. It seems Redhead Momma was having the calm before the storm, but what catalyst was pushing this ever-present danger? Surely, not slow, cool, low-pressure Dad.

* * *

Awake, awake! Young man Jay's mind leapt into action, yelling so loud the entire brood was now alarmed. Jay hurried into the living room as he heard his momma call out as never before. There, standing in front of the living room door was Redhead Momma, and this tropical depression was a full-blown hurricane. With thunder and lightning firmly in her hands, she yelled at the locked glass-paned door. "You leave, and you leave now!" was the scream that thundered from Redhead Momma's mouth. "I won't tell you again."

Jay's eyes focused on the door and back again to what he assumed was the posture of positive enforcement. Steely eyes that would make the dead scream in terror, a stance for battle that only those of the table round could identify. Heartbeats sounded as if a hundred feet below, hollow and deep—the sound of loneliness. Young man Jay's ability to focus on all that was taking place before his eyes. Ten years was fading fast. Light, dark, the beat of his heart!

Boom! A sound broke the masonry stature of the young man Jay, a force against the door of such startling vibrations it could be felt resonating throughout the entire room.

"Momma, what's wrong?" was the sound heard coming from deep within the young man once frozen in fear.

Then from outside came a sound so familiar and warm, "Son, open the door."

It contradicted all that young man Jay had known since this early rising.

It sounded like the whistling giant. "Daddy," was the sound of innocence coming from a confused child—not the young man he had so warmly become, but a timid little boy afraid of what was now becoming reality. Redhead Momma had drawn the battle line of defiance and cried out one last time for Giant Dad to cease.

"Open the door, son," was the call that seemed to come from so far away, as if it had sounded from another dimension altogether. "Daddy, I can't!"

"Listen to me, son. Open the door now." The storm within the room was now enveloping young man Jay; there was no way to avoid the debris of conversing with the darkness now surrounding him. In the distance, a calm voice directed him to obey the simplest of commands. Before his eyes was a storm of rage he had never encountered before.

"Momma's got a gun, Daddy. I can't open the door." Yes, there before young man Jay was the living picture he had seen for many years, those of which showed Giant Daddy and Redhead Momma time and time again in their Western garb on a lonely red dirt road with pistols in hand. A holster tied down on the leg of Giant Dad, and Redhead Mom proudly posed beside the man who had taught her to shoot so well. Standing quietly beside them as a speck in the picture was baby boy Jay, diaper at half-mast, gripping a bottle of the moo juice, Quite the family photo.

Family photo! Quickly looking to the right, young man Jay had remembered this photo was a time before the brood, the siblings, those he now spotted peering around the corner of the bedroom door. Easily, young man Jay motioned with his hand for them to back away from the center of the storm. Now with little ones out of sight, he returned to a reality that felt like the worst of nightmares.

2

GIANT DAD

"Jay, Jay."

"Yes, Momma."

"Pay attention to what you're doing, son."

"Yes, Momma." Jay no longer felt young or even alive for that matter. Paying attention to washing the car was the least of his worries. Attempting to act as if he was living was now going to be his masterpiece, at least he hoped to fool Redhead Momma.

"Isn't this fun!" Redhead Momma exclaimed with the cheeriest voice she could muster. All Jay could do was politely smile and say, "Yes, Mama." As Redhead Momma made her way back inside the house, Jay continued to ape the same motion over and over again, the whole time wondering, *Is this the day?*

Time is a strange consumer, sometimes fast, oftentimes slow. Time, a friend or foe? It passes just as thoughts, memories, today and then, those. Something was amiss. It was hard to remember how long it had really been. Jay had a calendar that seemed to have started this year. Who was his teacher last year? What did he get for Christmas? His birthday was not long ago. It was just before spring when all the pretty flowers bloomed. The white dogwood tree was Jay's favorite, as always, right?

It was another warm day of early fall in the South. Subtle breezes flicked at the ever so lightly changing leaves, blowing Jay's hair with a coolness that hinted at a summer coming to an end, a summer of milestones in the life of those who had lived the moment of the big bang. For some reason, Jay no longer felt young. It could be because he now was the oldest male of the house, but by far, he was the least in control, hating the sun for setting each day due to the fact that with nightfall came a time of sleep for some, nightmares for others.

This night was quiet. All were at rest excluding Jay, of course, whose mind kept returning to that awful night so long ago, but was it, really? Time, once again, a friend or foe?

The blinding sound of it all, yes, blinding. The gun sounded off with such force that Jay could no longer remember the day or night of it all, never even hearing the glass pane in the door shattering but faintly hearing the screams on the other side of the universe, screams of "You shot me! You shot me!" But why did they sound so far away? Everything at that moment was different—movements, sounds, sights, things seen and heard that will affect Jay for the rest of his days.

In the still of the night—time just as sleep is of no importance—Jay closes his eyes and once again tried to recapture the whistling sound of Giant Dad, the smell of hot pancakes and sweet, buttery syrup, and that smile. Oh, how Jay missed that smile. It was as if that light was fading from Jay forevermore. He could feel the coldness closing in, a darkness he enjoyed, and the color of beautiful red blood. This was where Jay now found peace alone at night in the cool of the dark, finally at rest.

"Jay, come outside for a moment," Redhead Momma said.

It was a relief from the chores inside the house, but probably, it was now to focus on the chores ahead on the other side of solitude. Jay liked the outside chores; he could be alone with his thoughts and work the hours away without any interruptions—questions from the siblings who are oblivious to the pecking order of the new establishment. They went about their playtime just as if it were any other day, annoying and young. Jay was relieved to see how happy they are, playing and laughing but always asking Jay what was wrong. "Nothing, nothing at all."

The sun was bright as Jay cleared the door. It was brisk but warm, a nice day for working outside. He smiled as the breeze once again blew through his hair, a familiar friend to which he was now endeared, touching him throughout the day, letting him know he was not alone. The breeze always seemed to stir when the darkness began to take over, that ever-present darkness. On the other hand, this day held promise as Jay rounded the shiny car in the driveway. Spotting Redhead Momma, Jay puts on his best artificial smile as to imply joy to the one he now so feared. No smile was returned, only the direction of a pointing finger to a figure that seemed slightly familiar. "Hello, son."

"Jay, come say hello to your daddy."

Jay heard the words, but all motor skills were gone. Breathing was an effort. *Standing, am I still standing?* was Jay's first thought of reality. This was real, right? Giant Dad was standing there with that smile that would light up the world, which could make a rainy Saturday fun with excitement, but this was not that day, and Jay had replaced that light. In his hands, Giant Dad had a football, brand-new. Jay could see it shining.

"Would you like to throw some, son?" Jay heard the words and could only slightly move his head in a positive motion. Stepping into the soft grass of the front yard, Jay received the first throw from Giant Dad as Redhead Momma went quietly into the house smiling at Jay, as if to say everything was now okay.

Back and forth, the ball flew as Jay began to feel the exhilaration of flight caused by the medial effort of his ever-growing arm. Giant Dad smiled at the effort of each catch and throw Jay made. The bright sunlight and cool breezes made each moment into one Jay would never forget, then the smile was gone. As Giant Dad held the football, he motioned Jay to come closer.

"Son, let me ask you something." As Giant Dad now kneeled down and gently put his hand on Jay's shoulder, Jay stood still as a mouse, fearing any motion might cause his demise. Here it comes, the darkness invading the light, the wonder of moments enveloped in a void of expanding tension, a tension that could be heard in Giant Dad's voice: "What do you remember about that night, the night your mom and I were yelling at each other, the one where I was outside? Do you remember?"

Did Jay remember! The words cut as a dull blade, dragging themselves into the darkest chambers of his mind. Nausea took the place of smell. The pain cut so deep into his mind that for a moment, he prayed for the blinds to be closed forever. The time of reuniting was now washed away in a sea of death and loneliness. The vision of beautiful red blood flooded his senses. "Nothing, I don't really remember anything," was the faint voice heard in the distance, the quiet voice of the dead.

The once-so-contagious smile of Giant Dad now took on another look altogether, a smile of self-worth that Jay had not seen before, victory of cheer but yet with a sneer, a smugness as to believe that Jay was such a fool not to remember the most traumatic episode of not only his life but of any life his young mind could imagine. Yes, there would come years of learning that would overshadow the evil bestowed, but it was not this day, the day he had hoped for. For so long, he had dreamed of the flash of light and deafening sound of thunder that had wiped away the mind of years before—before the beautiful red blood. He had hoped it would all just go away.

The grip's firmness on Jay's shoulder broke the numbness in his aching mind; thankfully, the grip was strong enough to keep Jay from the dizzying sickness attempting to take him to the ground, a place where gravity called with amazing sound. Focusing on the moving lips of Giant Dad along with the smile that would never look the same, Jays acting skills came into play as if he understood the verbal onslaught coming his way.

Attempting to show a pleasant smile, Jay was beginning to sense a growing problem, a need, a swelling of emotions that needed to release. "Think quick," was the sound that come from the inner chambers of Jay's darkened mind. "I'm just so happy to see you, Dad," was the words heard in the falsified distance as the overwhelming tears streamed down his face, hugging his dad with all he had, hoping he would not see through the disguise of pain as those words filled the air, piercing into Jay's consciousness.

"I'll make you a deal, son, I promise I'll always come home, never will I be gone that long again."

There was no reply.

3

FAMILY

Excitement was in the air as the young siblings giggled and laughed as Redhead Momma called out, a cow. Traveling was always entwined with games of challenge, fun for the whole family; this one was a favorite of all. Looking intently across the rising horizon, all scanned to find the next wanted item to obtain another round of laughter. Jay sat, quietly focused on how different the scenery had become since leaving the old place of nightmares. Continuing to bring the best of performances to the overreacting crowd, he played along but wondered where this hilly road would end. To end, it was a thought that consumed Jay all day and sometimes all through the night.

Grandma and Grandpa's place! This was finally realized as the scenery became familiar, a dream from long ago. It was a dream or a memory that Jay could somehow pull back from the bottomless pit of his mind. A memory, no doubt, but where had it been? Should this not have been one of the happier times of his young life? "Well, we're home," Giant dad said.

"Oh, the place looks just like I remembered," Little Sister proclaimed.

What! Jay thought. *Little Sister remembers this place*! Sure, the trees, the long red dirt road traveled just before arriving, familiar, but remembered! Jay sat stunned as all jumped out of the car, wanting to know what Giant Dad meant by being home. "This is now our new home. We bought it off your grandparents," Giant Dad explained. "And we'll live here for a while until we build a new house later on. Get out of the car, son. Go check out your new home."

New home, this place was smelly and old, with red bricks of the mountainous region that stretched as far as the eye could see. The red dirt gave every hilly bare spot the look of dark-red blood. Problem was you might only see one or two houses in the scoping effort, but the beautiful red blood was everywhere.

It has three rooms of moderate size. The last on the left was Jay's and his younger brother of three years, a great difference from almost twelve to nine, yet he was a good kid, just spoiled by Redhead Momma, her little baby. Sister siblings had the room to the right. It was still so close you could smell and hear everything. This was going to be torture. Looking outside the window, Jay noticed the drop-off viewed as the backyard. The inquisitive side of Jay always won, a true explorer at heart. Excitement and danger were his best friends, and he knew one day they would all die together. The drop of twenty feet could only mean one thing, a basement! Why didn't he remember the basement?

Jay found the mysterious door just past the bathroom, leading back into the confined kitchen space. Holding the doorknob, Jay knew he needed clearance to proceed. Opening the door, smelling the musty dirt-filled darkness, Jay calls out, "Dad, is it okay if I look downstairs?"

"Sure, son, just be careful. Those stairs can be tricky, and the light switch is there on the right." Jay flipped the switch to see the steepest stairs he had ever encountered. Gently stepping onto the first step, he heard a sound that could have come from the TV show called the *Munsters*. His blood raced through his body as once again, his lifeless existence surged back to life.

The basement was old just like the rest of the house, but there were shelves and boxes all over the place. Boxes were hidden behind boxes that only the fearless of climbers dared to seek out. Row upon row of beans in jars, tomatoes in jars, and the smell of what seemed like death. Though unknown to Jay, the smell of death, this odor must surely be close. It was something he had never smelled before. Turned out some of the beans didn't seal right and spoiled. Ever smell a jar of green beans gone bad before? A first that will never ever go away.

Climbing the shelves to reach the secrets of boxes hidden behind boxes, Jay was now feeling more alive than ever. This dark basement was new, the scenery new, the long red dirt road so hilly and lined with trees of all types, the likes of trees Jay had never seen before. The house was old but full of recently unviewed things. But why was all this new. He had been here many times before, right?

Speaking of unviewed, Jay had never seen the likes of what he now found in the box way in the back. Being carefully hidden so far from sight, he knew it would hold a treasure of unspeakable gifts, gifts so amazing that Jay slipped and fell back to the concrete floor. Before he slipped in shock, Jay had spotted a view of something new and never before seen by this twelve-year-old man, well, almost twelve.

Checking quickly to ensure that no one was coming his way, Jay slowly began the climb back up the dusty shelves. A spider ran across his hand but was nothing compared to the adrenaline pulsing through his veins. It was a moment to consider the Langley beauty that raced before him. But now back to the real adventure. Grasping firmly to the top shelf, Jay pinned his body between the Heater duct and cinder block wall, reaching once again for the box of flashing memories that would change his life forever. There in his grasp was a world unknown.

Fall had come and school began just like in the other parts of the world Jay had lived in. This was so different compared to what Redhead Momma had often spoken. "This was going to be different," she explained in as soft a voice as ever heard by their spirited mother. "We are calling this area home from here on out."

The "out" Jay was looking for sure wasn't here. He had envisioned a world of great excitement, not hillbilly livin'. Time would tell, and the master of theater would continue to enthrall the audiences with such performances that inevitable fame would claim his encore body long before the sleep of cool, dark death.

Once the school day had ended, Jay would rush from the grounds, heading toward the long red dirt road that would carry him home to the land of exploration. The red dust puffed beneath his feet as he ran jumping and dodging to miss the many rocks that littered the road. It was said that during the winter months, the dirt would be covered in rocks, and these were those left from the year before. Getting home was met with the question of who might be attending the proceedings this lovely fall day. Mom or Redhead Momma, it was a mystery.

The freedom of country living was beginning to grow on Jay. He loved the forest, the trees, and the coolness so deep within—as if it was alive and part of him. Deep into the woods Jay would go, the creek with majestic sounds could calm the darkest of hearts. The farther the better, as he sought to once again live his life. There would always be a kinsman relationship with the wilderness that lived and the wildness that lived within Jay. This he felt deep into his bones, as deep as the darkness that flows. They would always be one.

A new meeting was arranged this early fall. "Reunion" was the name explained by parents who no longer indulged in the party-town life. We will visit the strangeness of this topic at a more convenient time, but now, they must prepare to attend the family get-together. Loaded in the car, they headed deeper into the mountains. The leaves were becoming so beautiful in this part of the world that surely angels must have painted them. The ride was fairly short, revealing a group of family members who lived not far from where Jay now called home.

Arriving on hillbilly hill was table upon table of covered dishes that turned out to be food, lots of food. Then came the shock of all life, people who knew them, but they had no clue—except for Giant Dad and Redhead Momma. Everyone here in these parts seemed to have a double name. Jay's turned out to be Jaybo. "Is that little Jaybo?" came a shrill of excitement as the largest woman he had ever seen came at him with arms open wide and the darkest set of teeth scaring the movement right out of him. Next thing Jay knew, he was swept from the ground at such lightning speed that he was sure his clothes were left behind. Kissing and squeezing with such emotion that Jay knew for sure he had drawn his last breath—this was not the first kiss he had imagined.

Greetings faded into the past, and so many yelling at Jay, "Don't you remember your cousin this, your second cousin that, and how could you forget your uncle Dirt Clod and aunt Skeet?" So many people talking so loud Jaybo was going to lose it…

"Hi, Jaybo. I'm your uncle Red."

Uncle Red? Here stood a kid the same size as Jay that turned out to be only a year older but with deep eyes and a smile as if put on, kind of like Jay's.

"Let's get away from the crazies," Red almost had to yell.

"Please call me Jay."

"I'll do it," Red said. "I hope someday you'll be able to call me a friend." He hoped. Could he sense Jay's disdain for all things he had observed so far this beautiful fall day? Nothing personal, but Jay has a safety net he keeps close, just in case. Red knew the area well, and like a flash, the boys flew through the woods, stump jumping and laughing and rounding trees with the agility of young bucks that also called these woods home. Faster and farther they ran, leaping across creeks four feet wide, adrenaline flowing, freedom blowing through their hair, more alive now than memory allowed. *Take me now, God!* was the heartfelt cry screaming within the mind of young Jay. *If you're there, please take me now!*

Red had a real smile on his face as the boys came to a sliding stop. Jay no doubt had one on just the same. "Man that was great," Jay exclaimed. "You really know these woods, Red!"

Both boys gripped their knees and attempted to get more breath in what was available: an old, dead fallen tree leaning over became a great spot for the boys to take a squat. "I love the quiet here in the woods," Red softly stated.

"I need it, you need it, Jay, I know what you've been through, and I'm here to help, if you'll let me."

Jay's mind started spinning. *What's Red talking about? What does he know? He couldn't know! Who is he!*

"What I'm about to tell you is top secret in this family. We can talk to each other about it, but what you and I have seen must never be spoken of in front of the family."

What you and I have seen? Jay thought. *What the, who the, where in the world does this guy come from, and what the fuzzy caterpillar is he talking about?* "Okay, sure," said Jay. "What you and I have seen we can tell no others."

"I'm serious," said Red. "This is not to be taken lightly. We know too much, and we've both seen too much. We're in this together until the end, until our last breath. I got your back. You've got mine." Red took out his pocketknife and cut the palm of his hand. He then gave the knife to Jay, cut his own palm the two gripped hands, and looked sternly into each other's eyes. Now it's for life.

4

FAMILY BONDS

Red and Jay had a lot in common, to say the least. It turned out that dear old Uncle Red was Redhead Momma's little brother. As a matter of observance over the next chilling winter, Redhead Momma had quiet the brood, brothers, and sister all over trailer park hill. Amazing. Jay had never even seen a trailer, but now, they were all over the place. It seemed a lot of Redhead Momma's family lived on this one dead-end road that slowly climbed the mountain across from the patriarch's house.

Redhead Momma was different up on the mountain. She demanded respect from all, and all gave freely. The hillbilly family knew she was the great provider, the one who had left the mountain and seen the world. She was now from another place, another state that might as well have been another universe. Her language was different. Jay would risk his life at times by giving her that look, the look she hated, and she wanted to rip off of his face. It was nothing more than an attempt to understand this Southern dialect, but to her, it was the face of the man she once loved deeply, but now, she was still with that man, Giant Dad. Her scornful gaze would fall next in line to the man with the same name. Oh how she hated him. Jay could see it in her eyes. As his performance would reach a thunderous applause, he would smile and calmly as the dead would say, "I love you, Mommy," to which she always replied, "Love you, baby" or "love you, honey," never using his name, never getting that close. Names were used to scorn.

Winter, cold, and lots of snow on the ground. Giant Dad had a great idea to teach Jay how to hunt rabbits. This was exciting, as Giant Dad was going to spend some time with Jay away from the family, bonding—that's what this is called. Layered in clothes with plastic bags over his tennis shoes to keep the wet snow out, Jay bounded outside beside Giant Dad who now held in his hands a magnificent item, a shotgun.

Following Giant Dad into the woods with an air of excitement, Jay knew all too well the area they were trudging through, then Giant Dad spotted something. "Come here, son." Giant Dad motioned with excitement. "This is a rabbit trail. See the prints in the snow running off in that direction?"

Jay was smiling ear to ear as he knew they were now closer to the rabbit and Giant Dad showed him how to hunt. "You take off following those tracks, quickly now, and I'll meet you back here, and we'll get that rabbit."

You see, a rabbit runs in big circles, and Jay later found out that this was the job of the dog, normally a beagle, which would run the rabbit around the circle, and the hunters would stand there and shoot the rabbit as it ran by. So he learned the lesson of hunting, freeze being your dad's dog while hunting rabbits in the winter. Now that's called Southern bonding.

Finally, summer had come, and Redhead Momma was great for allowing Jay to escape her domain, allowing freedom in the form of family, hillbilly family. She had no problem dropping Jay off in the mountains and leaving him there to run wild as a buck with the rest of the clan. Grandma and Grandpa were so detached and old that as long as Jay was with the brood, all was good. Freedom's first taste at such a developmental stage of one's life, yes, freedom to live as the nature of the beast now called, free to expel the scent of suffering upon the most beautiful of landscapes, the mountains. Home at last.

Red and Jay became as close as brothers; they were in fact blood brothers struck with a deal to hold in confidence the things that must never be spoken aloud. Red's experience put him right up there with Jay, and even though Red was much younger, eight at the time of the shooting, to see someone you love dearly get the trigger pulled on them, it was traumatic to say the least.

The ability to share experiences was a great relief to both of the young developing minds; however, the road to understanding love was so clouded; it was as if you were following someone down a red dirt road on a hot summer afternoon doing fifty-five, peaks of it every once and a while, but making it out clearly never happens until you run right into it. Then it's too late, it just hurts, and so goes life. Jay and Red enjoyed their time together; it was as if they could read each other's minds—both understanding that sometimes it's nice to just sit in silence, listening to the creek run, letting the pain leave with the wind gently blowing through the leaves. Freedom, oh, to ride on the wind, to be as the breeze, no one knowing you're even there until you're gone.

That summer, Jay met a new friend on hillbilly hill, a little old man that normally said nothing at all, even more quiet than Jay. He was holding on to something but allowing no one to know. Little Old Man took a walk with Jay that hot summer day, strolling down the road, turning onto another road, and finally a short ways up the old dirt road, they came to a stop. "Look there," said Little Old Man. "You see those watermelons up on the side of that hill? Let's sneak in there and get us one."

Jay's heart leapt with the thought of it all, "sneak in there." Jay's grin from ear to ear gave it all away. He had allowed someone to see real emotion, but there was no stopping him now. "Okay," Jay replied, anxious to try anything that could make him feel alive.

Walking back down to the hot black top road, smiling like the joker, Jay and Little Old Man made their way back toward the home front with a delicious surprise that could be shared by all. As they rounded the last curve near the house, Jay saw it—Redhead Momma's car. Panic began to set in as Jay started mumbling to himself—his shirt, a new Sears and Roebuck red-collared pullover that Redhead Momma had clearly told Jay not to get dirty. He was holding a watermelon fresh out of the red dirt field tightly against his chest. Little Old Man could clearly see something was wrong, "You okay, son?"

"Jaybo, what have you done?" came the new hillbilly name that curdled Jay's blood.

"Momma, we were just walking up the road."

"Shut up!" came the scream that meant it was time to get torn up, Normally on hillbilly hill, due to showing dominance, this would call for a hickory switch and an innumerable amount of lashes, never less than ten, but man, it could get bad really quick. Jay sat the watermelon on the porch and walked closer to Redhead Momma. She could clearly see the red mud stain. Jay stood there, waiting for the first slap against his face, as was the normal routine for Redhead Momma. Jay had even seen her slap her brothers, one who was near twenty years old. Jay didn't care at this point—at least it was some form of contact from Redhead Momma. Some is better than none. Jay went dead inside as normal and began his performance of sorrow and regret, if they only knew what he was truly sorry for.

"Hold on there, little girl," came the calmest words Jay had ever heard. "Don't you lay a hand on that boy. Me and him was having ourselves a good time, and you're not going to spoil it. I'll buy that youngin' five shirts if I have to, but you don't touch him!"

"Yes, Daddy," said Redhead Momma. As her tone changed, she placed her hand gently on the side of Jay's face. "You go ahead and help your grandpa cut up that watermelon, son." Grandpa, this was the man always working or sleeping, never getting to really know him these past few months, but now…

Jay spent as much time around Grandpa as possible, but it was very little compared to the amount he was home. Grandma was also there, and boy, was she the opposite of Grandpa. He was quiet and didn't waste words. She was large and in charge. Jay knew exactly where Redhead Momma got her temperament, including her sisters, aunts—all of them were very redheaded and full of fire. Jay learned over time that their kids and himself had a lot in common, especially when it came to getting torn up. Grandpa and Grandma kept talking about something called church. Grandma was very excited about this thing called the Holy Spirit. She'd get so excited that you couldn't understand a word she was saying, for it all just sounded like repetitive gibberish, but man, was she excited.

5

SALVATION

The summer went on, and things were starting to change. Giant Dad had found that attending church made him feel better and that it could help the whole family. Not sure if this came from Grandma and Grandpa, but he seemed to be serious about it. One Sunday morning, the clan attended its first-ever church. Man, was this different. Jay was seeing more people in pretty clothes than ever before, dresses to the floor and lots of men with ties around their necks and some of them with smiles so broad it was frightening. Jay didn't realize someone could show that many teeth to strangers they'd' never met. It was all wrong. Jay could feel it. Being dropped off into a group of young men, Jay found himself in a small room with a few other boys and two adults who started jabbering just like his grandma would do. Jay was amused, trying to confuse someone with an IQ they would never obtain. Jay just smiled and eased the minds of the performing cast, amusing, very amusing. Suddenly, the door flew open, and there was Giant Dad with a look on his face Jay had seen many times before, He knew the jibber jabbers were not well liked, and Jay was quickly removed from the performance. Giant Dad was upset about them attempting to shove something down a child's throat. He continued speaking very loud as one by one, he gathered his progenies and made their way out the door into the bright Sunday morning daylight. At least this time, it wasn't Jay's fault.

Giant Dad decided to take the family to a new type of church. It seemed this one went on all week long, Monday then Tuesday, everyone sat in the same area, and after some very catchy songs, this fat guy would get up and start yelling and sweating. The more he yelled, the more he sweated. Pacing back and forth, the fat guy screamed. Jay could see Giant Dad was very entertained. He even said some words Jay had never heard before. Then some other guys were calling out the same words: "Amen! Halleluiah! Praise the Lord!" Jay was fascinated, the cause of such random responses. Grown men yelled back at the fat guy sweating up front. What was the point this guy was attempting to get across?

Each night of that week, people were invited to come forward, many did. Monday night, three people were up front crying and grown men shouting, "Thank you, Jesus," then laughing and shouting. Jay looked over to Giant Dad, attempting to gain insight to the circus before, but all Jay saw was this smile on Giant Dad's face, a look so unfamiliar to Jay that he quickly turned away. Jay was sure Giant Dad had seen him, but there was no way Jay was looking again.

It was Wednesday evening, and Jay finds himself in the front seat of Giant Dad's truck heading back to the church. There was this tension, something Jay could not put together. Giant Dad kept looking in Jay's direction then said, "Son, what do you think of the preacher's message so far"? Maintaining the role of innocence and youth, Jay's quiet reply only stimulated the conversation: "Preacher, is that what he's called?"

The explanation over the next several miles fascinated Jay. A man called, as Giant Dad put it, to tell the truth of a man named Jesus. Now Jay was no stranger to the baby Jesus born in Bethlehem. Every Christmas was a celebration of candy nuts, new clothes, and a toy or two. It was a beautiful time with a tree inside the house and colorful lights inside and out. It was a very pleasant time of the year except for the last two years, the big bang. He missed Christmas all together, the move. Jay's universe was still spinning out of control, but he was always able to hold it together around people, who were just people.

Back to reality, Jay finds himself attempting to understand what this preacher was talking about. It would be a lot easier if he would slow down and stop everyone from shouting at the top of their lungs, "Amen" here, "praise the Lord" there. "Glory" was the newest one for this Wednesday night. These guys are complete idiots with no understanding of proper sentencing. With all that was going on, it would take a miracle to ever get the point this fat guy was trying to make. In any case, Jay tuned in and started to put the whole mess together: *key ingredient, Jesus, salvation, redemption, forgiveness, and eternal life, what?*

Now wait, a "coonskin cap" moment: *Eternity, where did this come from?* Jay now realized that some claim eternal life, and that meant locked in this existence of maddening role-play forever. *No way, not going to happen, what the hell! Hell, is that what he said? Now what's this so-called appointed dispenser of prophecy spilling, hell? A place of fire that tortures but not consumes, eternal screaming and biting, a place where there is no peace, only suffering?* Welcome to Jay's mind, well, except for this eternal fire thing.

Jay listened that Wednesday night, and parts of this message or sermon, whatever, were intriguing: eternal life and heaven or hell. Giant Dad had that same weird look on his face that made Jay feel funny. Was there something Giant Dad had not told Jay? Something he wanted him to do?

On the way to church Thursday night, Giant Dad once again engaged Jay in conversation concerning eternity. "You have to believe, son," was Giant Dad's response to the fat preacher man.

"What do you believe, dad?" Jay asked with true inquisitiveness.

"Me, I believe God loved me so much that he sent his one and only Son, Jesus, to die on a wooden cross to pay for my sins. This allows me to have eternal life with him once I die here on earth. You see, son. Jesus loves us so much that to keep all of us from going to hell, Jesus the Son of God, took our place and all the sins that go with it. He paid a price so all who believe can have everlasting peace and life with him and his Holy Father God. No more pain, no more suffering, no more death."

Jay's mind was reeling.

The fat preacher was working up a nose dripping sweat that Thursday night. The windows were open, a slight breeze blowing, but hellfire and brimstone were flying all over that country church. Jay locked in to every word. Giant Dad and son truly had a bonding moment in the front seat of that pickup truck, his words ringing ever true as the preacher man was letting it fly. There was a pulse that night along with the echoing words of Giant Dad causing Jay's heart to plummet through his shoes. The floor was vibrating. The yelling of the men and women caused a flush unfelt before, a pressure, a gripping in Jay's chest and mind. If he didn't know any better, one would have described it as a "*Holy Ghost experience*"!

Friday night was different. Giant Dad didn't have as much to say on the drive over to that country church, and Jay was too busy attempting to digest the previous night's mysteries. Jay thought of those feelings, those words. *Was someone really willing to love that much, forever, and never leave them alone but go with them always even if they were as screwed up as Jay?* That's what the preacher is saying. He's said it every night. He said it was for all who would call on his name, Jesus, the Son of God. All would receive salvation and never be left alone again. Something about a helper, a Holy Spirit, would come and be with them always. Holy Spirit, Grandma and Grandpa talked of the Holy Spirit. That's when Grandma got so excited. Was all this real? Could someone really love a mess like Jay that much?

It was the same song every night, slow and steady, "Just as I Am." That is the song. There was something about that song. Jay stood there with everyone else, gripping the seat they call a pew, attempting to tear the wood right off the top of that seat. Jay once again felt the stare of Giant Dad. His heart was beating through the floor, and he dare not look. That look. What was it all about? What did Giant Dad know? A battle for breath was now consuming the thoughts of Jay. His body temperature rose, feeling the sweat as if the fires of hell were licking the bottoms of his feet. "Let go;" came a voice so loud and clear that it shocked Jay into looking at Giant Dad. *What did Giant Dad say, "Let go"?* Giant Dad stood there as tall as ever, but his look, a look that will never leave the mind of this impressionable young man for all eternity, compassion—no, wait, Jay saw love. He saw love in the eyes of his father for the very first time since that night of darkness, the place where Jay liked to hide. He felt safe there in the darkness.

"Let go," said the preacher man in a voice Jay had become accustomed to. "Stop trying to rip the top of that pew off and set yourself free from the bondage of sin that now has a grip on you." Jay now stood more confused than ever, looking up at the sweating fat preacher man. *Was it him who said let go just before he said let go?*

Jay's grip grew even tighter as the night seemed to go on forever. *How long was that fat guy going to keep talking, and how long was this song going to be sung?* Jay, now sweaty, was sure the devil was pulling at his legs, the pew starting to crack, and sanity was losing grips with reality just as his hand was losing grip with the pew. The heat, the sweat, this was not normal, and Jay knew something had to give, and it was Jay. Deep inside, a peace came over him. *Where is he? Who is that talking?* Jay thought. *Such a calm voice, one of understanding, one of compassion, where did the song go?* It was as if Jay's ears had closed, and everything around him became so bright. Then the words "I love you" came as Jay's heart broke into a million pieces.

"I'll make you a deal," the fat preacher man yelled from the front, shocking Jay back into the here and now. "If you'll stop trying to tear the top of that pew off and just walk down front, I'll introduce you to a Savior that will love you forever. He will never ever leave you. Jesus said in the Bible that 'I'll never leave you or forsake you. I'll be with you always.' If you'll let go and accept his sacrifice on that old rugged cross, his blood washing away all your sins, you can become a new creation in Jesus Christ."

Jay looked to Giant Dad once again, Had he accepted Christ, the love of Jesus? Is this what Jay was seeing in the eyes of his dad? Thinking back, ever since their arrival to the red dirt road, Giant Dad has been ever changing, going on Sunday mornings to what now seems evident, church, and other than his normal morning whistling self. There were noticeable changes. He didn't argue as much with Redhead Momma. Once he even said he was sorry to one of his sisters for being too rough and just upset. He hugged her and told her he loved her. Not the normal thing for Giant Dad, not a real "touchy feely" kind of guy.

"Let go!" came a voice so clear and deep. Jay was still staring into the eyes of Giant Dad. Seeing the love of Jesus, Giant Dad lifted his head as Jay let go, the pew no longer holding him back as he floated toward the front of the church.

Time was standing still, movement deliberate, but unavailable to known human touch. Tears welled up inside of Jay as all the pain he could remember came rushing to the surface along with his broken heart of a million little pieces. Not wanting to cry, to show weakness, this was not part of his well-programmed performances; he was actually losing control. His heart ached so deeply that the unreachable darkness was being confronted.

No! This was off-limits to any and all. The deal was salvation, forgiveness. All Jay had to do was believe and cry out to the name of Jesus to be saved, and this is the words of the fat preacher man—nothing about giving up the hatred that stirred so deep within, the love of a coming, painful, exhilarating death that would someday wipe away the scared mind of a man no longer allowed to speak the unspeakable. No, that was not the on the table.

As Jay fell upon his face covered in snot and tears, someone placed their hand upon Jay's back. Jay could only hear the cries coming from within *I am evil, Jesus, a sinner hated by all, one who is unlovable, one who is not worthy to be saved, let alone loved by the Son of God. Please save me, please save me.*

Then sobbing turned to peace. Jay had an experience so real that it could have only been from God. It was so intense that all around Jay no longer seemed to exist. The same thing happened when Jay was baptized a week later. As he came up from the water, he felt a presence come over him just as the fat preacher had said. *This relationship was personal, just for me.*

6

NEVER ALONE

Time now buzzed with excitement. Jay had a Savior, and no one could take that away from him. Giant Dad said it was his personal relationship with the Holy Spirit of God that came over him during his baptizing. They now finally had something they were both excited about and could share. The difference this now made throughout the entire family was that everyone goes to church every Sunday morning. This church had around a hundred people in it and another fat preacher named Big Mac. He had a wife who played the piano and a son named Little Mac who was exactly Jay's age, twelve. Jay got along great with Little Mac, and the beginning of a great friendship was now on the move, and boy, did it ever move.

Summer was still stretching on, and amazingly, Jay was having a pretty good time running the hills of the south and just trying to be free. The chains that still had him bound in mind seemed to tighten every time he thought on the darkness of days gone by. "Some things will never go away," he consoled himself. "Just learn to live with it."

Amazingly, Redhead Momma allowed Jay to spend the weekend with Little Mac and his family. He just had to behave and see them at church on Sunday. Jay figured this additional trust came because of the preacher man status and Little Mac being a preacher's son. This was all new to Jay, so he was sure to pay close attention to how a preacher's son would perform and act. Jay could use some of this persona to carry him through the darker days and years to come. The act Jay saw was something he never expected or had attempted to prepare for.

Little Mac and Jay had a great time riding bikes down old dirt logging roads, coming upon old shacks and barns, while still standing, No one was sure how.

They explored everything and anything that was so worth exploring. Imagine when people actually lived out here, no power, no TV, working hard every day just to survive. Times were changing fast. It was now the seventies, and progress had moved so quickly during Jay's life that anything seemed possible. Mac and Jay headed back toward the house with eyes full and minds dreaming of things to come: *First, let's eat some supper.*

Supper is a new word now used in these parts of the world. What used to mean dinner is now supper, and dinner is now lunch. Crazy, man, it made no sense. Mac and Jay finished supper and headed back to Mac's room. Goofing around and throwing raisins around like basketballs was now more fun than Jay could ever hope for. Mac really liked basketball, and Jay had never played the game, which would change if Mac had anything to say about it. Doing his best to mimic Mac, Jay took what is known as a hook shot from across the room. Mac was lying in bed, yelling out the countdown, "Three, two, one." Jay let the basketball raisin' fly, soaring through the air toward Mac, then bam, right up the left nostril. Mac was freaking out, gagging and choking, attempting the one-fingered side blow, nothing. That thing was jammed in there.

After some toothpick surgery, all was well once again in the land of basketball stars named Walton and Thompson. Their imagination was allowed to set them free to be famous and far from there. "Settle down now, boys," came the call from Momma Mac. 'Guess it was time to come back to reality, but oh, how Jay enjoyed the role-play of a famous college basketball player. This night would change Jay's focus of the future, but his focus at that moment was really about to change.

Mac threw Jay a book, a soft cover, a small novel that looked really worn. *A strange way to end the day*, Jay thought, flipping through the pages, it was evident he had never read one of these—curse words in almost every sentence, saying things never thought of by a man of twelve years. Jay continued to read. It was of men and women, and it would cloud the Holy right out of Jay. It was amazing.

Many things happened that weekend, first time ever for a couple of things, things that gave Jay confirmation that he truly was a man, but just missing a few steps to make it official, as the little worn novel explained. Those words seared into his mind, and little did he know, the effort to replace them with words of light could only be obtained at very short intervals. The wide road was before him, and happy to be on it, Jay did not realize the darkness he tried to hide so deep was about to embrace him forevermore. The destruction of spiritual warfare had begun, and the battle was that of the flesh, a battle faced by all and conquered by few.

Church life continued, and Jay was happy in his role as the new preacher's son. Yes, Giant Dad had changed so much that Big Mac and some of the other *brothers*, as they called each other, ordained Giant Dad as a preacher man. Why not? He was always reading a bible and going to church a lot more than just on Sunday morning, so we all started going a lot more, which was okay with

Redhead Momma because she liked the attention of a preacher's wife, for a while anyway. On the other hand, Giant Dad loved preaching. He would yell and holler, sweating and pacing, hitting the wooden Bible holder stand with such force it would wake up the old folks. He was alive, no longer the victim of the big bang that hung over him and Jay as a cloud of persecution. Giant Dad had found his way out, and he was living. Jay, on the other hand, could feel himself falling deeper into the darkness, alone with no one wishing to talk of the mighty storm that destroyed so much. They act as if it never happened. Jay just kept on acting.

Preaching at every chance was the new life and times for this new hillbilly family. Jay was always excited to tag along with Giant Dad as he made his way around the evangelical circuit. Everything moved so fast, tent revivals with sawdust floors, and almost no late-summer breeze to lick the sweat off from the crowd. People were getting saved in the name of Jesus by the bunches. Jay's spirit rejoiced with the new saints as angels in glory rejoiced. Yes, Jay was becoming a spiritual warrior but was not sure how. He was so alive when reading his Bible, electric while in prayer over words that convicted his heart, ready to be a full-blown man of God.

School started as quickly as it ended. Everyone seemed so excited to see each other, not Jay. He was from a different kind of school, one where you had to "move every other year" kind of school. Jay would wait to see if someone at the new schools would laugh when the teacher first called his name—anyone who laughed would get it at recess. These days, Jay was having a little problem that everyone kept asking him about: where he went to school all those years. Jay had no response, everything from ten years old and back. Nothing.

Mac was at the same school and talked Jay into trying out for basketball. Jay was all for it. He and Mac were now pretty close friends and enjoyed hanging out. Mac was a clown and was not afraid to fight, just like Jay. They were a pair not to be messed with. Once making the basketball team, Giant Dad put up a goal at the house so Jay could practice. He even came out and showed a couple moves to use on taller players; one was the ever famous hook shot that almost ruined a perfectly good raisin. Jay was just glad Giant Dad took the time.

That year in the sixth grade was amazing. Jay made the basketball team, and everyone started to know his name, everyone in a little country school, that is. The backboards were wooden, and the gym was old and sweaty, but when all those people gathered inside during the winter, the thunderous sounds that reigned pounded to the beat of Jay's heart, the cheers as a basket was scored, the frenzy at the victorious buzzer ending the battle. Yes, this was good. But this excitement was to be measured, this revival of feeling against the darkness, against the emptiness that Jay had so loved to embrace. Yes, there is Jesus who is changing Jay's life more and more at every meeting, but you must be willing to meet with holiness, and sometimes it's just too hard to return from the dark, so comforting, personal gratification, hidden in boxes on the very top shelf to little worn books that changes one's life, imagination to condemnation, what a wonderful ride. To see in pictures what some believe is love from the highly hidden boxes or to read what others describe as love in the little worn books was wrong but somehow so very exciting.

Wrong kept ringing in Jay's ear as he continued to study the works of sixty-six books called the Bible. Deeper and deeper, Jay would continue on his path to righteousness, studying the New Testament, the words written in red. Now this was life changing. Here, Jay could finally see what needed to be underlined as proof positive, *love*. Jesus is love, a man described by many but only found by those who would stop and listen. The Christmas story was now becoming a light focusing on the eternal, of mankind, and his need to be delivered and *saved*, as Christians put it. Page by page, Jay became closer to Jesus as he taught the disciples in Matthew chapter 5, and even though he understood so little,

Jay began to *know* the Savior that now enveloped his life, a holy presence that traveled the same roads as all the redeemed.

Prayer! This was very important to Jesus, and so Jay made it important to himself, asking no one questions about the Word of God. They were buffoons of the lowest order not even wanting to share a hug of brotherly love, church members afraid to share knowledge or artificial love. Giant Dad was no better. Even though he had love for Jesus, he had no hands-on emotions for any of the children where he called home. In church though, he was different. He smiled a lot and hugged on some of the members, calling them brothers and sisters, laughing and slapping each other on the back, standing around out front before the preaching, smoking cigarettes and talking racing. Was Jay missing something?

Into the Word, Jay climbed, talking with his holy helper that Jesus had sent him to live and understand the Christian life. *Christian*, a follower of Christ, Jay liked that title. The Bible even told Jay if he obeyed the words of Jesus, he would call Jay a friend. Jay would never attempt to call Holy Jesus a friend, never bringing Jesus down to such a lowly level. Jay was not too far down for Jesus to help him; he just didn't want Jesus to know how much he enjoyed it there. Sometimes staying for days before calling to the name above all names, he was always there when he called. Jay prayed that he always would be.

Living in the love of Christ was invigorating. Piece by piece, Jay discovered what true love was all about, Jesus, who will never leave us or forsake us, a promise to never be alone, to always be loved no matter how messed up he was, and boy, was Jay messed up. This was not always so in the world of the mortal. One day, people love you, and the next day, you're a target. Jay read this over and over again in the Bible. This guy named Saul was real special. That's when Jesus jerked him up and kicked him so hard it even changed his name. Now he was Paul, knocked that first letter flat out goofy. Paul goes on to really great things, but this one line he said, "I love the Lord with all my heart, but it's this flesh that I battle with daily." This guy knew what he was talking about. He wrote so many great letters in the Bible, but Jay believed Colossians is the best reading he have ever done. It all comes down to Jesus, the one true love.

Jay hit his knees even harder. This time, it was after a pretty good whooping; a hickory switch was the deterrent of choice. When will they learn that the act could sustain all attempts of domination? Crying, screaming, running in circles, all to the delight of the ring masters, Jay would perform, and the pain continued to become his very best friend. Seeking no retaliation from above, Jay was just thankful that Jesus always loved him, and when he prayed in desperation of loneliness, he was always there. Not there like some may imagine, for this had nothing to do with imagination—the helper was there. The presence of his holiness was more comforting than the gentlest touch his mother had ever given, and those were very few and far between. Treated as a criminal for leaving the bread wrapper untied, the punishment was a beating. Jay was the biggest and could take the lashes better than the little ones. Who left the bread untied? I guess we'll never know. Comforted in the presence of his Holy Spirit, Jay cleaned the blood from the back of his legs and laughed a little. They didn't know his personal relationship had gotten so close. Now he knew he was loved truly. For the first time, he knew he would never have to suffer alone. This was the deal made that night on his knees, in his room, to a Holy God who would never leave him alone.

7

POLAR OPPOSITES

Jay now turned thirteen with little to no fanfare from any and all. It was just another day in the country, and Jay preferred it that way. It seems when attention is warranted to someone other than Redhead Momma, life can become a little uncomfortable. "So you're a big teenager now, turned into a big man, is that right, son?" Redhead Momma mockingly proclaimed, attempting to rile a response worthy of the abuse to come.

"No, momma," Jay quietly stated as he looked at the floor, knowing any eye contact would set off the already irritated boss of the family. Anyway, how dare Jay have birthday on one of her days? You see, every day was her day in the land of the redhead momma.

How did this switch get turned on? Jay thought. He was getting tired of apologizing for everything and anything that upset his momma, always looking for confrontations, anything to light the fuse, three hard slaps across the face and the yell "Why won't you look at me!" This took Jay off-guard. The slapping in the face hurt like nobody's business. Redhead Momma was short but very strong, country living, working a hard life on the farm with plenty of rivals to defeat. She could be merciless. To fake cry or not, Jay never knew which way this storm was blowing. Here again was the woman who hated the man. Only one problem, Jay was just the substitute. The man she really hated would be home later, and he would get his share but only verbally. You see, Giant Dad was now a preacher, a man of little to no violence unless Redhead Momma lit the fire in him.

Cursing and screaming continued in Jay's direction until the words he longed for came bellowing into his face, followed by multiple slaps. "Get out of my sight," Redhead Momma screamed. "You disgust me! If you ever look at me like that again, I'll kill you. You hear me, you little hellion?"

Enough was enough. Jay turned and walked away. Redhead Momma followed him down the hall, punching him in the back and screaming things that Jay just blocked out, still attempting to reach around to slap his face some more. She loved to slap Jay in the face. I guess that kind of love was better than no love at all.

The redhead storms became more frequent as Jay found his peace from reading and praying and growing in faith, a union he had made that was never broken. He was always there, living in the light. Jay liked to call it a peace, a joy to be loved and wanted. Sometimes even the church members would pretend to love him, but Jay saw through that in a minute, they were Redhead Momma's friends, and with that, they must stay loyal. It was always amusing to Jay when his momma would introduce the brood. He was always listed last, and his name was, in his momma's words, "This is my little hellion." Jay thought that was his name up to around eleven, then he figured it was just a term of endearment.

Jay called out in prayer time and time again, and as always, the holy peace was there, a comforter, a healer, a friend. Jay had become very close to his Holy Spirit friend; he was allowed to tell him all. Nothing shocked Him, as he always understood no matter how dark the conversation would become. The Holy Spirit would never leave Jay alone in the dark. He was always a light that Jay could see and find his way out again, always there, the love of Christ, a feeling that could never be undone, the greatest of all time. Jay wept. This love was so real, but how, he was so despised and hated. Yes, that was the word used time and time again, "I hate you, and you don't deserve to be loved." But Jay was loved from above.

Crazy thing about a mother's love and the word *crazy* is literally used here; it can change as the sky, from dark and cloudy to bright and sunny in a micro minute. With no advance warning, Redhead Momma would show up bright and loving ready to take piece parts of the brood on a wild and fun-filled day. During school, she would just let the little ones skip with no worries in mind. She would pick a kid or two, and off you'd go, shopping, or McDonald's, and just having a great time. Only one rule was that you had to lie and act like you were sick the next day. Never bring this up to Redhead Momma; she can substitute a slap for every offensive gesture.

Life with what we now know as a bipolar mother was always interesting especially when raised as a poor country girl, the "poor me" stories over and over again along with an ego of beauty unmatched until this very day. Was Redhead Momma pretty? No, she was beautiful. Even Jay could see that. Long red hair, great build on a woman, if a son may say so himself, but those eyes could cut through a room and put all on alert, piercing brown that held one's attention of amazement, a walk and stature that commanded respect. Yes, Redhead Momma was a true force to be reckoned with.

"You ready, Jaybo," came the put it in high-gear request.

"Yes, Momma," was the safest response for Jay as another weekend of freedom was now at hand. "*Back to the hills we go*" is the cute little song Jay sung in his head as they drove farther into the country. Making their way toward one of the main roads, a car quickly pulled out in front of them. Redhead Momma lay down on the horn as the gentleman in front of them politely gave a one-finger wave. Words coming out of Redhead Momma were burning up the air. Jay knew the storm brewing, and the low pressure was moving in fast as the car in front came to a stop at the newly installed red light. With Jay's intellectual mind of thirteen years, he attempted to calm the storm beside him.

"Momma, it's okay. He doesn't know what he's doing," Jay blurted out.

No response.

Momma's face now matched the color of red Jay had learned to love so much; she was now a full-blown tornado, so powerful and yet so unpredictable.

Reaching under the seat as she left the car in park, Redhead Momma made her way up to the unsuspecting soon-to-be unconscious driver. With a flash of silver, the twelve-inch crescent wrench flew through the air, firmly encased in the eye of the storm, allowing the free end to smash the unsuspecting driver in the head.

Calmly reaching into the car, Redhead Momma put the large sedan into park, turned, and then made her way casually back to her own luxurious Buick. Jay wanted to melt through the floor and disappear into a puff of smoke that lazily rolled off the cigarette Redhead Momma had just lit. Not a word. It was as if nothing had happened. She pulled around the unconscious man slumped over his steering wheel and drove off down the main highway without a care in the world. There was no storm, not even a drizzle of rain from what was once a raging F-5 tornado. This was the woman who feared no man and would kill any, and all at the drop of a hat, Jay had great respect for his momma and an even greater fear. He knew she meant what she said, and pulling a trigger was just a day in the hay. Survival was the name of Jay's day in the hay. He must become the loyal performer or a statistic as the man in the sedan. Lights, camera, action. This would be a masterpiece, and Jay's life depended on it.

Seeing Uncle Red waiting in the yard with that big hillbilly grin was just what Jay needed. "Grab your stuff and go on," Redhead Momma sweetly spoke. Jay looked to see a beautiful smile, one any man could fall in love with. It was peaceful as if nothing had happened twenty minutes ago, nothing out of the ordinary. What in the name of Cooter's cat? Jay's mind ached with delusions of his mother at that moment, *Sweet, no way,* but this was no act, here before Jay sat the destroyer who was happy to set fire to all debris left behind. Cool, calculated, she was the force that controlled the darkness deep inside of Jay, not her actually, but he now knew, he was his mother's son.

Jay had a lot to share with his uncle Red. So much had been going on in his life that he had caught up with Red on a lot of the new more interesting topics, girls for one—but not to leave out the relationship with Jesus and his Holy Spirit. Red was right on track with the entire conversation, and the young men just laughed as they went from one arena to another. Fascinating how two separate guys could view such complex subjects such as Jesus and girls in the same light. Jay was mesmerized by the similarities that drew the two worlds into one. Now was the time to find out exactly what it was that made Jay and Red so alike.

Red was a lot like Jay when he started to talk about that day, looking off into the distance and then just letting his gaze fall to the forest floor. His words were soft and quiet, speaking in a tone that was very familiar to Jay, the tone of being there, a place you never wanted to go again.

"It's been a long time since my sister was shot," Red started. "I don't know exactly what day it was, but it was raining. I was playing on the front porch. Guess I was around eight years old when I heard these crazy noises coming from up on trailer park hill, screams and words. I don't remember. Nothing out of the ordinary, really, stuff I'd heard a hundred times before. But there was something different." Then Red paused, and the woods became quiet as Red and Jay sat on their favorite log; it was as if every animal and insect had stopped to hear Red's recollection of that terrible day. Jay knew the pain Red was feeling. He also was at that moment in time when the memories become so real that you just sit and watch as the reel unwinds, clicking in time, Jay's time, Red's time.

The woods were so cool and beautiful during the summer months, hanging out on that log next to the swift running creek that came out of the ground just about a hundred feet up from where Jay and Red were sitting. Cool, clean water. The boys both took the opportunity to wet their whistles before strolling along the creek. Downstream, they would go as Red slowly began recalling those horrific moments in time. "She wasn't married long, just a couple of months at most, lived in the first of three trailers up on that hill, screaming and running. She came barreling down that hill so fast her feet couldn't keep up with her. Right behind her was my newest brother-in-law, chasing and yelling, calling her terrible names. As she got to the bottom of the hill along the road, she fell hard on the ground. Then he stepped over to straddle her, still standing. I could see something in his hands. Sister was lying on the ground, screaming, 'Please don't kill me. Please don't kill me.' He shot her six times in the head, right through her hands."

Red was now crying, and Jay cried right along with him, "No one will talk to me about it," Red exclaimed. "No one." Jay understood as he hugged his hurting blood brother. Yes, Jay understood.

8

JUDGMENT

Jay and Red ran those woods like it was nobody's business, throwing diesel cocktails off the I-40 bridge at three in the morning just to watch the eighteen-wheelers blow through there with horns a blasting and cop lights a flashing. Sitting high up on the overpass known as hillbilly road, the boys had every advantage in the world when it came to getting chased. Fear was not an option or even a consideration at this point of the boy's lives. Living free or dying trying was the hillbilly stump jumping way.

Now Jay also had some additional "redhead momma" brothers. These guys were not as young as Red, and boy, did they like to see how far Jay would go. You see, these boys were ages between sixteen and twenty, with anything and everything becoming fair play. Smoking white owl cigars until Jay was so dizzy, things were flying out of his ears; it felt like it anyway. Drinking white liquor known as lightning was a real favorite of Jay's, Man, it made you feel so warm inside. Jay would just sip it as Red stood by and watched. One thing came to be known about Red; he didn't partake, and that was that. On the other hand, Jay loved to push the limits, and his uncles loved watching Jay's destructive ways. They would push him into fights with other boys on the mountain, and Jay was all for it. Age wasn't the issue, and winning wasn't always the case. He just felt free. Every time he would strike or be stricken, he felt more alive, numb to all that was going on around him, a different feeling that had been prepared from all those years of standing there and taking the blows. Jay's uncles had taught him, "If a man's talking, he ain't fighting. Strike while the mouth was moving." Jay enjoyed that summer bonding with his kin, learning to live life fearless, to love the taste of the blood that saturated his mouth time and time again, knowing now that nothing could stop him, not a man, not a bullet. Life was great, and Jay planned to live it free or die trying.

Summer living was gone in a rush. That thirteenth year of Jay's life, so many things have changed while spending quality time up on hillbilly hill. Jay had become a true stump jumper, a man of the woods, well, almost a man. The hidden boxes and the little worn novels were sure reminders of that. Jay loved to return to the peeks of those shelves. Way in the back, he would grab a dusty old box and reach inside to unveil the wonders of the greatest creation God has ever made, the flesh. So powerful an image, fascinating to the point of not being able to look away, getting closer as if to see the pictures come to life, the lines the curves going places and taking Jay's mind right along for the exhilarating ride that he hoped would never stop. Whose would these have been anyway? Grandpa?

The conviction Jay would fall under was in no way strong enough to keep him from frequenting this new and exciting world; it was "natural," as his uncles put it, same with his pal Mac. "We are human," Mac would say, "and this is what humans do. God created all things, and this is just one of many wonderful thrills of nature." Jay had no problem with that, and so went the turmoil of man and flesh, Jay had a feeling this was going to be one long road. Thank God, he didn't have to travel it alone, for the bumps in the road of flesh, sooner or later, get the best of some of God's best.

Another weekend with his pal Mac, Jay was living the fun life. Actually, any part of life away from the eggshell walking existence of polar town was a true blessing. Away from home he could breathe and be more like the created character so many seemed to love, Jay, of course, knew he was not actually loved by these people. Sure they laughed and smiled, allowing Jay to cut up at every opportunity but always keeping a deeply respectful attitude was the true weapon of Jay's arsenal, only he was aware of the battle taking place, the battle of one's self-depressing mind, the darkness within. *Never let them in, they cannot be allowed inside.*

Sunday morning came at Mr. and Mrs. Mac's home. Jay was awakened by the normal Mac household shenanigans: Mac's sisters squealing at their little brother, Mrs. Mac attempting to get them all seated around the table for breakfast while juggling the circus of cooking and a lovingly supportive wife to Mr. Mac. Things seemed quieter than usual, but who really knows when you have so many in such a small area? "All's well when fed well," Mrs. Mac would say. Seemed like a wonderfully wise woman to Jay, always smiling, always pleasant to Jay. She even attempted to touch Jay on his cheek one time. Jay flinched as her hand drew close. He saw the pain in her eyes as she quickly pulled back her hand. She meant to caress. Jay was unaware of such contact. He had seen it, but to feel it?

Mac and Jay sat where they always sat in church. Sunday school was over and now was the time to scope out the hot chicks all dressed up in their Sunday's best. The services started out just like all the other times: stand up, sing a song; sit down, choir would sing a song; stand up, sing another song. These Southern churches were all alike, sing about Jesus, talk about Jesus, but after

Sunday, you really didn't hear much about Jesus. Sure Jay's Dad would study alone, but to get religious around the polar storm was asking for a fight. Let's remember who's number 1 around here, and it sure wasn't Jesus.

Jay wondered if it was different with the other members of Preacher Mac's church. Looking around, Jay could see the faces of many of the members, but something was wrong, some seemed shocked, and others started crying. Jay attempted to focus in on what Preacher Mac was saying, but he was now crying also—not just a little, but a lot. Looking at Mac sitting beside him, Jay saw a jaw-dropping expression on Mac's face. Literally, his jaw was hanging open, and his eyes were welling up with tears. *What the heck is going on?* Jay thought. what did preacher Mac just say? "Sorry, I'm so very, very, sorry."

Ever hear of confession is good for the soul? Jay was hearing it now and was not sure how any of these words could be considered as good. Crying and pointing toward the cute lady playing the organ and then pointing back to Mrs. Mac on the piano, Jay was starting to make sense of all the now-tumultuous activity surrounding him.

It seems this confession was one of the flesh, and Jay was getting a firsthand look at the destructive power of every man's weakness. Jay's Dad had told him of a quote by a Mr. Graham, "The sins of the flesh will take down 75 percent of God's good men," and Jay would learn to respect the prophecy of this great man, as this destruction is a comfort to no man.

Jay would miss the freedom of running wild around the household of the Macs, as the resignation of a once-powerful man of God was circulated throughout the small towns of those Southern hills. Jay was no longer to associate with that type of people. "That type of people?" This reassured Jay to never let them see the real man. They thought Mr. Mac was evil; he was just human and needed a hug in a time where not even his own children wanted to hug him. Sure Jay understand the shock of it all, but now the sin was out in the open, the condemnation, the judgment, and abandonment by those who had used the most misused word in the world, *love*. Mr. Mac was still a Christian! Didn't that mean anything! Jay had grown in the Word of God, his fascination of someone that came from royalty to die for the sins of the wicked people whose reflection is of all mankind. Wicked when left to our own ways of doing things, sacrifices for self-worth and unspeakable pleasures. *Had not this man confessed his sins before the righteous? Why were they now crying out to "crucify, crucify him"?*

This experience led Jay into a study so deep and private that he dare not share his findings with anyone other than his own personal comforter. Jay loved the way the word described the spirit, *helper* and *friend*, his friend to which he could lean to cry and to contemplate the sweet surroundings of death, the truth that lay before him was from the beginning of time. *Truth*, such a powerful word. It says in John that "God is a spirit, and he seeks those who worship with him, those who worship in spirit and truth." God the Father wanted to personally worship with him, *spirit and truth*. Exactly what does that mean? Jay knew one thing from his newly ambitious study of God's Word. Forgiveness was not an option. *How did so many who had been in churches for so long miss this command? And who are these so-called Christians, followers of Jesus Christ!*

The fallout from the Mac fiasco turned Jay into a worshiping and studying Jesus Christ protégé. He himself would know the words in red with such a love as to emulate the precious beautiful red blood that flowed down Calvary's cross. Jay consumed himself into the Word that summer, laying in the woods in the heat of the day and read from a little New Testament, the testament of Jesus and the Holy Spirit of true love, a God who loved the world so much that he allowed the most precious of all love to bleed the beautiful red blood at the hands of men just like Jay. It was Jay that day who put this love on an old wooden tree. Jay said the words, "He died for me."

Jay would not talk about the preacher Mac mistake and how it changed his life, as all the ones who needed to know already knew, and they knew from that time forward, Jay would never look at the fallen as the ones he'd seen before. There would be no judgment coming from this shattered vessel so broken that only in the eyes of Jesus and his Holy friend would he ever seem normal or loved. Jay made up his mind that he would be a messenger to all who would hear the truth, not of judgment, but of truth, the truth that would shake the foundations of the world. When not speaking of the words in red, he would do as those same words directed. His yes would be yes and his no would be no. Anything more comes from evil. Let them hit you if they must, steal from you, give it to them, love those who hate you, bless those who curse you, and pray for those who persecute you.

Jay could now see through his friend, the Spirit, Preacher Mac on his knees, praying for those who now persecute him. Still, Preacher Mac was a forgiven son of God!

9

CHURCH LIFE

School year begun, and Jay and Mac were now big-time eighth-graders, rulers of the halls, the subject matter of whispering girls at every turn. Mac was allowed by his folks to attend his last elementary/middle school year here in the valley of the hills. Why not? Mac had gone to this school from first grade up, and Jay knew it had a lot to do with his heavenly Father blessing him with a comforting companion, one who, on some levels, lived in his own new personal chamber of torture. *Welcome to the comforting halls of darkness,* Jay thought. *No matter how much you fill your waking days with light, when the lights went out, the darkness would sooner or later creep in. Stay awake as you might, wheels turning, speaking to the friend who'll never leave you, but this darkness is just too deep, just too deep...*

Fall meant one thing in this part of the world, preparing for basketball, and Mac and Jay had fed off each other so much that they both were now ready to shake things up and shock some coaches. A new coach was in town this year, and he became a great teacher and respecter of the round-ball sensations. These boys were good, and along with a deeper walk with Jesus, Jay had a light about him that attracted all. His love through the eyes of Jesus had transformed him into a compassionate healer wanting to take the pains of all he encountered and place them in his own place of darkness, a place where they would never escape. Never speaking of his darkness, Jay sought to help others just as Jesus had done—only one problem, Jay was not Jesus.

The year flew by, and boy, was it an exciting one—school dances, a successful B-ball record, and a coach who advised Jay to work hard through the summer. He had a feeling Jay could really be a great basketball player. Really, *great* was a word Jay was not used to. Jay liked to think he was great; it had a nice ring to it.

Mac and his family moved just as they said they would, farther into the mountains, not far from hillbilly hill, but it would be a long time before Jay would see his dear friend again. *At least we both have Jesus,* Jay thought. *Never alone when you have your best friend with you.* Jay's friend was always there; he knew Mac's was also. Giant Dad now had a church, one more toward the city, about a thirty-minute drive from the red dirt road known as home. Jay never really felt at home, but boy, was this new church thing going to be something, and new was not it. It was a rundown little white church right off the main highway, about a quarter of a mile away from the famous crescent wrench incident. Man, was that bringing back some memories for Jay.

Jay learned real quick that being a preacher's son was meant for those whose dad had their own church. Once Giant Dad had that distinction, it gave Jay a special distinction also, as a rebel. The term "You know those preachers kids" would become familiar fast. It seemed everyone had a closed opinion about them, as if the recognition was in some way a deception to their dependability as a true Christian. Jay would play along without confronting the issue with idle chatter, continuing to pull those of suspected darkness ever closer to his realm of light, and come to find out, there were many enticed.

Summer was a busy time for a pastor and his family in a small Southern church. There were revivals to start the summer and said to be revivals to end the summer. In between, there was vacation Bible school, and Jay was quickly learning what it meant to be a faithful member. Sunday morning and night with Monday night visitation, then Wednesday night services along with Thursday night prayer meetings. Jay was encouraged to go wherever Giant Dad went. They would talk of the Word, and Giant Dad would look surprised at the comments from his thirteen-year-old sitting there next to him in the front seat of that new Chevy truck. "You been studying the Word of God, son?" Giant Dad asked with a grin. He knew good and well Jay was studying; he just didn't know how much, and Jay was not about to let this conversation go too far as to give anything valuable away.

Conversations over the next couple of summer months would continue to bring smiles to the face of Giant Dad. Riding down the road to visit some of the members was always a special time for Jay. He would see his dad's face light up when speaking about how God was working with so many hurting and confused souls. Salvation was the true light calling his dad, preaching and seeing souls saved. Giant Dad would preach so hard that ten minutes into his sermon his jacket would fly off, and he'd loosen his tie, just a little, and still had to maintain that look of what Jay like to call "A Preacher Man," one called by God, a man who would walk through the fires of hell to save one more soul for the kingdom. Jay loved this man but could not really show it. The acting role of love was fine for now. There was no real love to be shared, as he saved it all for his friend, his Savior, the only one who truly loved him.

The summer was coming to an end; it was one not so spent on Hillbilly hill, and it seemed Grandma had been talking a little too much and got Jay and his uncles on the wrong side of Redhead Momma although she took delight in the fact that Jay was now confrontational and offered advice in how to knock their blocks off, as she put it. "You got to hit them first and hit them hard," was the advice Jay was happy to take. Now he knew where his uncle got the "If his mouth's moving, he's not fighting" idea. Amazing the wisdom of a hillbilly woman. Of course, those words would never leave Jay's mouth aloud.

The distinction between a preacher's son was one thing. On the other hand, a preacher's wife in a small country church was like a queen of the ball. She was fussed over, and every hypocrite in that place thought she was the saint that came marching in. The verbal trash talking that would go on Sunday mornings was right next door to blasphemous in Jay's mind, talking of people who weren't there. You'd better be glad you were there, or they'd be talking about you. All the men in one circle and the women in another standing outside, smoking their cigarettes, talking racing and women and who was dressed like a Jezebel.

Jay's impressionable teenage mind was trying to hang with the men, but the conversation was not what his best friend had ordered. *Where was the concern for the lost, the hurting? Was that talk only for inside the church*? Jay drifted away; he and his best friend.

Now after church, the ride home was always great. Giant Dad wanted Jay to count how many times he would use the word *and uh* or if he slapped the pulpit too hard. The Holy Spirit was leading him, so slapping the pulpit was going to happen. Was it just too hard? This was a happy time with Giant Dad and his younger brother of three years. They were men bonding and talking about God, feeling the comfort of the holy helper, their friend, until the turn.

Making that right turn onto the red dirt road always brought silence to the chatty trio; actually a duo, as little brother would contribute only as a ten-year-old could, which most times left Jay and Giant Dad in stitches because that boy would say the funniest things, but not on that red dirt road. They were closing in on the final curve leading to home. "Get out of those church clothes and get ready for dinner," Redhead Momma would call out. Every Sunday, there would be a beautiful roast, mashed potatoes, green beans, and biscuits. The house smelled great from everything slowly simmering as the family worshiped at church. All settled down with the blessing said. It was now time for the real feast.

Giant Dad got to eating without ever looking up as Redhead Momma began her north of the pole banter: it was this one and that one and" how could she wear this or wear that? The nerve of them acting like they are Bible-believing Christians, we know what they really are." It was a feast for the gorging as she tore apart any and all who had fallen in her sight. She was the imperious of all domains, a force not to be tried or tempted, the calm before the storm and the storm itself, if anyone wanted to know. No one was that brave, especially Giant Dad, but Jay, poor, sweet Jay.

10

MOMMA

"Oh, Momma," came Jay's words of light, "didn't Daddy preach a great sermon this morning?" Jay loved the way his dad preached, such power and spiritual conviction, pacing back and forth as his hand would fly through the air among the cries of "Amen, brother," a fierceness that made the devil shake at the awesome power of a Holy God. All was quiet, as no one attempted to look Jay's way. Down at the end of the table, opposite of Giant Dad, Redhead Momma sat on the left side of the soft-spoken preacher man who said, "Why thank you, son. I really enjoyed the Holy Spirit this morning. It felt like a good message." At least Giant Dad had tried. Jay was thankful that he pulled the live fire away, but now, the crosshairs were on dad, and Mommas verbal gun was always loaded.

"Well, what you need to do is let me at that graying hair you've got there. You're starting to look like an old man up there, prancing around in those colored suits, waving your hands around so everyone can see your sweaty armpits, yelling so loud no one can understand a word you're saying." On and on she went, trying to drive the fun out of anything that didn't include her, starting in a calm tone then escalating into a good old-fashioned butt chewing. That woman was born to kick tale and take names. If there was ever a fighter, it was her, and with that ego, she would tell you real fast how beautiful she was and how every man on the planet was flirting with her, trying to get her to come home. "I never wanted to marry your daddy in the first place. I didn't need him, and I still don't need him. Every good-looking man around was chasing after me, and I didn't want or need any of them either."

Redhead Momma would go on with these little tirades and always end the way she wanted: everyone kissing her butt, telling her how beautiful she was, sneaking in a good-looking man comment toward Dad every once in a while, hoping she would allow it, attempting to save some face for poor old Dad.

He just smiled and would tell her how much he loved her, and he did. Jay never understood this. He could feel the pain of past years swell up inside of him and was not sure who the man would be to wield the redemptive power. All he knew was that that day was coming, and it was coming fast.

Jay had to give credit where credit was due. As he aged, his momma instilled in him a great desire to work. Why, at thirteen there in the South, you could start working as soon as you got your Social Security card. Jay got his and was allowed to work part-time after school, bussing tables at a restaurant just a couple miles away. "You make your own money, you can buy your own style of clothes," Redhead Momma said. This was 1973, and clothes were changing fast, coming out of the 60s. Jay was all for not having his momma buy him the oversized jeans that he could grow into or the ugly plaid patterns of hillbilly's best. No, sir, Jay wanted to have a little style when he started high school in the fall, so off to work he'd go every Thursday through Saturday night, a working man, thanks to his redhead momma.

Work was always easy for Redhead Momma; she loved to talk, and a beautician was her calling. Talking with a cigarette hanging out of her mouth with the ash always at the breaking point, she would go on and on. The topic of conversation in a beauty shop, just in case you don't know, is the last person to walk out the door. It always amazed Jay at how all the women knew something about the other women who just left, and not realizing that they were the next in line as soon as they left. Did they actually believe they had nothing to talk about?

Redhead Momma opened a new beauty shop in the basement of the redbrick house on the red dirt road. She was not a real educated woman; she had to leave school at twelve years old to help work and take care of the hillbilly brood. She never made it back to school, but Jay always admired the drive and intelligence of this bipolar woman. She had a chip on her shoulder and every right for it to be there. There was no harder worker than Redhead Momma, and no one could deny her business sense. All she needed a chance.

Country living is said to have great advantages for long life and health. This was not the case of Redhead Momma; she had known the doctors of the South the whole time growing up even before the many years of travel up and down the Eastern seaboard. This is where Jay had learned to talk differently. With their slow draw and intentional slang, Jay was often irritated with the length of time it would take to form the simplest of sentences. It was like they were on some of Redhead Momma's pills or something. Jay could not believe the amount of pills she would take, pills to go to bed, pills to get up, pills for headaches, and pills for anxiety, pills for everything under the sun. You needed it? Redhead Momma had a pill for it.

Legal? Not a chance. Jay thought. *How could anyone be allowed so many pills and none to fix the real problem?* Redhead Momma was not tired and sure didn't need a pickup. She was wound so tight she'd spin through the house like the cartoon Tasmanian devil, a devil that could switch gears in mid-spin and come out the other side, slinging a venomous string of words that made all aware there was no place to hide. No matter where you went, she would find you, and it was always best if she didn't have to look too long. Volume along with the demeaning words just got to the place where Jay would step out and meet the evil head on. Might as well, all the good anger was saved for him anyway, the one she truly loved to hate.

Jay knew Redhead Momma had the family doctors in her pocket. Why not? Jay was born on Dr. Dillon's desk a cold February morning thirteen years ago right when a snowstorm had hit. Redhead Momma had to dig the car out just to get to the doctor's office and ended up giving baby Jay pneumonia. So the story goes. Tough, no doubt. She loved her family enough to kill for it, never question it, bipolar crazy as a bag of bats. You better believe it. The only problem was everyone was too scared to confront her with it. She told everyone what to do, and if you questioned it, like Jay was prone to do, you pay the price of the crazy dance. Jay was learning to enjoy the dance, the taste of blood, the feel of it running down his back, the warmth and beauty as it flowed down his calf, the pain becoming more and more a comforter that Jay would learn to love, a special bond.

Now the language was Jay's favorite part of the dance. Redhead Momma would get so wound up the hillbilly would just flow from that little fiery woman. She could cuss and then try not to cuss so fast you thought she was talking in tongues. Now this is a good place to point out Redhead Momma's Church of God upbringing. You see, she could get the Holy Ghost with the most. Was Redhead Momma a child of God? Jay had heard his momma pray with the best of them, sincere, heartbroken for those she loved. She was just bipolar, and no one could help her. The pride of that woman would reflect in the image of Jay for the rest of his life. Jay knew the craziness that wanted to escape into the light, but he was determined not to let it out. This might be more than he could bear. He had to keep it in. The confrontations Jay had with his mother were only because he was so much like her, as giant dad would say.

"Son, you know what your problem is? You're just like your momma," he could hear his dad say over and over again, attempting to console a bruised and battered Jay. He felt for his son, but was not willing to cross that line. Who could blame him? Redhead Momma slept with the same pistol she shot him with under her pillow every night. Jay always wondered how disturbed someone must be to sleep with a gun under their pillow. Now he knew. He had found it while snooping around. With great knowledge comes great responsibilities to right the wrongs, and Jay thought he was just the man.

The thought that he was the man was an issue. This next idea of Jay's was so unbelievable that Jay knew he was losing his mind just thinking such thoughts. But enough was enough, he couldn't take it anymore—living as a coward every time Redhead Momma would walk by, flinching due to expectance of multiple blows to the head, the continuous verbal assault of such demeaning topics as to belittle everything Jay was going through, the accusation of becoming a man of no use to her or anyone for that matter. A lack of intelligence at every opportunity was her cry to Jay, "How stupid are you, boy!" At that time, Jay could not see the pain in Redhead Momma's own life, the lack of education always hanging over her head. All Jay could feel was the anger deep inside, so deep it had joined forces with the darkness within. A plan to end the suffering was in play.

11

TO KILL

Jay and Little Bro became very tight throughout that year, Jay fourteen and little bro now eleven. Jay remembered that age well, the age of forgetfulness. It was the time of Jay's life where all began but were temporary at best. At least with Little Bro, he could laugh at the goofiness of youth. Something Jay did not remember, *goofy*, never, not unless he wanted the unwanted attention of Redhead Momma. That was something Jay was definitely getting tired of. This, however, was not the fault of Little Bro or any of the other siblings hiding throughout the house. They all would get their share of slaps and three swats with a switch ever now and then, but Jay's was different, and he understood why. Heck he was told enough.

No doubt about it, Jay was his dad's son and was becoming more like him every day, seeking the relationship with God that was not available to him in this dimension, wanting to be free, to live where love always was a dream. But with the Holy Word, it was to come. He promised becoming a man of God, and doing his will flew in the face of Redhead Momma. To worship her humor, to laugh when she laughed, and to be silent as she spoke, never looking at her with that look, the one Jay so proudly owned but paid a hefty price for, the look that could start the wheels a turning, the mercury rising, and the special love train rolling down the attack track.

Attack was the thought running through Jay's mind as he sat crying from yet another senseless beating due to boys just being boys. Little Bro was starting to toughen up and enjoyed roughhousing around with Jay. It was fun in the house, the boys' first mistake. You could hear Redhead Momma coming up those stairs, cursing everything from man to beast, demanding to know why such stupid little children had to make so much noise in her domain. "Momma, we were just playing around," came Jay's defiant response, one that was not well accepted.

Later that evening came the reason for Jay's painful turn of heart, a turn never expected; then again, the beating to come was not expected either. He could hear Redhead Momma screaming at Giant Dad concerning the disobedient attitude of their eldest son and demanding discipline to correct the errors of Jay's ways. Little Bro sat quietly beside Jay as he awaited judgment from the unjust, not sure what to say. Jay told Little Bro he should go watch TV for a while and that it was best to be out of sight until this was all over. As Little Bro left, Giant Dad entered the room. "Talking back to your mother was not the smartest thing to do," Giant Dad explained as he shut the bedroom door. Jay sat quietly, knowing an explanation would get him nowhere. Redhead Momma had spoken, and Giant Dad must obey to avoid the wrath of Mom. Jay always hoped someday Giant Dad would stand for what's right and not just what keeps the peace. *Didn't he see there could never be peace as long as chaos controlled the house*? It seemed clear to Jay, but who was he? Just a whipping boy.

Little Bro sat quietly, attempting to comfort the fractured pride of a boy's love for his parents. Hate is such a strong word, but it was the one burning through Jay's mind at such volume that all else vanquished within the sobs. *Why did he have to do it?* Jay knew Giant Dad was aware of the truth. Little Bro had even put in a good word to Giant Dad, but this could change nothing without the consent of Redhead Momma. Jay was still pleased with Little Bro, so Jay sucked it up and calmed the outer storm from its rage, only to release a deviant plan that would seem insane. Jay would soon learn how loyal Little Bro was, confiding in him the plan to kill, to free all within the walls of crazy town, but would Little Bro go along?

The next week was all about getting alone out in the woods and speaking the unspeakable. Little Bro seemed intrigued at the possibilities of a home without parents who believed in belts and hickory switches, real freedom to grow up happy, and laughing without worrying if it offended Redhead Momma. Could such a life really exist? That's what Jay was selling, and Little Bro was all in.

Summer was coming to an end, and Jay had an exceptional three months off from school. Why, at the end of middle school, Jay was but five foot nine inches tall, and now he had jumped to an astounding six three, averaging two inches per month throughout the summer. *Skinny* was a word most would use looking at Jay, but being allowed to purchase his own clothes, he easily perceived a stouter frame than that of 160 pounds. Excited of high school, Jay knew what must be accomplished if all were to work in his favor, ridding the family of the evil sadist who shared the same abode.

The night had come, and all was falling into place as Giant Dad and Redhead Momma left the house. Watching as the truck drove up the red dirt road, the boys anticipated what was to come. They would return during nightfall, which works perfectly for Jay's plan. Sister siblings, none the wiser, would stay in the living room as Jay and Little bro would hear something outside and go to see if someone were attempting to break in. Jay grabbed the pistol from under Redhead Momma's pillow, and Little Bro carried a single-shot 16 gauge shotgun. They quietly snuck downstairs and out into the yard. Knowing the expected time of their arrival, Jay positioned himself behind one of the large oak trees, breathing or attempting to grab a breath. He told Little Bro to stay hidden until Jay opened fire. The final countdown.

Breathe, Jay thought, *just breathe*. But that was easier said than done. Jay's heart was beating out of his chest just like the night he met the one he loved and who would always love him. "Not now!" Jay shouted in his mind, attempting to override the Spirit within. "I have to do this. I can't take it anymore. Either they die or I die. What's it going to be?" Jay continued to battle within, heart racing, mind swimming, and Little Bro. *What!* Jay thought. *Little Bro should not be here!* This was so wrong that Jay's spirit blasted him for getting the innocent involved with such wickedness. "Want to be a man?" Jay heard this as clear as if Jesus himself were standing right beside of Jay. "Then don't use a little boy to do what a man must do."

Truck lights were coming down the red dirt road; it was Redhead Momma and Giant Dad returning home. Jay could recognize that Chevy anywhere—a beautiful, new pickup bringing Jay's internal battle to an end. Jay knew he was outsmarted by the one who loves him so, never raising opposition during the entire planning stage. Even in the woods, it was as if Little Bro and Jay were all alone and left to devise the perfect crime to free the ones they loved. Thankfully, true love won out that night. The battle raging in Jay's mind was futile. He had no comeback for the love he now felt for his little brother. *Is this why they had become so close*? Jay remembered how horrible the night Redhead momma shot Giant Dad, and now Jay was putting a gun into the hands of the innocent. He could not. He would not allow Little Bro to live in the darkness that Jay found to be so comforting. There was not enough room for both of them. Jay thanked the Holy Spirit and stepped from behind the tree.

The lights from that Chevy taking away the darkness showed a tall silhouette of their oldest son standing there with a plain outline, excluding the pistol gripped firmly by Jay's right hand. "What's going on, son?" Giant Dad asked as Jay called Little Bro out from the shadows. "We thought we heard something messing around out here, Dad," came a response from Jay as calmly as he could. Of course, his sisters would back their story up, knowing it was the reason the two went outside in the first place. Giant Dad and Redhead Momma had a strange look on their face, as if they were running additional story lines through their heads, wondering what the boys were really up to. "Well, did you see anything?" Redhead Momma asked.

"Not really," said Jay, "but we heard something take off through the woods when we came around the front. That's when we saw you and Dad coming home."

"Good job," Redhead momma said. "It's nice to know you boys will protect the house when we're not here. You get that gun out anytime you need it, okay?"

Jay was dumbfounded and numb. How he ended up in the house is still a mystery. But Little Bro was safe and never said a word. He knew he loved that kid, but this required trust, and now Jay knew that Little Bro could be trusted with anything.

12

FRESHMAN

School was once again in, and for the first time since living, the country life, the palace of education was not within walking distance. The school bus was now the embarrassing mode of transportation Jay required, at least until he turned sixteen. At fourteen, however, the needed assistance was in the form of a big, ugly yellow bus filled to the brim with various-aged young men and women looking for the excitement of a new year. What dreams would come as a high school student? Oh, the spotlights to shine, who would be the next country cousin Casanova? Time would tell. Now at seventy-five inches, the accommodating roof height of the seventy two inch ceiling would require Jay's head to be bent down to stare at all the seated future classmates. Jay could see in their eyes the look of amazement, towering with that smile that could light up the darkest of day. Years of performances had prepared Jay to shine like a shooting star. Girls giggled while boys looked away. Jay was too much to take in larger than anything in their life was now bequeathing a safe passage not allowed to all freshmen.

Jay walked the hallways of hope to be high with such an air of royalty that the majority would pause, stop, or just move completely out of Jay's path. His reputation preceded him. Some knew him on the church circuit as the bad boy preacher's son while some knew him from his days up on the hillbilly mountain where he left an impression of one not wanting of personal attention. Mainly, they knew him on the basketball court. He had made quite a name for himself the last few years, but now, he was there before them. They knew him, but they didn't know him, asking if this was the same guy from last year. Jay just turned on the performance, and all recognized the light, the spiritual light Jay wished all could have, the light to hide away all the pain. He always wondered how the rest of the world masked the pain of life and living and sometimes living without really having life at all.

Now that those early fall bus rides were starting to become fun, Jay had made friends with this little short kid named Dave who really only lived a couple miles from Jay. After school, the boys would meet at the elementary school's outside basketball court and work on some B-ball. Dave was really pretty good, and it helped Jay work on a lot of his more technical shots that were sure to impress during the highly celebrated basketball season. Dave was a funny guy, and Jay was able to relax around him, *a new friend*, just what Jay needed. An interesting thing about being the last to be picked up and the last to be let off was getting to know the bus driver who was a junior. She was pretty and had a lot of curves and liked the conversations Jay and her would have once most of the other kids were gone. Jay had a way with words due to him always performing for the masses, never allowing the real Jay out—the one he protected must never be allowed to surface. If so, he surely would rule all who placed their trust in him. Domination was the game, and a winner must be humble and surprised at all the accolades. Jay had the humble part down pat; he was the master of identity illusions. Now you see him and now who the hall of holy is that?

School took an interesting turn as the varsity boys head basketball coach stopped him in the hall and asked his name. Jay proudly divulged the information to receive question upon question on who his relatives might be. Lacking the ticks of a clocks opportunity to answer, the coach proceeded to name some of his uncles on his dad's side and even named Giant Dad as previous dinosaur-age players he had the privilege to coach. As usual, Jay was much more intelligent than the portly basketball enthusiast. He just smiled and answered yes to the question of interest to play in the upcoming season. Jubilantly departing, the coach now seemed to be having one of those really great days. *You're welcome,* Jay thought, thrilled to bring some additional light to another gloomy day. Noticed by the elite then to be praised by all, Jay could hear the applause.

With school starting back slowly, the overhyped sideshow of church life was now finally coming to a manageable arena. Sure, everyone still attended the Sunday services, but a lot dropped out of the additional fellowships during the remainder of the week. Jay was still thrilled to accompany Giant Dad every time he headed out the door, and even Little Bro was starting to tag along to the merrier points of arrival. Wednesday night was when you really got to know the people of a little country church. Their kids who attended schools were not your own. It was a mixture of minds and ideas that fascinated Jay. The depth of some youth needed testing, and Jay was always testing, saying things to just to see the response. Nothing vulgar. Jay was always complimenting, watching to see what type of a reaction was produced if it was natural or how did they handle it when he would stand close, looking down into their eyes, touching them on the shoulder or brushing the bare skin of a hand. All was a test, and the human laboratory was amazing to Jay.

Giant Dad was quiet as he and Jay proceeded to visit the home of the "near dead." Jay thought it funny. *So close to an ending but on the edge of the eternal knowing*. Closer to actual living than anything ever described to man before, the thrill of stepping into the eternal dimension. Oh, how Jay longed for it. Never feeling loved or wanted on this earth, but there, he knew the lover of his soul and longed to be in his presence. This was not Jay's day; it was the nearing of a fellow member of the church. So many throughout this world would journey home on this night, but not Jay; he had been shown many things, and going home was not one of them. Thankfully, he was allowed to tag along with one of God's great warriors. There would come a day Jay hoped to be as valiant. "Son," Giant Dad broke the silence, "how would you like to preach for me one Wednesday night?" Stunned beyond words, Jay looked in the direction of this mighty man of God and wondered if the words just spoken had truly been said at all. Calmness came over Jay as he heard himself respond positively, "Sure, I think I'd like that." Giant Dad just smiled and nodded as they turned into the drive of the soon to be traveling saint of God. Tonight, another warrior would be called home, a job well done.

Jay's freshman year at hope to be high was starting out fast. On the other hand, his personal journey of faith was a war within one's self on a daily basis. To define or even attempt to find the line that joins the dual existence was so clouded that the daily doses of pouring rain only made the addiction of creating the greatest persona of all time an exhilarating challenge that Jay came to love. Yes, the word so far from his darkened existence was now coming to life in a way only hoped but never expected. Was it possible that Jay could maintain this light of faith and still control the darkened desires that would stir so often in a man of such a young age? To love something was to *own, possess, control, abuse, neglect, and cast aside* once drained of all human emotion, except one, all that could be left was the sobbing empty hull. This is where Jay found peace in his darkness. Empty, sobbing alone, he would meet the one who loved him so, who died for him to take away the sins of the world. Only broken in his presence was Jay allowed to exist. Anything else would require *"the end."*

Jay's freedom at hope to be high allowed an air of royalty that suited him to a tee, tall and good-looking, a striking smile that left young girls giggling and older ones wondering. He paraded his lovable charming persona to all areas throughout. His presence demanded acceptance, and with acceptance came jovial banter that all would enjoy so greatly that departing was always resounded to "Come back anytime, great to see you, and have a great day, Jay." Teachers, coaches, principals—all respected the light that was in this tall, handsome, warm, welcoming young man. Jay was a part of youth they wish they could all revisit—to be just a freshman and yet to be so popular with everyone loving them except the upper class boys, as they knew what Jay was up to better than Jay knew himself. They had been there to some degree. They knew the power he could possess, and they hated him for it. But hatred, this was something Jay loved to live with, what he enjoyed. To be hated was to live life to the fullest. The more he was hated, the more he could love himself, all of him, the greatest to ever darken the hallways of hope to be high.

13

THE ATHLETE

Hope to be high was a standard high school for country living in the early seventies. You had your homeroom where things got started. Bells would ring, and out into the day, all would go looking for the next great adventure at their new home away from home. Jay loved it here due to the intellectual vacuum that has made the majority of students babbling messes. He loved to walk up to perfect strangers and starting a conversation of life's intimacies while gently placing his hand on some area of exposed skin. Their reactions were amazing. Some would almost stop breathing while others would respond affectionately, exposing a wanting that Jay enjoyed very much, allowing Jay access, if wanted. Making a note of the more free-spirited females, these encounters between classes became the most fun he would have throughout the day.

Gym class at hope to be high was a wonderful time of day, guys against guys all seeing who was the biggest and the toughest, strongest or the fastest, letting the coaches who mainly taught these classes see the prospects of future school victories. Jay had been reassigned in his gym class, and now he knew why. It just so happened that he ended up in the class taught by the boy's varsity coach, wanting to see just how good this freshman was firsthand. No problem, Jay would end up being an athlete of his dreams, a contender who would not stop, one who must exceed all expectations; Jay had to. He never competed against anyone else. They were all losers. Jay competed against his own darkness. "You crybaby, you sissy, you'll never be anything. You are worthless. I hate you. Get out of my sight." Jay would prove to the world how great he was. All would love him, and all would call his name.

Ego is not the word for Jay. He was so far past that, as all would proclaim. He was something they had never seen before. All sports or any sport, he was the one they wanted and soon to be picked as captain to all competitions. Jay was adored as a leader, especially by the other classmate boys. Jay knew what to say and how to address the sensitive issues. He had heard so much negative banter that offending was the last thing on Jay's mind. He carefully nurtured the shy and damaged, knowing how they felt and where they came from, building the egos of the good but not so good to a place where their confidence was beneficial to all. Jay wanted to win more than anything else but was willing to lose for the experience of elation on the faces of those who rarely did. Jay was thrilled to celebrate the less celebrated. He knew the joy of finally being accepted. His holy acceptor was his joy.

The varsity coach made it clear that Jay was not to play football due to the possibility of injury just before the worshiping season. Basketball was worshiped and on a level that left everything else behind here at hope to be high. Even though Jay's athletic ability in football was amazing, it was a sport not really celebrated. The varsity football team had not won a game in a decade or more, and Jay agreed the benefits of worship was too great a risk to miss out on. During gym, the guys would attempt to talk Jay into joining their losing efforts, but Jay's deal with the head coach would stay where they both wanted it, behind closed doors.

Football season ended, and tryouts for basketball began. Jay was advised to try out for the junior varsity team of freshman and sophomores. No one had ever made the varsity team as a freshman. Jay did as advised but would shock the J. V. world as they knew it. All the work Jay and little Dave had put in was about to pay off. You see, no one knew Jay's potential. He practiced and worked like no other, driven by the internal burning fire to succeed, and to prove once and for all that defeat was not in his vocabulary.

Making the J. V. team was cake for Jay. He worked harder, longer, and with a light of joy that confused the rest of the team. They thought, *Why was he so happy all the time?* The coach was rat racing them to death, trying to get them to quit, and all Jay could do was cheer everyone on—so positive that he wanted all to make the team, but only twelve would be picked, who would have the courage to dig past the pain, a feeling Jay loved so dearly that to feel it was to know he was alive. Living between life and death was a world of pain that was embraced as a long-lost love. To feel its ever bitter breath upon his life was to inspire greatness at every turn, to be more than anyone else, to never pause at the edge but to gleefully leap into the unknown. This was something so foreign but yet inspiring to the rest of the boys that with all they had left was to leave something more precious than gold on that cold gym floor, a pool of sweat identified as themselves, knowing they could have tried no harder, giving all in return for nothing—nothing is promised, only earned.

Team cuts were now final. Starters were identified, and of course, Jay was immediately picked as one of the two captains. There was no doubt to where the light shown brightest. The exemplary athleticism on display was a joy for all to see, but all was not available. Jay knew better than to flash brilliance in the presence of the common. This would be unveiled during games of importance, allowing praise from all in attendance but with just one jewel at a time. Everything at once? No. They were not deserving of such greatness. They would gladly take what Jay would give them and love him the more for it. Face it, it's all about the love, the love that stained the darkest walls was a love worth sharing with all. Oh, how Jay loved to hate them all.

The gymnasium would be electric on game nights. The girls would play first, and by the time the boys got out there, the place would be rocking. At seventy-five inches, Jay was turned into the team's center, a position normally held by the tallest of the squad as well. That just happened to be Jay. He would guard and play inside where the main battles were, and truthfully, Jay enjoyed every elbow thrown as well as received. Much could be hidden with the correct body placement.

The four-month season would fly by, and with a winning record, Jay had made the local papers almost weekly. Using different strategies and shots, he elevated his game to the joy of all who attended the weekly worship meetings. Jay loved to read about himself weekly and basked in the brilliance of self-worth for only him to see. In public, Jay was as humble a person as any would ever meet, jovial and loveable, complementing any and all but himself. They could never see inside what Jay already knew. He was the one chosen to be elevated for the greatness of mankind. How great was yet to be determined.

The junior varsity season was over, and a first-ever occurrence in the round ball temple was about to take place. The head coach for the boy's varsity squad still had the playoffs to attend to and needed some young athleticism to overcome a portly squad who, though efficient, could barely clear a ten-inch vertical. Up came Jay and the other J. V. captain, a guard. This was a first for this educational institution. No freshman had ever played on the varsity, and that was the last of that saying. Jay attempting to fit in along with his humble personality was accepted by all, and all loved him as if he had been a part of the team the entire year. Things were quickly changing, and Jay was going to be in the center of it. The boy's team did well but was soon knocked out of the playoffs. Jay should have been given more playing time, was the way he saw it, but all was fun, and the bonding was fantastic.

The varsity girls still playing meant a road trip, so the guys got together on the country club golf course from a back road with inside information revealing that after the weekend tournament, kegs of cold beer were still left on the course. This was a first for this impressionable boy who would turn fifteen in a couple of months. So why not have a beer or two? What could it hurt? But could it remove the hurt? As glass by glass, the elated feeling began to dominate and would release a new side of this celebrated young man, a side of want and need, a new darkness that had a required taste and that required tasting a lot more.

Jay put the old charm to work, and seeing he was now part of the varsity team, his parents allowed him to go out of town with the supporting fan base that mostly consisted of older classmates, including cheerleaders and pep squads. This was going to be exciting and life-changing for Jay, just being voted the best-looking male freshman along with some advice from an upper classman. Jays top-shelf days of snooping and hoping was about to become reality. His friend had told him who and why. All Jay need do was to accomplish the mission. What could go wrong? Everything was lining up, a little too perfectly. This new darkness was at work here, and Jay was just too naive to see it. He truly believed he was in control.

Conversation after conversation, Jay was convincing his dad that the true path was the only path for him. Memorization, application, and covering fornication became the confused road that Jay would travel publically and privately. Girls were now starting to notice a change in the looks Jay would give them. Six months ago, it was cute and funny, but now they saw the eyes of a man wanting to get out of the fourteen-year-old prison. *Trapped* was the word best used to describe the pent-up frustration of this raging hormone of a man. Feelings were overwhelming, spiritual callings almost hypnotic, the road less traveled peaceful and inviting. It was one Jay had come to rely on, to rest on. The shady lane of truthfulness was a place he was well familiar. It would not be enough.

14

TEMPTATION

Jay enjoyed preaching every once in a while for his dad at the little country church. He was spirit-filled and even teaching Sunday school classes when needed. He loved to study his Bible and the closeness with his Holy Spirit was amazing, Jay often wondered if everyone had a relationship like his, but he would soon learn that the relationship is an individual thing, personal, very special. So loved by Jay, he wished he could stay this close forever, famous last wish!

The weekend for the big game had come, and Jay's freedom was riding out with a group of kids who had turned an old school bus into a traveling recreational vehicle. Along for the ride was an upper-class girl, the one his friend had mentioned. She seemed great, and everyone was having a good time on the road. That's when the farm came into view, Boone's Farm, that is. For those unfamiliar, rejoice, for the multitude of apple, strawberry, and grape harvesters, welcome to the messed-up mind of youth. The petting game became popular with Jay and the pretty upper-class mate. The more farm, the more pets that were allowed out to play, chatty chickens, groping geese, playful licking puppies, and then the big pig, and we'll just call him Jaybo.

The fans arrived at the hotel where the roving RV parked to allow access to the multiple rooms of students there to pray for the team. Jay, on the other road, decided to hook up with a pal who just happened to not only have a room but also was known to weed the garden for his favorite farmer friends. Looking to get in a little extra work, Jay thought he would attempt this weeding thing. They all got together, and once the weeds were put together, they decided to set that weed on fire. Next thing Jay knew, he was lying on the floor of the hotel room, door open, classmates walking by to see the weed jobs laughing uncontrollably and wrestling with a couple of girl weed assistants. *Man, this was turning out to be a great day*, Jay thought. *For everything, there is a season.*

Seeing as how the big game wouldn't get started until the next afternoon, the laughing season went on well into the evening. It wasn't even seven, and Jay had accomplished more debauchery in the last ten hours as to change his reputation forever in a "good" way, some would say. Many desired this way, but this kind of darkness was new to Jay, Jay welcomed anything that made him feel alive or loved, and both of those items were quickly checked off his list. The things they all wanted to do were a fresh new atmosphere with a lustful space of freedom to be welcomed by all. Breathe deep and take the plunge, show no hesitation. It was new. Jay wanted to try anything that could change the hate he would feel, the hate he always felt.

The evening dance continued with a beautiful tempo well into the night, spirits flowing, gardening of weeds at different intervals, burning the fires or, as some would say, the candle at both ends. In the midst of this tango of life, Jay ended up needing a shower in which one young classmate he barely knew was more than willing to share her room for such a ritual cleansing. Her roommates were out and about on the dance floor of life, allowing Jay the opportunity for a shower serenade. It was truly music to the rhythmic ears; a pace and tempo that would become classic one day, a masterpiece as it would be retold.

Opportunities for a memorable evening spanned well into the night, making the rounds with an attitude of gratitude, groping willing participants here and even more willing participants there. Jay knew this weekend would be marked with those known only as legends. Masses from hope to be high would speak of this fornication fest with sounds of reviled amazement in their voices and looks of wanting in their eyes. Oh, how they would dream of ever having the opportunities to become one of the endeared, one of the few, the famous, and to be the leading man of the show. The performance displayed was a far cry from the top dusty shelves—a star was born.

"Larger than life" was now the reputation that followed Jay around. So many things had happened during that weekend trip, and now when people saw him, they were into his personal life, knowing things that Jay enjoyed doing and wanting to be a part of his world. Problem was that he was not in control of this new world. It was different. Yes, he excelled in his multiple performances throughout the past weekend. Even now, many new older and bolder girls were confronting him on the evaluation provided for them from his farm-friendly classmate so much to the point as to enquire a time slot for themselves. Of course, this elevated the "already way too elevated" ego of this superstar, allowing him a confidence he really did not need, but so goes life, and here comes Mr. Fantastic!

Fifteen came without any fanfare except from the ones who liked to take his mind off of reality. Jay had come to learn that the time spent playing on the farm was a time that the painful reality of life would fade into a distance. He, of course, would excel at all his efforts, performing to the best of his abilities, wanting to always be loved and adored and once receiving the applause and adoration, would turn cold to the audience who just moments before had loved him. He knew this type of love was not real, but it felt more real than anything touchable here on earth. It was addictive. He had to have it. They clamored all over him, praising and wanting to be next to him, to love him, to love the performance, but all Jay could do in sincerity was perform. He was good at it all as it consumed him.

Would this world of plays become the avenue of escape from the darkness of years gone by? Would there ever be a theater to which Jay could finally take one last bow and then walk quietly into the normal world his inner being called for on a daily and even more frequent basis? The world of truth that all who were close to him avoided like the proverbial plague, the taboo of truth. It seemed as the darkness of the road he had just recently embraced was nothing compared to the avoidance of truth. Over the short span of Jay's life, he had seen truth met with condemnation, a passed judgment without thought or, as the world he often confided in always stated, prayer. Where was the prayer?

The remainder of his freshman year was quick just as the descent into darkness. Time was now a blur. Things were happening so fast that reality was taking on a life of its own, and at the same time, fantasy was consuming the idle thoughts left behind. Jay was becoming so encased in the perverse battles that the role he once lavished was now drifting farther from sight than at any time before. He actually felt as if he might lose this cherished light forever, replacing it with desires that controlled almost every waking thought. How had he fallen so far so fast? Where was the bottom, and was it avoidable? So many questions, way too many scenarios that continued to play over and over in his ever-storming mind, but the war now was with this man. No other way to say it. He was now performing as a man, and as with men, there are *consequences.*

Summer had finally come, and Jay was more determined now than ever before to seek the light, to become one with the true love of all creation. He dug into the Word to find his foothold, something that he could carry in his heart that would make a difference in the battles he so easily lost. Surely, he was not in this alone! Here, here is the Word, the truth, the Bible had the truth. He read the words aloud to himself, "If you love me, keep my commandments. And I will pray the Father, and he will give you another helper that he may abide with you forever—the Spirit of truth, whom the world cannot receive, because it neither sees him nor knows him, but you know him, for he dwells with you and will be in you." Jay would come to love the words written by John the beloved, the Spirit of truth. Yes, Jay had received Jesus during that hot summer revival, but it was the Spirit of truth who came and indwelled with Jay. He now had the strong foothold of truth, but to always keep the commandments of truth, this would be the catalyst of many internal wars to come, and for a fifteen-year-old with the darkness of pain that none should ever have to bear, he would submit time and time again to the siren of darkness, battling, praying, and cursing the day he was born. Longing for an easy way out, any way out. The torture of being hated and yet being so loved was a madness of performances that masked the truth of who Jay was and now had become. He sat alone contemplating, peace, yes, eternal peace.

15

PEACE

Summer of sweet fifteen, Jay's time, the time of year where this larger-than-life personality could finally seek the path of truth, and hopefully, somewhere down that long spiritual road, maybe he could find peace. Jay could let the macho guard down and be the humble portrayer of love and understanding; he received such gratification from serving others, helping ease their pain as if to reduce the sting of suffering. This was not a cure but an avenue that he loved to take, to see in the eyes of the elderly a joy of being recognized once more as they once were. Each of them having a story to tell, and Jay was so willing to sit and listen to the amazing tales. They were great in their own time, celebrated by churches, cities and governments, leaders, and bands of warriors, facing death and then coming home to live as if what they had accomplished, or what they had went through, never really existed at all. Jay could see those familiar stares, ones he also shared. Even though young, Jay understood the distance, the look of unbelievable days gone by but still so close and real its powerful hold could consume the spinner of yarns into a statue of silent stone, alone there in the darkest of minds.

Studying his weekly lessons in preparation of the upcoming Sunday, Jay found great comfort in knowing he was bettering himself and living as the good book stated he should live, keeping his eyes on Jesus and in the Holy Word. Giant Dad, being a great example of this, always studied long hours throughout the week even so much as to bring wrath from his redheaded companion. He had become so accustomed to the verbal attacks that Giant Dad could quickly change course to direct praises of beauty and supreme holiness to the altar of egos, Redhead Momma. Jay was astounded and encouraged to see the manipulation of this maniac of alter egos, first hot then cold, and before too long, if you knew how to play that favorite song, you could see the ego of the most loving mother in the world. Yes, she was the greatest of all loves. Just ask her bipolar self and stand by.

Jay's attention to this metamorphosis could possibly allow for a future with a lot less confrontations with Redhead Momma. He watched as Giant Dad played and swayed like the cobra, moving slowly back and forth, deadly but, for the moment, not feared. It was all done with a lot of lies with a little bit of truth thrown in. Giant Dad would allow the harshest of words concerning spiritual growth and just how great of a man he thought he really was in that little backwoods church. Why, without her, they would have kicked you out a long time ago, as she had stated. Giant Dad just kept that wonderful peace about him and agreed. "Yes, dear," he said as humble as any man he would ever see. But at fifteen, Jay hated her for berating Giant Dad like that. Jay didn't mind being put down like that; he deserved it. He was breathing and was hated for it. It was just her thing—so insecure but then so arrogant as to defy the world along with its creator.

The regular routine of summer was laid out as a perfect play. During the week, Jay would work on the chores Giant Dad assigned, marking off the trees in the adjacent woods he wanted removed along with digging up their roots, tilling the entire area and planting grass. Normally, around a half acre was the goal each summer along with the garden upkeep and maintenance of the remaining front and backyards. Jay enjoyed working hard outside in the woods every day, a place where he could always meet with his helper and talk to the one who knew Jay better than he knew himself. It was peaceful at times, then came the play called twister.

You could hear the screaming and yelling coming from inside the house, and who in their right mind would want to jump into the eye of the storm? Why, Jay of course. He had come to realize that serving meant where he could help the most, and if Redhead Momma was having a spiritual ego of crazy, it was Jay's responsibility to confront the mental demons and serve as a distraction away from the now-cowering brood. Redhead Momma spotted Jay as soon as he came in the door, sweat covering his shirtless seventy-five inch frame, tall and skinny, the perfect target for an already out-of-control Tasmanian momma. With leather belt in hand, she was demanding to know who was making all that noise. Jay believed the noise in her head would get so loud as to drive her crazy.

Jay often wondered if the battles he faced in his own mind also consumed the mind of the sometimes very lovable redhead momma. Did she actually believe no one loved her? He had heard her say as much on multiple occasions to Giant Dad. Accusing him over and over again of never having loved her and stating that she didn't need anyone to love her, which of course was the cue for all the little subjects to state their rehearsed lines of adoration and once again allowing this storm to calm and the peasants permitted to return home from the spontaneous worship service. When calm, she was a saint, but there was something within that drove this beautiful redheaded woman into the scariest of people you would ever want to meet. The eyes were steely, her demeanor strong and unshakable and harder than anything you would ever volunteer to go up against.

Back to reality, Jay recognized the upbeat tempo of this storm out of control. He needed to act and oftentimes would without even thinking, attempting to take the storm in his direction and most times succeeding. "Please calm down, Momma," Jay heard himself belt out probably a little too loud, but it definitely worked, as the wind was changing, and the storm was headed right up Jay's tornado alley. Guess the word *please* was missed all together. Eyes of fire focused his way with words of venom spitting into the heart of Jay's soul. He kept his calm. Seeking a truce of peace was his only option available. But she did not allow it on the bargaining table. Her arm quickly drew the belt thorough the air, and with nothing more than reflex, Jay allowed the belt to wrap around his arm, jerking it out of the storm's eye, standing defiant against the destructive F-5 with eyes of fire all his own. Jay demanded the same intensity as his mother before him. Erecting himself to a height of domination, Jay saw her look of amusement; she seemed pleased with herself as if this entire act of defiance was, in some way, planned the whole time. In her squirrel cage, the nuts were abundant, and Jay felt as if he just stored a great load himself. Man, this was crazy!

Peace now restored. Jay once again worked the day away while having a conversation for the ages. He needed something explained, so he talked to the Holy Spirit in truth and understanding, then all would be expedited.

Would it all make sense? No way. Jay was still getting acclimated to the hot and cold side of talking with the Spirit. Sometimes it would come to him as clear as the wind blowing past his ears, and other times, nothing, just peace which Jay greatly enjoyed but still needing answers to so many questions. This day, the question was how long he had to live. Everything got calm so quickly. Redhead

Momma returned to her gossip shop and not heard of again. Jay enjoyed the hard sweating work, and even Little Bro came out to give a hand picking up some of the freshly tilled rocks as to say, "Thanks, big brother." It was a good feeling, but answers did not come. How can one have peace without having the answers?

Jay worked until dusk alone, seeing as how Little Bro got bored with rock gathering fairly quick. Oh, to entertain the mind of a twelve-year-old, one who just turned twelve by the way. Jay drifted away, remembering the years of not too long ago, a time that was blank to Little Bro and very dark to the remembering minds of that life-changing moment. Jay knew one sister who remembered, but the little sis had no idea. She would remember bits and pieces and sometimes inquire of these fleeting shades of light just to be assured by the older two that it was nothing more than a nightmare, one lived by Jay each and every night. But now, there was someone to talk to, one who knew the truth, the comforter that would change the way Jay looked at that horrible night, that night of screams and blood. Crucify him, crucify him!

Blasting through to reality, Jay looked this way and that, attempting to control the ability to breathe while the screams of the masses cried out to crucify him. A dream, a nightmare, where was he? Still in his room on red dirt road. He was not the one being persecuted. Jay took a deep breath, attempting to understand he was home in his room with Little Bro fast asleep close by. Then remembering bits and pieces of the horrible nightmare, one darker than any Jay had before, the innocent Jesus saw him so clearly, not saying a word as the throngs of people cried out to crucify him, a sacrifice to be made. Just as a sacrifice of that terrible night, it had to happen. Without the big bang, there would have been no salvation, no directional change of so many, yet how many more to come?

Jay sat in the dark, contemplating this new revelation, running the events of those long-ago weeks over and over in his mind. Holy Spirit, what would life be like if those events never took place? Praised as the one to provide, but in reality, just as life goes, the provisions or the ability to provide were all false—man attempting to glory in himself, believing he is more than God, placing himself upon an undeserved throne when he should be kneeling at the throne of good and just. Only one is worthy to be praised, and it is not mankind.

Jay's mind was afire, his understanding coming into focus. It had to be the sacrifice of man's own ego to allow humble access to another wise egotistical world. God had provided a way to work good into the life of these who had lost control, never truly realizing God was in control the whole time. Jay's excitement was too much to contain. "It had to happen this way," he told himself. "Salvation would come to many, but at a cost. There was always a cost." Giant Dad took the shot that Redhead Momma delivered so that not only this family, but many more families would one day be delivered. Jay thought of those he had already seen come forward for salvation at the calling of God. What about the families that Jay would touch, being used for good in such a dark world that sometimes the darkness is used for light? This was amazing. This was the peace of mind Jay was searching for to combat the darkness so deep within. He was on his way to a glorifying relationship with the helper who would never leave or forsake.

Life is just not that simple as Jay would find out. Yes, there was peace in knowing God's will for salvation and how he could use evil for good, but there is no magic button to erase the trauma of such a young mind, especially with a mind no one wanted to talk with. *Attempting to bring it up will cause more harm than good*, Jay thought. The dark voices had no problem with allowing peace in worshiping; they were powerless to stop it, but living life day-to-day was an area disguised as of peace, quiet and beautiful. Jay would learn just how beautiful and peaceful the roaring lion could be.

16

ALONE

The mind of fifteen-year-old Jay was in no case the same mind as most his age, and summer made it that much more difficult. The conversations within himself raged from, *Holy Father, will this insufferable condemnation of a mind ever turn itself from darkness back into light?* Understand this, the war that rages within the darkened mind of a combustible youth will in time implode or explode. Just pray you're not standing nearby.

The weeks ran pretty much the same during these hot summer months. Jay was doing the assigned chores Monday through Wednesday, allowing the middle of the week to require a filling of the spiritual tank. Jay loved going to church on Wednesday evening, singing some good old hymns about when we all get to heaven right down to the sweet by and by. Preaching was always special with Giant Dad giving as good during this meeting as with any other. Jay loved the way the Holy Spirit would take over after a couple of clumsy joke-filled moments. Then hold on to your seats, the atmosphere would change; the intensity of the words that carried a calling to all within hearing range and this range could have been across the road at some points. Clear and intentional, the Word of God would flow, hitting its targets with such accuracy as to see the initial impacts as those just speared would shift and cast their gaze anywhere other than back into the holy light, the man of God's direction.

After the preaching was over, choir practice began, allowing the youth some time to get better acquainted with each other. It was during this time that many of the member's children sought to learn more about Jay.

Yes, they all had heard their parent's comments while reading the evening paper describing this amazing athlete and the praises of hopeful years to come. That was their parents' opinions, and Jay was exceptionally gifted at knowing the true person just by having a five-minute conversation. Parents are rarely true to their individual form while discussing other people, as all saw need to disguise the otherwise obvious, veiled to reveal themselves in a positive light, the whole while condemning the actions of others unaware. "Self-righteousness is not an option," as the preacher man would say. We must all rely on a redeemer.

Hanging out with the youth was always playful and entertaining. Jay so loved the young girls as they would get in small groups and giggle to such a crescendo of excitement, allowing all to know that these only dreamed of that very first kiss. So cute and adorable but still the same hunger that resided in Jay would size up the possibilities for the future, knowing good and well what a difference a short amount of time can make. This specific type of calculation was a never-ending disease that controlled the inner darkness of Jay's mind; it was an attempt to seek out love in the physical form that was an illusion on red dirt road. Done with the familiar "show me yours, and I'll show you mine" of kids play with family members. This world of darkness was the unimaginable vulgarity of the adult lifestyle, one so dearly embraced by Jay but alone to deal with the consequences of an overriding hunger whose consumption would eat away at the very soul of this young convert.

Alone once again with thoughts of Wednesday evening's possibilities, today was the beginning of a weekend full of promise. Working on Thursday evenings meant freedom for high-charging Jay, and he had gone from bussing tables to assistant head cook in just two years. Assistant head cook sounds pretty important, but really, Jay just got to make the hush puppies, French fries, and those skin-burning livers. Man, did they like to pop hot grease. Great thing about it all, Jay stood at a window, leading out into the seating area where the waitress would pick up the freshly ordered seafood, and on display, that's right, was seventy-five inches of adorable.

Jay worked very hard for the money he made, so posing and flirting was not an option. Jay had to be the best at everything no matter what. He would give all or die trying. This was the world of Jay's mind that left him deeply alone to weigh out the consequences of each and every action. Of course, this won him additional accolades—ones he really didn't need. He knew if he could please the unappeasable country dad, he would leave everyone else ecstatic. Normally, it would take three attempts to please this difficult man, but as life would disclose, it was well worth the aggravation, for Jay anyway, or as he would come to be known "Mr. Perfect." With everything having to be just right, it was his special, crazy little world, and only he alone could make sense of it all, magical.

The display at the fish restaurant was only to allow pleasant viewing for the masses of young to old ladies. Spotting a hardworking man at such a young age caused minds of possible outcomes to develop and to imprint trustworthiness. This plan was developed so quietly and secretly with such precision as to not alarm the ever-trusting ladies in waiting but allowing positive thoughts throughout their homes and even into their rooms of dreams.

Jay amazed himself over and over again with how easy it was to paint a deceptive picture that all would want to buy, to touch, to own. To enjoy the painting was possible. The picture was so perfect that it left most men doubting, but ladies, they would covet to own it one day, if not for themselves, then for the ones they loved—so close but just beyond reach, retracting of fingers just to feel it slip through their wanting hands. Never would this perfect painting be owned, just out of reach forever.

He was amazed at how simple it was to contemplate the total dominance of the female species and how satisfying it had become to use the false love they offered and turn so quickly what they believed as beautiful into the emptiness of reality. This loveable return was corrupted and damaged beyond all they could possibly believe even to the point that, in many ways, left them believing it was their own inability to appreciate perfection that caused this turn of event.

Each weekend was becoming the same, working through Saturday night, messing with the waitresses and revealing the not-so-shy young man they hoped Jay would be. Jay allowed them peaks into the maze of his mind but only deep enough to intrigue; anything deeper would cause fear to quickly consume the calming effect. Intoxicating as it was, the darkness of the solitude would expose the raw edges of adulthood that was Jay, the impossible one to love. Without this hope of love, or the illusion thereof, all could easily be lost, the play that must be performed to the individual and must not lose its potency for fear of multiple critics. The illusion of love Jay had lived with this his whole life. Well, what he remembered and now just wanted to embrace the loneliness that he had so endeared. Holiness verses darkness, how they were not the same was definitely a miscommunication in Jay's mind. Both requiring dependence, how could there be one without the other? Even the good book said it was impossible for mankind to rid himself of the evils of this contradicting world. Knowing full well that the term *mankind* meant women just as men allowed Jay to dive even further into the lonely darkness in preparation of his next performance. This had all become one large game to Jay, playing his part with such internal applause that within the confines, he had become the greatest to ever perform. Watching the population through these rose-colored glasses allowed for some of the most amusing of times there alone in Jay's mind.

17

SUNDAYS

There was always something about that seventh day of the week. Jay loved it, as it was a time of reflection and singing songs that worshiped a Holy God along with a Savior. The songs of hope and faith that could ease the pain of this earthly existence, promises of a land far away where there would be no more suffering—oh, how Jay would sing to the rafters these songs of faith. It was faith believing that had so dramatically changed his existence those few years ago. Enabling a relationship beginning in sacrifice, entering into knowledge of a guaranteed never-ending relationship with a holy helper to guide and assist. Through his studies and with an unending desire to accompany the preacher man where ever his next calling was to be, Jay absorbed and became dependent to the promises of the Holy Bible.

Studying was a celebration for the weary mind of Jay, allowing him to see the failures of so many but still receiving the grace promised by such a loving God. A God who so loved the world that he sent his one and only Son to redeem the creation that mirrored this eternal existence but who also had recklessly denied the path of holy being called out by the great I AM. To read some of the passages was not enough, Jay had to start from the beginning and follow through to the end, the end where he had studied but more confused himself than at any other interrelating point. Revelations was not the easiest of reads, so for one who seeks truth of all things and internally decides his own importance to these findings, Jay decided that Genesis, the beginning, was the logical starting point.

Deeper and deeper he would go into the Word of God. Preacher Man Dad had said that it was the inerrant word, no mistakes, and true from start to finish. This was turning out to be one summer of reading for the ages. The creation of all then came the fall—mankind at fault for disobeying, jealously, coveting, and drunkenness.

Jay was so deeply entwined with every word he was reading right up to the point of Leviticus, Numbers, and Deuteronomy. So many times he almost bounced his head off the supporting desk, or should he say the snoring desk, because this was rapidly becoming a true snooze fest.

What happened to the excitement of the worldwide flood that has left sea sediment on the highest peaks of all the mountains of the world? The covenant with God and the newly named Abraham whose family would be greater than the stars of the sky or the sands of the sea. The "near sacrifice" of his son at the place of the once Holy of holies of today, the deceit of a twin brother named Jacob, and the changing heart of his elder twin Esau. The name given to Jacob there in the desert before confronting his twin brother Esau—to actually be named Israel with the clouded actions of life chosen by one so esteemed left Jay confused. How is it possible that God could use such men as Jacob? A name in Hebrew which means deceiver, then Joseph with his coat of many colors became one of Jay's favorite stories, a story of truth and love that God had used for good.

The studies found Jay so involved with adventures of Moses, the Egyptian Hebrew prince who obeyed and delivered the chosen children of Israel, so as one would expect, Jay jumped the books of boredom, promising himself and his Holy Spirit to return and study again one day soon, not too soon. Remembering the exciting, fifty chapters of Genesis, Jay longed to see the interactions of God Almighty, and the best of the fallen men he would use to accomplish his will. Joshua was the mighty warrior of God who would fail to obey the commands of complete destruction. Judges would come to monitor the evildoing of man and attempt to stay within the laws of Jehovah while at the same time, some would fall to the desires of mankind with not even the vow of the Nasserites holding one of the more famous of them to obey the will of God. Failure left and right, Jay would see more hope in the women God used to develop faith for his people. Ruth, not born of Israel, would become the lineage for the greatest of all, Jesus! Over and over again, the same truth was revealed. It was not man who was prepared to serve a holy God, but a holy God who prepared the inadequate of mankind to serve him.

Sunday after Sunday of that summer drew Jay deeper into the Word of God. "Was it Old Testament God, or was it New Testament God?" some would ask as Jay so enjoyed discussing the Word that so enveloped his waking hours. To discern between old and new testament God is to say there are two different Gods, which is insulting to the original interpretation of one true God. God is God, and that's that—one Bible, one Father, one God. Sure Jay got the funny reference of going Old Testament on someone, but this was no laughing matter. This was the Word and working of God. Talking, reading, studying with a new best friend, the study Bible, understanding the revelation of a devout man of God coming into the world through the brokenhearted prayers of Hannah, a mother that was willing to give her son Samuel over to the priest Eli for a life of devout service, a service that would bring to pass the greatest city of all, the City of David, Jerusalem, the city of kings, the place of promised restoration of our returning Lord, Jesus. Man, if that don't light your fire, then your woods all wet. Come in out of the storm and find rest here among the truth, the living Word of God. Oh, how Jay loved it.

Sunday would be the starting day for those great old country revivals. Jay and Preacher Dad would get there early, setting up the Sunday school classes and finding a quiet place to pray. Preacher Dad always said that "if you're not willing to pray about it, don't blame God for not showing up to it." Jay loved to see Preacher Dad's eyes light up when talking about revival. Jay knew why amazing things would happen during that weeklong glory fest. Sunday afternoon with dinner on the grounds, tables lined up under that big oak tree with good food from all around, families' finest of vittles to the joy of every boy and girl, a blessing of such proportions that everyone would be smiling ear to ear as the first gospel quartet was just starting up. Now for all who are familiar with a great gospel singing, you know there is nothing to compare—even for a liberated mind such as Jay's, there was no defense. The music would get to playing and the singers to singing and about ten minutes into it the Holy Spirit to flowing, and everybody wants under the spout where the Holy Spirit poured out. Little miss old timey would get to shouting, and her hair would unravel and fall almost to the floor.

Why, she used to scare the devil out of Jay until he got used to her, and now he just waits and holds on.

Revivals every summer had been Jay's favorite for the last three years, anticipating the angels of glory in celebration of those new to the redeeming blood of Jesus Christ now having a relationship with a Holy God who would not leave us in the dark on the price that had to be paid, telling us point-blank on what it takes to become a Christian, a follower of Jesus Christ and not leaving us blowing in the breeze with the rest of the world who now declared that just being good was good enough. What in heaven's name is good enough? How cruel of a concept had the evil one come up with, good is good enough for heaven, an eternity with a Holy God who cannot and will not tolerate sin. How many lives would be lost to the fires of an eternal hell thinking they were good enough?

Jay knew the easy line, as did the rest of mankind. None of us are good, and everyone knows it. We have all lied to make ourselves look better, told that special someone things that we really didn't mean just to get our way. The girls with the fake crying to manipulate the men of their lives, from stealing that cookie to murdering someone with just the words of hate. We all have sinned and fallen short of the glory of God. Jay was just so grateful that there were those brave enough to face the deceptive evil lies and preach the truth in the life of Jesus Christ. "Thank you, big, fat sweaty preacher man, "Jay could hear himself say as tears rolled down his face to the second verse of "Just as I Am," knowing his prayers were answered, drifting back to the days when Jay's faith in prayer would become unwavering, at home in that red brick house on that red dirt road.

18

HOME

At the place where most called home was this never-ending battle for dominance, to be holy or get the holiness kicked out of you? With each moment of arrival, the same tension would develop deep within, and just as spinning a roulette wheel, all would wait with abated breath at the ticking time bomb of big red. There was no denying that the ruler of the house was Redhead Momma or as the remainder of the hillbilly family so endeared to her the name Big Red. She was larger than life, and if you enjoyed life more abundantly, it would behoove all to pay a tithe of welcome to this ever-present deity.

Preacher Man Dad was so devoted to the love of his life that to sicken Jay was to speak lightly. Over and over again, we would hear how the meat was cooked to tough only to hear the sugary response of "No, honey, this is delicious and very tender," and Giant Dad was right. If there was one thing that hillbilly woman could do, it was cook, good. No, it was great. Jay quickly admitted that this was the best of both worlds—not only did Big Red cook the main meals great, her desserts were worth fighting for, and if a pie hit the table, it was a done deal. Delicious! Still, over and over again, the game to please would be played. "I'm getting fat," Big Red would exclaim. "Oh no, Momma," one of the siblings would exclaim. Normally, the one closest due to cautionary survival of protecting one's body from harm. "You look great, yeah, Momma," the others would all chime in. If you knew the rules, the days were pretty normal, well as normal as living in a crazy house can be. A well-protected crazy house at that. Since moving to the red dirt road and attending school here in the country, not a single strange kid had ever spent the night. Big Red knew the rest of the world was not like ours, and she was sure to keep it out and never let anyone in until one day four years ago. Big Red wanted to bring a baby to this humble home. Jay was very confused during that time, and this was not helping matters in the least.

"How would you kids like a new baby in the house?" Jay remembered Redhead Momma saying. Sure, he was only eleven at the time, and none of the kids really knew what to say. Normally speaking to Redhead Momma was a gamble anyway, but this topic of conversation was right out of the *Twilight Zone*. Jay knew Redhead Momma couldn't have any more children. She almost died during a hysterectomy. She told that story every other month just to let all know they were lucky to have a momma at all. "Sure, Momma that would be great," Jay proclaimed, knowing this was the response she was looking for. The smile on her face let everyone know Jay had made the correct response while Dad just stood there, silent and smiling.

They came home from school a week later, and Momma was motioning for all to be quiet and to follow her. Back into Jay and Little Bro's room they went, and lying on the bed was this little red head sticking out from under a blanket, but something didn't look right. This baby was larger than a newborn, and then

Redhead Momma pulled back the cover. Jay and the other siblings stood there amazed at what was before them. Sure they had seen babies but never one like this. Redhead Momma sat down beside Baby Red and started to explain all they were seeing. Even an explanation was going to leave more questions than give answers, and all were dumbfounded as Momma explained.

Baby Red was a water-head baby with a tube running from her head down into her stomach. Her head was disproportionate to the rest of her body as to cause a gasp from Little sisters. All were instructed to be careful. Pulling the covers down a little more exposed a scar running across the lower back of Baby Red. "She was born with an open spine," Redhead Momma calmly explained and then removed the remaining cover to expose little feet facing the wrong way. Her feet were backwards. Jay's mind spun, feeling this wave of emotion rising within the normally composed performer. Tears welled as Redhead Momma explained that the doctors didn't believe she would live long, but she was family and was now home.

What had Jay just heard "she was family," what Redhead Momma meant by this was that Baby Red was her sister's daughter's child who didn't want to keep Baby Red because of birth defects. If there is one thing Jay knew about his momma, it was you did not mess with blood kin, and that was that. If they needed a whooping, then she would whoop them, but outside of the family, they all needed to steer clear of the big red tornado when it came to defending those she loved, and yes, in her own crazy way, Redhead Momma loved on a whole other level—one Jay never really understood but also never questioned.

Baby Red became the center of attention at the redbrick home. Doctors said she'd be lucky to live six months, so into the circle of prayer she was laid every night as the entire family held hands praying for a miracle. This would become the home Jay always loved to remember. Redhead Momma with a love so great that to hear her pray to this day would be like living in the presence of a saint. She was so different when praying for those she loved, and she loved to pray; it was as if when she spoke to Jesus, all the crazy was pushed aside, and the peace of heaven would overtake her soul. Jay loved his momma so much when she prayed; he had even heard her pray for him, and it wouldn't be the last.

Over and over again, the prayers of the humble with broken hearts were answered by a wonderful heavenly Father. Baby Red continued to live, going through multiple surgeries to turn her feet back around. She was such a strong little girl there in her half-body cast they ended up breaking and setting her feet three times before leaving them alone. Without feeling, she was paralyzed from the waist down never able to control her movements of nature, always depending on a good sense of smell and some discreetly placed protection. Over the years, Jay attempted to maintain his feeling for this new little member, not wanting to allow anyone in. It never worked. Just as Little Bro was allowed in, so now also was Baby Red. She loved Jay so much, and she made him laugh with the prettiest smile you ever saw. She was a great addition to the home.

The spiritual side of Jay developed so greatly during the younger days of Baby Red. The prayers along with the faith that Giant Dad and Redhead Momma would show put a grip on Jay's life and would never allow him to be the same. Living now in a home of good and crazy, years of developing faith confirmed, Jay had seen it and lived it, softening to the siblings but always performing for all else. There was laughter and goofing around until the noise got to loud, and off the fantastic road, this cruising set of crash-test dummies would fly once more, knocked wildly across the yellow line into oncoming traffic of the Big Red called Redhead Momma.

Things at home were pretty quiet as long as Jay and Little Bro stayed out of the house working or playing in the woods. Little Bro had grown to love the cool of the woods just as much as Jay, running up and down the creek, chasing snakes and trying to catch them up by their tails and popping their heads off the way Dad had showed them. Dad liked to show the boys things that needed to be kept from Redhead Momma, and they knew perfectly well what Dad meant when he said it. Little Bro sometimes would slip up and mention things that were not to be mentioned, but normally, Jay could catch him and cover. Little Bro was doing pretty good for a twelve-year-old. Wait till puberty hits, and then we'll see if his mind gets clearer or just a whole lot darker. *Prayerfully, not like mine,* Jay thought.

The darkness was always more prevalent while Jay was at the redbrick home. You see, living in the country, he could never escape the day of the big bang—that shattering moment that always found Jay alone and left him feeling as if he always would be. There was nothing earthly to combat the darkness. Sure there was prayer and meditation on the Word of God. This would always allow for some peace, but to maintain that pose of defense was impossible. Here at home, there were so many occasions to remind Jay that he was just a finger pull away, and the darkness kept this thought running through his mind night and day. Jay had seen it in his nightmares and even on the face of the one he loved to hear pray. The darkness was here to stay, and Jay was beginning to like it that way.

Reminders of darkness could be contained while working hard at home. No complaining, Jay knew better than to complain. If he wanted to hear about hard work, all he had to do was mention it, and off to the illegal labor camps we would go. Big Red had a story for everything, talking about supporting your entire family. Why, no one would have existed if not for Big Red back in the day. She was all in all the greatest woman to ever walk the earth, and with this, you must believe that without her, there would be no existence.

Now one thing Big Red did not like was the neighbors up the road letting their chickens get out. Those little beauties loved to trot down that red dirt road right into Big Red's garden for some beautiful, ripe tomatoes. The boys were directed once and for all that this must come to an end and to let Big Red know the next time they saw those chickens. It was a hot summer day, and Jay had just got through mowing the two-acre yard when here they came, trotting with delicious tomatoes in their tiny little minds. Jay found great delight in Momma's diverted anger; as long as it wasn't on him or the little ones he loved, he was more than willing to spill the beans. Once the chicken alarm sounded in hair-gossip central, Jay went back out on the front porch to spot the little unsuspecting invaders, oblivious to any surrounding danger. Jay took a seat on the handrail as he heard Big Red stepping out the front door, and then there it was, raised and pointed, tracking the bobbing bodies of dark and white meat. Jay now was beside the pistol of darkened fame. With such steely accuracy, the trigger was pulled, and the first bird flew wildly into the air, never letting up. Big Red reacquired her next target and, bull's-eye, another direct hit. Those two chickens were at least fifty yards away, trotting down the dirt road at an impressively hungry pace had just dreamed of their last meal. No doubt about it, those years long ago practicing how to shoot that gun had stuck. Shooting someone through a glass door was one thing, but this was a feat worthy of the lone ranger. Jay's mind spun wildly as those echoing blasts resounded throughout the valley. "What a shot, Mom!" Jay heard himself yell. "You killed them both with just one shot each." Jay was amazed and realized Big Red could hit whatever she wanted. Running was out of the question.

19

SUBSTANCE

Tenth grade had finally got here, and Jay thought no more freshmen crap—back to a place where adoration along with flirtation flowed like the biblical milk and honey. The place where everyone knew his name, as the new freshmen would whisper at his passing, wondering if they could ever become the greatness that was before them. If everyone only knew how messed up the mind of Jay had become, searching for a conscious light while walking in an ever-pressing darkness. The greatest performance from the world's greatest performer was yet to come. Everyone anticipated, soaking in the beautiful smile that told all there was some remote chance for even them—they could be the next in line, *to love the unlovable.*

This school year would get a quick start into the epic. All throughout summer, Big Red maintained the reins of freedom, allowing only the basic of prison breaks, and she would allow them as long as everyone knew she was allowing them. Dominance was drug for Big Red, and it was her personal little stash, she had to have it, and everyone knew she was willing to kill to get it and keep it. Things were cool as long as no surprises were thrown her way, and plenty of foreknowledge was delivered. Momma could handle that, but you come up on her at the spur of the moment, a stupid rookie mistake, as only one was allowed to ever tread these angered halls. That was Little Bro. Momma loved her little baby boy, and Jay knew better than attempt to use him. That would call down the thunder, and Jay had enough of that storm to last a lifetime.

Hanging out in the halls between classes, it was great to be with his little buddy Dave again, funny as the last time he'd seen him up at their old hangout. Playing B-ball was allowed by Big Red. She knew how good her son was getting. All the praise coming out of that gossip hair shop and Redhead Momma could take no credit for any of it. Jay was going to be special. Everyone knew it, especially Jay.

Seeing old friends once again was a delight. Easing Jay's mind as to realize all the work that had been put into last year was still viable. Still months away from the arena of worship, Jay had plenty of time to make his presence known, taking on some new classes this year, making life as easy and stress-free as possible. Typing seemed like a good idea: a class full of friendly girls and only a couple of guys who were comfortable enough to take it. This would be Jay's first year at art and drama though. It seemed easy enough. Drama would be right up Jay's alley, so easy to perform and to show what they all wanted to see but keep the best just out of reach.

Jay believed in testing to see where people stood, how close you allow them, what are the key words used in the telling of their lies, and how much pressure could they handle when reality sat right down in their lap. Everyone cracks. Everyone lies. All are deceptive in motives, and Jay was overjoyed at knowing the truth. This would always be Jay's drug of choice, the truth, and no one was capable to provide this drug on a full-time basis, but Jay would continue his search.

Art was a strange class. The teacher right out of college was very pretty with country road curves. This would be a distraction except for the fact that something was different about this young lady. She was shy and hiding something. Her stance was always defensive, attempting to hold up her voluptuous frame, but Jay knew this was not the reason. She was keeping something pulled deep inside and was afraid it was going to get out and destroy her. Jay was fascinated to the point of befriending but ignoring the outside beauty—it was the inside. That was where the real person lived, and Jay would find her out. The rest of art class composed of freshmen to seniors, and the mixture was a grab bag for each class. Now the projects were on the level of elementary age, absolutely childlike attempts to pull life out of the class and into the art. You could do stick figures and make good grades in this class, just like Jay wanted it, nice and easy. With these classes and the couple of had to haves, Jay was going to make the best out of the years to come.

Jay never needed to take home any books for the mandatory classes of English, math, and sciences. These were easy enough to just pay attention while in class and take the tests. A passing C was all that was required of the home Gestapo. As were easy in the fun classes, so Jay's report card actually looked pretty good, and that was all he needed to slide by and keep the warden off his back. The one thing about the redbrick home dictatorship was that if you seemed loyal to the leaders and accomplished all that was required, the allowance of freedom was granted to an extent. It was a very tricky balancing act, but the thrill was just how high you were willing to balance. Jay had no fear of heights and truly enjoyed the rush. Something was becoming a big problem.

To enjoy this rush, this feeling of exhilaration required much more than just the natural ingredients produced from within the human body. Sure adrenalin could be obtained by asserting dominance over the masses in anticipation of retaliation, but the problem being was that the reputation and pure stature of Jay were enough to ward off most any and all responses of aggression. He found force was not the best way to gain all he wanted from the people. Acting had an effect on all. The jovial responses Jay was so quick to come up with allowed everyone the opportunity to participate in the deliciously humorous life and times of this budding star athlete.

Jay was friendly and sociable to one and all, seeing no disadvantage to separate tall to small or thin to round. These were humans, and all felt pain. Jay understood pain like most others would not. If happiness was based on feelings, then bankrupt would be the condition of the financial institution known as Jay. Pain replaced love. Words were of no comfort due to all being tainted in lies, truth not to be found anywhere, from anyone. Jay knew the price to be paid for getting his hopes up. He knew he must always show the fictitious funny man to all who would pay the admittance. The show was worth the price for the attendee, but the performer who gave all would end up costing a little more than he had to give with each performance. In time, there would be nothing left, just the hull of a man with the desire to cease to exist until the final curtain.

Handling the throngs of hope to be high worshippers along with entertaining the fish fry crowd was taking its toll—especially during the week when it was time to allow the real Jay a chance to mingle with the holy of holy rollers known as brothers and sisters. Jay loved going to church, bowing his head and reaching for the always accessible holy one. Repentance was all that stood in his way, so with little effort due to minor teenage sins, Jay could humbly repent and access the real and one true love. God's provision of His one and only Son as a sacrifice made worshipping simple with humble repentance. Jay could get right back in there and really enjoy the relationship of truth with God.

Some Wednesday nights, Jay was allowed to preach. Man, was that a rush for a fifteen-year-old. There was such a great difference if Jay was prayed up and living right, but if he had active sin in his life, he might as well been out on a deserted island all by himself, words falling flat with no spiritual lift at all. Sundays he assisted in teaching classes and enjoyed being close to God, and in his relationship with the Holy Spirit, here was the true friend walking with him along the way, and some days, that way would get cloudy or even have a storm of evil move in, yet His Spirit was never really far away; it was only as far as Jay had traveled in the wrong direction.

Friend of farmers rural and domestic alike, Jay made it a point to assimilate with the varying groups, if for nothing else, to help control the weed epidemics in hillbilly holler. He was just trying to do his part, and as time went on, additional problems needing his service were developing at a very rapid pace. Once you're in, it identifies you as a potential experiment for the greater cause, and if there is one thing Jay likes, it's to experiment. And why not? There was nothing here holding him back from seeking a deeper understanding of the entire existence. Seemed like a lot of fun, and if Jay was going to be judged on the merit of his willingness to party with the people, he would be found guilty of loving every minute of it. Jay enjoyed it so much that the remainder of his sophomore year flew by in a flash. Jay was now sixteen and driving, working a four-to-midnight job, playing basketball and living the high life. The clock was ticking.

Ticking is putting it mildly. Jay was so far out of control that his closest friends began to warn him of a big crash coming. Of course, this was in the minds of the weak, so Jay rested when necessary and then put on the old black jetpack when he needed it, even had a name for it, a black beauty. Once Jay got his hands on the black beauties, he was good to go—talk about filling up the tank with high test. Those little beauties would send you right down the road. You just had to watch out for that fifth-hour curve. You're going to crash, just depends on how hard. They even came out with another called a yellow jacket. Jay felt pretty good with his yellow jacket on—not as tough of a crash and a smoother ride. These were always handy right before halftime. Coach would be screaming for everyone to get on the boards like Jay. "Rebound, rebound," he'd cry while Jay was just waiting to go. They even started calling it that, go.

After basketball season, Jay had kept all the secrets needed to succeed. Some of his closer farmer friends would enquire about his commendable efforts, and Jay would allow a peek inside but never truly an entrance. They could see what Jay allowed, and he was sure they got their money's worth. After all, this type of entertainment was worthy of a front row seat and the applause of courts and kings. Jay was now on a journey to becoming dependent on additional measures to allow performances to go into his later teen years. Weeding and brews were now so normal that additional items would need acquiring to pick up the lively pace, how far to drive and at what price.

Going all the time was the call from the wild. Jay at seventy-five inches and a slight but visible mustache could now enter into the new and exciting world of disco. Clubs were gearing up, and dance music was everywhere. Along with Jay's ever-multiplying talents, he came to find out that rhythm was way too easy and that the heavy beats of disco clubs called to him as a long lost beacon. Jay was made to boogie, and everyone was quickly identified as a dancer or not. Jay was a great dancer, effortlessly moving to the beat. He had found some excitement to hold himself over for a while. *This can be big,* Jay thought.

Wonder how big?

* * *

Summer nights arrived, and Mr. Smooth Sixteen was a runaway train. Working in the yard during the day, Jay developed a nicely shaped and tanned physique from doing the same thing he did every year, making woods into yard. Cleaned up by 3 p.m. and at work by 4 p.m., everyone liked Jay due to his skills and hard work ethics. Everything was a competition with Jay. How fast, how far, and how many always made time fly, and once you had done your time, you were free to do other more exciting things. Work was what you made of it, taking breaks to toke one up every once in a while just made it that much more fun. Factory work was repetitive, but once you got the hang of it, you could do it flying by your heels, and that was often the case with this group of new guys, not from Jay's high school, but still they knew him. They just had no idea that in his time off from basketball, he lived this kind of life, loving life to the fullest. Jay wanted more and was happy for whoever wanted to come along for the ride. The faster the better. Jay had to be wide-open. Why, they would never know. They only knew it was exciting to be a part of.

The weekend nightlife was all that Jay could think about while out in that hot summer sun, cutting and tilling while in his mind, he was cutting a rug with a little miss disco pretty and then slipping into to the shadows for some love of the unlovable. He loved to share, just not commit. This was Jay's screwed-up life, and admittance into the realm of deep emotion was prohibited. No serious offers were ever considered, only the fly by night, just the way Jay liked it. To maintain this lifestyle pace was a trick in a hat; now you see it, now you don't. Worker, partier, ball player—all intertwined to perfection as long as the fuel held out. Now that could be a problem here in the South at times. Just so happened that the flows in and out of the county could be a little tricky, and Jay was pretty much relying on the black beauties and yellow jackets to complete the trip. Jay hated the thought of breaking down alongside the road. When the high pace of travel starts to slow down, the consequences are noticeable, and Jay did not like to be noticed in a negative light. He knew he needed better connections to maintain his high maintenance life, people he knew and trusted but out of his performance arena.

20

FAMILY PROVIDES

The relationships Jay had up on Hillbilly hill was about to pay off. A lot of people knew the clan, and as long as you were a part of the clan, a name was all you needed. Jay was very close with the shooters up trailer park way. After all, they were family. The gambler was Jay's uncle who chased down his Indian aunt, only one of Big Red's sisters with coal-black hair. Yep, she took the six shots to the head and still had a bullet lodged in her brain they couldn't get to. The gambler, well, he got out of prison four years later and kicked the door in on their trailer up on that hill. Door flew open. Shotgun went off, and the gambler ended up out in the front yard. Jay remembered seeing his scarred-up stomach that took the brunt of the blast. The judge in those parts put it this way: "You tried to kill her, and young lady you tried to kill him, now stop it!" So they did. They stayed married and had a couple more kids, some of Jay's cousins who related real well to the hillbilly way of discipline: hit them with something, don't care what, just hit them.

Now the shooting gambler and his shooting wife made Jay feel right at home. They loved it when the preacher's boy would come up and have some beer with them, and they never charged Jay a dime. This was a dry county, and gambling was definitely illegal. The trailer was just a cover for the multiple gambling houses they owned, and to keep everything on the up and up, a certain amount of funds were always donated to the local law. In the meantime, a special refrigerator was always kept full of cold beer, and folks would stop by all the time picking up a six-pack here or there, staying to chat for a minute and always being introduced to the tall, athletic family member. As soon as they would say Jay's name, everyone automatically knew who he was and associated him with the shooting gambler. Jay was family, and known as one to leave alone. It was good to have an uncle who had to kill a couple of would-be robbers over the years. This association was just what Jay needed to open some energetic doors.

Uncle shooter also had a lot of trucker friends, and why wouldn't he? Here in the South, trucking was a great life all its own, and if you wanted to meet some real characters, you were in the right place. Thing about this group of guys was the lack of sleep. These guys were on the road to make money, and that did not include wasting time counting sheep. Oh, they might see sheep along with flying turtles and snowstorms in the desert in mid-July but only because these guys pushed the limits so hard that they had their own language. Everyone in the South had a CB radio, and for all who dared to converse with these truckers, they would be treated with some of the South's finest verbal ballroom dancers. Even came out with a movie called *Smokey and the Bandit* to help out the less fortunate Northern CB enthusiasts. Yes, sir, the South was a land all its own, and if you fell into the right crowds, anything was possible.

Jay's efforts into this new adult world opened door upon door for whatever Jay needed, and what he needed was the substance of longevity, the magic "mush," as would be commanded by the furry ones of the North. This was the avenue less traveled, and Jay felt right at home living on every corner. Family had come through and now tightly associated with the hillbilly clan. Jay was free to obtain and often discounted deals that would keep the Jay train rolling down the track. The needed fuel came at very little cost even to the point of experimenting on some of the new stuff being passed around, and with Jay holding tightly to his self-destruct button, he was all in.

Connections firmly established Jay was ready for a summer of fun. Sixteen with his sophomore year very successfully behind him, it was now the first summer of real freedom allowed by Big Red. As long as Jay did his work and paid his own way, everyone was cool on allowing Jay the freedom to go and come as he saw fit, and Preacher Man Dad's rule was always be up and ready for church each Sunday morning. Not a problem, Jay still loved to worship; it was his time to thank the one who truly loved him. Without this love, there would be no reason to hold on to existence. So every week, Jay would call out, but lately, he heard no response. He knew he was loved by the holy one; he just couldn't hear his voice any longer.

Jay knew why he could no longer hear the voice of the holy—he was nowhere near holy, and when you allow static to get between you and the receiver, you just can't hear. Jay still had the Word. How he loved to read it when he was coming down! Landing in the realm of reality, the place where normal people lived, Jay had given up on normal months ago, and Little Bro was concerned about his big brother. Jay needed to be careful as to not allow him to travel this type of reckless road. He was still so young but growing fast. Jay had a great fondness for him just as the rest of the family, but Jay saw that look in his eyes, the look of worship, adoration, so Jay had to be careful.

Now this road to travel was becoming very difficult without Jay's own set of wheels. Borrowing Preacher Dad's new truck was out of the question, but being allowed to borrow the Buick was the easiest way to get on the highway. While washing Preacher Dad's truck on a very nice summer Saturday, Jay started up the wheels conversation during Preacher Dad's second inspection; it always takes three attempts to please his dad. Jay wondered where he got this perfectionist-compulsion lifestyle, but he knew it lied within them all. You could see it at every turn. Anyway, back to the wheels conversation. Preacher Dad understood the dilemma and offered to sell the Buick to Jay at a very good price. Jay was now on the road with a car holding a 430-cubic-inch motor that could get you from here to there in no time. It was a wild cat, and Jay liked the sound of it the very first time he put his foot on her. Man, did that cat purr. Jay was on the road.

Driving in the shoes of the humble but still aware of the star power he carried, Jay proceeded that summer to once again get closer to where he loved to walk, with the Lord. He knew the love that died for him on that cross put such a great value to his life, a price paid that made no sense. He was not worth it, and he knew he was nowhere near close to what one should call valuable. But still, Christ died for Jay. Jay would have gone to the cross for just one life, his.

Jay had heard preacher after preacher use these exact words, but Jay was yet to feel comfortable with this declaration. He definitely wasn't going to brag about it. It was so amazing to be loved that much. "Oh, holy God, why for me?" Jay cried within himself once again, falling face first at that country church altar, tears rolling and Jay pleading for an already forgiven heart.

God had forgiven him long ago, never to bring his sin against him again, yet this new life in Christ called for something so much more—to love as Jesus loved. Jay was in trouble, for he knew as the tears subsided and as he felt the touch of Preacher Dad gently on his sobbing shoulder, Jay could never love that deeply.

Jesus had a Father who was greatly pleased in him. Preacher Dad was torn between Big Red and preaching the truth, a truth that was very difficult to live when your living space is shared with the big red machine. This left little time for affection to so many household dwellers. Little Bro and Little Red always involved with the calming love they so needed, even by Big Red. The other two sisters took some abuse but not much. They were girls. Sure they got the switch with the best of them, but one thing was very different between all them and Jay, he was the one who defiled, questioned, and dared them to do it. "Kill me!"

"Kill me, go ahead and kill me. You wish I was dead anyway." Of course, the standard reply when confronting Big Red was as good back as anyone could give. Jay loved to get into yelling matches with his variable-poled mother, and once she tired of cussing and yelling, she'd go to hitting, but by this time, Jay was just too big and really didn't care. He would stand there with his hands by his side as she hauled back and slapped him across the face, yell a while, and slap again.

"I know you wish I was dead. I've seen it in your eyes every day since I was ten years old. That's why you can't stand the way I look at you—it's like looking in a mirror. It's the same way you look at me, but I don't wish you were dead. I just live like it," was Jay's response. Responses like this could easily go over the head of his minimally educated mother, and even once, he saw his mom start to break down, that was quickly changed, and the stubbornness took hold. Jay had this same ability, stubborn as a mule preacher, and Dad would say, "You're just like your momma."

"No, dad," Jay would respond. "I'm nothing like her."

Inside, Jay had to live with the reality of being just like his mother. Within him, he had an anger that raged, a hatred for life, not wanting to exist but rather to rule, to leave this world of condescending life forms in a heap of ashes while in victory, the taste of warm blood oozing from the ever-darkening form of life known as Jay, to transfer here to there in the blink of an eye, to actually be one worthy of the love that has made his life so valuable, but he could never find himself worthy, always chasing the dream of being able to love everyone just as Jesus. Jay would try, but his type of love was empty for the lifers of this world, and yet he would try.

The words Jay had heard his mother say over and over again became the deep battle cry of this young warrior. "I don't need anybody. I'll never need anybody." Jay not only understood this train of thought but felt to worship it and would keep the darkness of lonely pain at a distance. "Thanks, Mom." Jay hugged himself within. "The love I can never give will never allow a change to the emptiness of my heart."

21

FILLING THE VOID

Time is a void that consumes us all sooner or later. The emptiness of existence relentlessly hounding every waking moment while the sporadic nightly adventures take us even closer to the edge of a make-believe reality. Jay so enjoyed talking with Little Bro during their bonding time out in the woods even though through the expression on his face, Jay could see the blinks of fascination overwhelming the little guy. He might have caught some of the high points of the conversation, but Little Bro mainly just smiled and laughed when Jay laughed.

Today was one of those summer workdays that Jay enjoyed. A different tasking from Preacher Dad was always welcome, and as the boys worked, he was busy preparing for the Sunday morning service. Their mission was to get new poles for the grape vines. The old had lasted well, but it was time for new ones, so Jay and

Little Bro headed off into the woods with ax in hand to cut some nice green poles.

With the cool of the woods, they both enjoyed the solitude provided by the heavy foliage down along the creek. The boys had traced that creek upstream to find the beginning of it coming straight out of the side of a hill, a fresh spring spilling out of the rock and running down through their backyard way down through the woods into the river. There's always been something special about the sound of running water and how different it can be between a creek, a river, and the sound of waterfalls coming off the mountains. So special would these moments be, and oh, how the boys loved the opportunity to work close to one of the most peaceful sounds in the world, filling the void of a world full of turmoil. How soon can it all come crashing down? Before you know it, you can be jerked back into the realm of reality. This was one of those days.

Jay had the ax and was cutting on the side of the creek bank while Little Bro standing up top was gathering up some lose vines to be used for securing the poles to each other. Everything was going great; they had just finished chasing a water moccasin that got away, but man, it was always fun to run them up the creek. Those guys were fast, and if you didn't catch them just right by the tail, they could spin around and bite you, and boy, they knew they'd get whipped good if they were caught chasing more snakes. Redhead Momma did not like it at all. She hated snakes in general, but it was Preacher Man Dad who showed them how to pop their heads off, confidentially of course.

Jay saw Little Bro slip off the top of the bank and was sliding on his butt down toward the creek. It was funny, and Jay was busting a gut. That was until Little Bro let out a scream that startled Jay, then he saw it; one of the cut vines had stuck Little Bro through his shorts. Jay jumped up the bank in a smooth, quick motion, grabbing the vine and instinctively pulling the vine clear of his brother. Seeing blood run down from the inside of

Little Bro's leg, Jay grabbed him and started running up the hill known as the backyard, arriving at the top back drive that led around to Big Red's beauty shop. Jay stopped to check on Little Bro who was still in a lot of pain. "Let's see how bad it is," was the command from Jay. Little Bro dropped his shorts, and Jay was off to the races.

Running into the house, yelling, Jay was attempting to explain the predicament of his little brother and how he needed the keys to his Buick right now! Actually, babbling would be the correct definition of what Jay was attempting to do, scrambling his words, flailing his arms about, attempting to ape out the latest *Tarzan* movie with cheetah-like expressions. Preacher Man Dad's voice raised and cut through the air, "Calm down, boy. Tell me what's wrong with your brother." Jay looked at his mom standing at the kitchen sink then returned his gaze back to his dad, back and forth, attempting to put into words what delicately needed to be said. "What, son!" his dad yelled out. It was all or nothing—no easy way to say what needed to be said. Jay just said it…

Preacher Man Dad and Little Bro flew up that red dirt road, leaving behind the biggest dust cloud Jay had ever seen. Everyone was stunned and quiet, and even Redhead Momma had nothing to say. Standing in the front yard and watching the dust cloud settle, Jay turned and walked back toward the woods. Redhead Momma stopped him, asking if he was okay. "Sure, Momma," was Jay's response. "I'm just going to go down and finish cutting up those grapevine poles."

"You be careful, honey," she said as Jay slowly walked down the hill and back into the cool, dark woods. What had his momma just said? Did she just use a calming voice along with a sweet reference toward Jay? Was it that she could see the pain in Jay's eyes and the concern of knowing someone had gotten inside to the deepest voids of Jay's darkness, allowing the light of love to come seeping into a place where none was allowed?

Jay fell upon his knees, there in the cool waters of that creek. The sound of rushing water drowned the tears Jay had to release, a pain that was piercing into his heart, cutting so deep into a place where nothing was allowed to go. Jay cried out with a broken heart for the one he loved more than himself, one he would always have a special love for. Little Bro could never know, but now, Jay called upon the name above all names. "Make it all right," Jay cried. "Please, God, let him be all right," Jay knew Little Bro would one day be a wonderful father. He could tell by how much he loved his big brother. He has a special heart, and Jay wept for his healing.

There was nothing to do now but gather up the poles and vines and hauling them up the hill to the bottom driveway. Once there, Jay used posthole diggers to make the eight holes needed for the bigger poles then attaching them with longer, slimmer poles. Jay used the vines to tie everything together. It was good work and took his mind off of the possible prognosis. Jay stayed busy, attempting not to think of the hole pierced through his little brother. *He's to young,* Jay thought, *to endure such pain*. If only Jay could have taken his place. Just then, Jay's spirit reminded him of the one true love who took his place upon that old rugged cross so many years ago. This was true love, and now Jay felt it for his little brother.

Wait a minute. Jay just heard from his Holy Spirit. It had been so long that he thought the communication process was hidden by his darkness, and it was until Jay fell brokenhearted over the one he loved. With a broken heart, he called the God who knew what a broken heart was all about. God had to turn away from his son Jesus as he took the sins of the world upon himself so that any and all could have eternal life. God could not look upon that sin. It stormed, and the earth grew dark, but because Jay was covered in the blood of Jesus, God could look upon Jay and comfort him in his time of need. His Holy Spirit reminded Jay of the price paid in love, and that price was the true love of the world. So when one felt broken over the prospect of someone we love being lost, we can feel that pain to the point of holiness, allowing us to call upon the holy of holies. The veil was torn. Jesus had made a way. We just have to love them, as Christ first loved us. Through Christ, Jay now saw this was possible only through Christ.

Time would tell how well Little Bro healed. If it was any indication as to how quick he was to run though the woods again, he was feeling fine pretty quick. *That kid has guts,* Jay always thought. Jay could jump from a twenty-foot-high bank across the creek onto a sandbar, and Little Bro would be right behind him. The summer months were spent close to the house the year of being sixteen. Little Bro was thirteen but not sprouting like Jay did that summer before high school. Oh sure, he was growing but would not reach the great seventy-five inches of Jay and the preacher man.

Jay's height at times would confuse many, club owners, beer sellers, and even the cops. Preacher Man Dad was down on the back driveway with Jay helping change the oil in the wild cat when a police car pulled up behind the Buick. A police officer came around the Buick, introducing himself as Jay continued pouring some oil back into the car. Preacher Dad conversed with him for a few minutes, and they left and went on their way. Jay had just finished wiping any residual oil prints off and started to gather all the tools when here they came. Two cars flashed and doors flew open as they skidded to a stop. They jumped out with pistols drawn and yelled at Jay, "Don't move!"

Okay, Jay thought, *I won't move.*

Now Preacher Man Dad was stepping between Jay and the police officer nearest to Jay while Redhead Momma was coming out of the house. She was not happy. Everything was happening so fast—everyone yelling, Preacher Man Dad telling that cop he better quit pointing that gun at his son, and Redhead Momma was going to kick somebody's butt.

"Don't you point that gun at my youngin'!" she yelled. "You get off my property, and I mean now."

Of course, Jay was standing there with his hands up, thinking the hillbilly running days had finally caught up to him. Well, no matter what it was, Preacher Man Dad had left the gentle and the meek behind, letting that cop know he was going to have to shoot him if he didn't take that gun off his son.

Jay was not expecting this much commotion from his mom and dad. They were defending him and, with their own lives, had threatened to protect Jay. Why, it never crossed Jay's mind that they actually could love him as much as he now loved Little Bro—enough to give their lives for him. This was so confusing to Jay. Was their love really that deep? Jay had heard so many times the opposite, but now, where the bullets meet the blood was a stand, a stand of love that no one was allowed to harm their oldest son even if they were the law. Everything froze. Time stood still, not a sound, nothing but the piercing eyes before them. The law was staring at them, and Jay's mom and dad were staring back.

The sheriff pulled up, and boy, was he mad.

"Put those guns away," he shouted, breaking the silence.

"Preacher, I am so sorry for all of this." The law holstered their pistols. "These guys are supposed to be picking up Navy deserter, one who would have a lot shorter hair than your son who is also the county's best basketball player." The sheriff had two daughters who were very good at basketball and even went to hope to be high with Jay as his friends. Jay had even been over at the sheriff's house, giving his youngest daughter a ride home one day after school. Now that everyone knew each other, they were about to meet the real deal—Redhead Momma who was going off like a rocket. She knew the sheriff well, as they all sat together during the basketball games and was on first-name basis. The sheriff was funny, yes, ma'am this and yes ma'am that.

"I know and we are terribly sorry. "

Family life on red dirt road had changed. The cops were looking for some guy who went AWOL but instead found a family that could beat the crap out of each other, but anyone else had better think twice. They were a close family, and what happened with the family stayed with the family. Kin was kin. Jay first noticed this when Big Red brought Little Red home. She knew that baby was family, and no one was going to abandon her. It didn't matter if doctors gave her six months or two years. She was now three and doing fine, and that little girl was Jay's sister just like the others. Family, a small part of Jay now understood.

Jay's understanding of what family really meant was drastically changed that summer of sixteen years. Little Bro had become so close to Jay that he no longer even tried to hide his deep love, and don't get started on Little Red; she had a smile that would light up the world every time Jay entered the room. She had a demeanor about her, of love. No matter how she had to get there, she would get there, scooting along the floor, dragging her useless legs and feet the whole time with a big smile on her face, meeting Jay halfway for some hugs and kisses. She loved Jay unconditionally, and Jay had no choice. He would give his life for this little girl, if only he could take away her disabilities, but the way she was in God's eyes, she was perfect, a perfect little light who would love all—even the unlovable.

What Jay had seen with Big Red and Preacher Man Dad was enough to convince him that the love they had for him was real, no matter how little they wanted to show it, no matter if they ever talked about the night of nights that Jay relived over and over. Jay knew he was part of a family, a family who loved each other, but no matter how hard they attempted to fill the voids, Jay's could never truly be filled.

22

COPPERHEAD HILL

August was a hot month that year on red dirt road. The dust up and down that valley would just hang in the air to the point that having a clean car was almost impossible. Jay always kept his Buick on the lower driveway that led around to Big Red's gossip shop unless it was Thursday through Saturday. Those were the days Momma had women coming in and out from 10 a.m. until 10 p.m. every day. Jay had to give her credit. She could do up some country women's hair. They'd come in flat and leave dressed up and ready to go to church on Sunday morning. They loved it when Jay would come by the shop, but Big Red wasn't fond of it. So that was that. Only in emergencies would any of the brood chance a swing by. It's best to just let the excitable alone if you have a chance.

Now the women coming and going kept talking about seeing a snake; some even identified it as a copperhead, and here in these parts, copperheads are a common poisonous snake that you did not want to get bit by, and now that it was so hot, they had every reason to come out and play. Problem was nobody ever saw where it was going or where it was coming from. Jay knew these old ladies loved for Jay to stop by, and so he figured once the stories got going, they would say they saw one, and Big Red would call him in to look for this ever-fleeting intruder, scaring the women who now needed to be protected by the long, tall drink of water they could only thirst for. Jay loved to startle them with his understanding of sublime messages passed his way. Jay was no longer the little boy who would act shy if told how cute he was; he was now sizing up the women with a look of longing, if only they could trip the light fantastic to a day gone by where they were worth wanting. Fantasies, Jay understood them well, and he knew for a fact that if an age limit existed, he had never heard of it. Church ladies or not, a sweaty, dark-tanned shirtless man of sixteen years and seventy-five inches tall left them looking and wondering of days gone by.

Early Saturday morning came with great expectation. This was the one day of the week that Jay lived for. Summer chores done throughout the week, and everyone stayed clear of the Big Red storms. This could be one of those summer days that would go down in history. Jay had max freedom on Saturdays after working all week, turning woods into yard and then every evening heading to the cardboard factory for his regular-paying forty-hour-a-week job, Monday through Friday, four to midnight. Jay was a slave to the factory, but he made it all fun and excelled at everything he did. They all dug being around this mature man of sixteen. Everyone looked and talked with Jay as if he was some guru of understanding. Jay had learned to listen with the expectant face of receiving and understanding wisdoms beyond his years. Everyone could sense it. Jay was very special at comprehending no matter how deep or how dark the subject.

This was a great advantage that not many had acquired. Jay had looked at the world through speculative eyes ever since he could remember. Oh, that's right, the big bang. Jay would never trust what anyone had to say, but he remained to be understanding, allowing an admittance into their world without even cracking the door into his. He was a genius that was active in a performance for one or all. There were no boundaries he could foresee to ever hold him back or deter the accolades so welcomed coming his way. Jay was a force all his own, and all desired him in any way that would be allowed, at a distance, at a very great distance. You were allowed to feel as if you were close but always at a distance.

Back to Saturday morning and cleaning up the car for a hot night, Jay washed that Buick from top to bottom and inside to out. It had to be clean. Everyone who was anyone started out the weekend cruising the strip of cherry town. At sunset, they would line up fifty cars in a row, slowly cruising and talking trash, attempting to pick one or the other up with a new line, but the car had to be spotless and shinny, if any type of conversation was to be started and if started, side by side, could become the artificial affection Jay so loved—nothing permanent, just trying to feel, something, anything.

Jay continued reminiscing about nights gone by as he finished shining the wheels to the Wild Cat. Looking low, Jay noticed a couple drops of oil on the drive. He and Preacher Man Dad had just changed the oil a week earlier, the weekend of the Navy deserter. Jay could laugh about it now, not then though, and in any case, Jay needed to tighten up that oil plug because losing oil was losing money. Jay jacked the front up enough for him to slide under the car, wiping at the plug to see how bad it was leaking. Jay reached back to where he had laid his box wrench and retrieved the waiting fixer of the plug. All was going well. Jay tightened and waited, wiped and waited. Oil could be tricky and slow when it came to leaks. Jay knew it was best to get it right the first time. Preacher Man Dad and his three-times-a-charm routine had surely taught Jay that. Laying there, putting on the final adjustment, Jay was suddenly stunned. He didn't want to move. He was sure of what he felt. Only one thing could feel like that, easing its way across Jay's calf muscle. Jay took a deep breath as he glanced down to see one of the prettiest copperheads he had ever seen slowly gliding over his leg, five feet of muscle with a pretty brown pattern and a very large head that Jay knew all too well living here on the red dirt road. It was beautiful and mesmerizing as it glided with such ease like it was floating. That lovely female serpent not slowing one bit as she eased across Jay's leg onto the driveway from under the car into the very warm morning sun. How did Jay know it was a lady? Simple, ladies love the Jay man. A male would have bit him just for being such a superior male species, not the ladies. They all knew how special it was to get this close to Jay. She just smiled and went on her way.

By the time Jay started breathing again, getting to his feet from under that beautifully clean car was a cool, easy motion, leading him toward the garden just off the drive. This was the direction the brown slithering serpent was heading, but it was unlikely that Jay would find it. It took a minute or two to get the old heart kicked into gear. Jay was sure all would understand.

Looking and looking and some more looking took up way too much of the brothers' time that Saturday. For the life of Jay, he could not see where that snake came from. Now going was a different subject. Once you left the driveway into the garden, there was ample opportunity to disappear into all sorts of wild. Those woods on the other side of the garden were country thick, and even chasing rabbits was impossible out through there. You could get on your belly and see where small critters ran through but no man was to follow. Maybe a couple of deer bed out there, but they were off-limits to all. No one was to mess with Preacher Man's deer. So much for that hunt. They would all just have to wait until someone spotted it coming or going again.

After living there on red dirt road a year or two, Preacher Man Dad thought it was a good idea to get a dog, a collie-mix breed.

He was a good dog just the same but not too smart though as you would think collies should be; it must have been the mutt in him. Little Bro had brought up concerns about Joe. Yes, Jay named him Joe. Why, no one knows. It seemed good enough though. So now, we worry about a dog getting a snake bite. Sure enough, Preacher Man Dad comes home and gives Jay his single-shot 16-gauge shotgun and one shell. "Take this and go take care of your dog," Dad said.

Jay was confused. "I don't need a gun to talk to Joe."

"Just take it, son."

Jay stepped out of the house onto the front driveway and whistled for his dog. "Come here, Joe. Come on, boy," was Jay's normal call to this very lively three-year-old. Jay saw a dog resembling Joe slowly coming out of the woods, laboring to get anywhere and foaming hard at the mouth, snarling, growling, and just looking terrible. Jay's eyes began to well up as he slid the shell into the breach of his shotgun. Walking toward Joe at a quick pace and slamming the breach closed on his gun, Jay raised the release. He had said his last good-bye to the only dog he would ever own. Joe was a good dog.

Summer was almost at an end with Jay finishing up a new quarter acre of yard. The events of this past summer would hold strong in the minds of all who lived there on red dirt road. It was a summer of understanding, drawing closer as a family and realizing that not everyone loves in the same manner as others. Love was a differential that went from crazy to the cross—so hard to grasp but very thankful to have even if some of it was incomplete. How could it all be made whole? We look to the east for that day and listen for the trumpet sound—no, not the sound of a bugle boy trumpet, but the low, deep sound of the days of our Lord as it was heard here on earth. But now, with heavenly resound, glorious the love of that day will be, the one true love, Jesus, yes, say his name, Jesus.

Jay's thoughts ran holy as he continued his work there in the shade of trees that found favor in the sight of Preacher Dad. Jay loved to go to that holy place where he would find peace and understanding. Yes, Jesus understood Jay's pain and loss of trust in those who say they love you one day but then later don't.

"I saw it, I saw it," came the screams of little old lady number 5 of this Friday afternoon. "Jay, I saw where that snake went," she called out as Jay dropped his mattock and went flying up the freshly tilled soil.

"Where did it go, Mrs. Beehive?" Jay called as she neared the gossip shop without ever turning to see where she was going. She was not going to let that snake sneak up on her. That was for sure. Pointing to a little bridge going across from the back drive to the sidewalk leading to Big Red's shop, Jay stopped and wondered, *Is it laying up under that bridge*?

The two-foot bridge spanned the ditch that was used to let the washing-machine water run down the hill. Country living in the seventies, you had to love the ingenuity.

Preacher Man Dad showed up on the scene from all the yelling, and Jay pointed out the high points of the confused conversation. He was a man of God who seldom used colorful words unless he was talking about the lower South side of a Northbound Jay, then he could get serious, and now was a time to get serious. "Pull that bridge out of the way, son," Preacher Dad said. With that, Jay lifted up the crossing span and set it aside. That's when they saw it—the perfect place.

There in plain sight was a hole in the cinder block of the back driveway, leading up under the back drive. God only knows how large this den of unknown venomous potential was before them. Preacher Man sent Jay to let the ladies know to stay put for a little while and then get Little Bro and the shotguns. Jay sprinted off to do as his dad had said, adrenalin pursing through his veins with excitement in knowing he was about to see the little lady who had so fondly caressed Jay up under his car. "Today's the day, girl," Jay said to himself, giggling. Returning with guns ammo and Little Bro, Preacher Man Dad stood there with an eight-foot piece of garden hose and a can of gas. Taking his Remington semi-auto, Preacher Dad handed Jay the can of gas along with the hose. He then loaded his gun with five rounds, loaded Jay's 16 single-shot and stood it against the brickyard barrier, took Little Brothers 20 single-shot, loaded it, and gave him the gun, telling him to stand out of the way but be ready to shoot and not to shoot at anyone standing. Killing copperheads is what this was all about, and Preacher Man had a feeling there was going to be more than one.

Jay now did as his dad had instructed and slid the garden hose about two feet into the hole.

"Now remember," his dad instructed, "once you start pouring that gas into that garden hose, those fumes are going to burn the eyes of any and all snakes in there, and the protector of the den is going to be mad as all get out and come flying out of that hole, looking for a fight. Make sure you get out of the way when you hear it coming."

All sounded pretty simple to Jay: pour the gas and get out of the way. One, two, three, right? No, that's not exactly how it goes. Jay started pouring the gas nice and slow down the hose and looking over at Preacher Man Dad's nervous expression as he tightly gripped his shotgun, anticipating obviously more that what Jay expected. Then came the sound. Jay turned back toward the hose as he was hearing gas escape from the inside of the hole. Barely then getting louder, he heard his dad yell, "Get ready!" The sound that was growing was not gas fumes escaping out of the hole; it was that five-foot beauty hissing and coming up that garden hose in posthaste manner. She was moving, a mouth wide-open and a head that looked to be a foot across, which meant that Jay was entirely too close to this red-eyed beauty.

Jay put into gear as his left hand held the hose and his right hand threw the gas, and it was off to the races. Only problem was is that snake had a head start and was gaining on Jay quicker than he was getting away. *Boom!* Preacher Man Dad just saved Jay from having a very bad day by busting that beauty's midsection and knocking her down into the cutback grapevines with freshly hewed poles for the new season. Jay noted how nice the work was that he had accomplished and, of course, sharing props with Little Bro who had sacrificed so much that day. I digress.

The blast gave Jay enough time to clear the firing line while the almost-blasted half copperhead stood straight up off the ground about three feet high, and man, was she mad. That was until Preacher Man delivered round 2 to the head. Jay grabbed his gun as Medusa's head erupted. Poppa snake was next along with about eight smaller but just as deadly, booming and banging all over the place. Little Bro would shoot and forget to reload. Man, this was exciting, and next thing you know, the neighbors from up the road came running around the house to a backyard full of fun with their guns a blazing. It was a hillbilly good time right there on red dirt road. Next thing Jay knew, Redhead Momma was shooting from the gossip shop door. Now this was family fun.

The smoke finally cleared, and to count the deceased was impossible. There were snake pieces all over the newly plowed grounds. That yard was ready for planting with fertilizer freshly ground in. Everyone standing around had smiles on their faces. Preacher Man slapped Jay on his shoulder laughing with exhilaration. "That was a close one, son."

Jay smiled into the laughing eyes of his father. "Yep, I was never so happy to hear a gun go off in my life." Jay returned, always remembering the night he thought he had lost his dad, wondering if he had thought about losing his oldest son. There was always a teaching hardness about the preacher man. Jay truly respected him as a man of God; he just didn't know how to feel about the man as a father. There was no closeness there probably because he was raised that way—but maybe not, as they never had that conversation, not even there on copperhead hill.

23

WEEDS AND GRASS

One thing for sure as that summer came to an end was that Jay was getting plenty tired of hoeing weeds and planting grass. He was sixteen years old, waiting on his junior year of hope to be high school to get started, finding himself every day weeding the garden or preparing the new patch of used-to-be woods for planting. This routine was starting to get old, but there was some relief of humor stirring there on red dirt road that took the eyes of the adults off Jay and onto his sister of newly dating age. Some might even have called this courting, but no matter how you looked at it, it wasn't focused on Jay.

That Saturday evening, the young man had come a calling while Jay just laughed and held tight to the front-tined tiller for dear life. Why, Preacher Man Dad had even considered a front-wheel-drive push mower for Jay, but it was just priced too high. It seemed feeding the free labor was what pushed it just out of reach; well, there you go. Once again, his existence had been a burden, always something with Jay. Preacher Man Dad thought he was being funny, but Jay's sense of humor contained just the right amount of respect to keep all in the dark. Best thing for everyone is to stay out of Jay's dark.

His tiller had hung up and, as many times before, would stop and pull a rock or a root free of the tines and get back to doing what was best: working the hours of slavery away. It did make time pass, but this was no ordinary rock; it was a chunk of quartz larger than a soft ball. Jay shut the tiller off and propped it up to get a good grip on that rock, twisting with it and barely moving. The rock was stuck but good. Jay knelt down on one knee to give it one last jerk, and that's when it happened. That tine in a bind let loose and pinched Jay's middle finger nail so hard that a surge of pain shot up through that man, and he was flying straight up into the air, coming down face first into that freshly tilled ground.

Jay's time on the tiller was now over, and nice and clean was not the way to describe this handsome young man. He made his way through the living room, and sitting there was sis and her new beau. Jay nodded in the direction of the guy he barely knew, but knew he would kill if he hurt that girl one little bit. Jay could not help the rage that was inside of him. It always wanted out, but this would not be wise. This rage was damaging, and someone was going to get hurt if released. Jay held it close, maintaining a persona of goodness and endearing qualities, performing just as he always had, not allowing anyone to see. Jay didn't like what he saw; he adored it.

Heading up red dirt road nice and slow as to not get the pristine Buick dirty, Jay was being distracted by the throbbing coming from the middle finger of his right hand. Okay, let's change the word *throbbing* to the most painful heartbeat ever. Jay cursed the beating of his heart as he turned around on the hard top at the end of red dirt road. Pulling into the drive, he was having a hard time with anything to do with that right hand. This kind of throbbing pain was new to Jay, and allowing it to continue was not an option. Ever heard of the old phrase "Want me to show you something that will help you take your mind off that pain?" Jay was all for it as he entered the house in obvious discomfort.

As with all the siblings, they were very tight. Having to walk on eggshells together all their lives, his sis could easily see the distress on Jay's face, and knowing he would rather die than return home once away in freedom's breeze, something was terribly wrong. Asking the obvious, the new boyfriend stated he could help Jay out—that he had been there before and it would make him feel like a new man. This peaked Jay's curiosity, and not being the most trusting of people, he knew his sister very well, and if she liked this guy, there had to be some redeeming qualities. Jay sat down with a new hope of feeling some relief, as that finger was killing him, turning black under the nail with a beat so loud he was sure the windows were going to bust out. Now Boy Toy had pulled out his sharp pocketknife and started a drilling process right over the deep, dark spot on Jay's fingernail, then released the hounds, and that blood pressure let off, and sure enough, Jay felt like a better, new man. Boy Toy said that you could even heat a needle and do it without the drilling pain. Jay kind of missed that pain now. Well, not really, it was a little more intense than he wanted to go through again. Jay liked the new guy in his sister's life. He just didn't know how much he was going to change her. Jay would keep an eye on this guy. One can never be too careful when it comes to boys chasing girls especially if the girl lived on the red dirt road.

Jay could just tell that Saturday night was going to be a good one. He met up with little Dave and one of his farmer friends, and off they went to do some more garden weeding and made for such an enjoyable night once they got the weeds all burnt up. All they needed now was some cold ones along with some hot ones, and they would be set. Now this could be difficult with little Dave. Let's just say his "smooth" was a little rocky, and his landscape, a little barren except for a dirt clod or two here and there. That boy was shaped like a pear, but funny, Jay loved that guy, and when he got toasted, he was like a walking vaudeville show, so much fun to be around, just hard to get hooked up.

Cruising with a cold six and some red bug eyes, the night was smoothly going just like planned. Jay was out to have some fun, and that did not include the Don Juan actor he so often allowed himself to become. Nope, he was with his pals laughing, and that was Jay's favorite state of mind. What a wonderful release laughter was—to feel silliness coming on and just bust a gut laughing at any and all of the entertainment there on cherry town road. Little Dave was so funny whenever they parked to talk trash to the hotties passing by. That boy would have two cold ones and get as loopy as a drunken monkey. He was the master of his own mind, assured to the point that he could have any girl he wanted, and this was entertainment. Now his farmer friend was not big on the cold ones but always had a snort or two of the lightning. Jay liked the lightning. That stuff could warm a corpse right up onto a dance floor. They would hit that every once in a while and drive around burning some tires. Well, it smelled like burning tires if you get the drift. Saturday night—with the guys until getting spotted by one of those, the ones who believed Jay owed them something—Jay had already given the best. The rest was his, and he shared it with no one.

On the other hand, little Dave was quick to invite the pretties over for a round or two of bantering. He even thought it was intelligent conversing, but to Jay and the farmer, it was a hoot and a half of the most jumbled-up mess you ever heard. Those girls would look right through him and want to know why the attention meter from Jay and friends wasn't pegging to the pretty and delicious. It's not that Jay wasn't hungry, insatiable of an appetite was well known of this traveling one-man show, but tonight was not that night. Jay had killed himself all week weeding and bleeding, and he was now going to enjoy it with no strings attached, which is the forte of any and all of the little daisies. Now little Dave was so funny that the flowers faded and turned to get away in which Jay was quick to inquire where the loves of his life were going. "Please don't leave me here in such desolate abandon," he called out as he almost fell off his freshly waxed Buick, laughing. This was a great night. Jay knew it would be.

The party went on until the dawn, and Jay made his way back to red dirt road. Slipping in quietly, he would head off for a couple of hours of sleep until time for church. "Is that you Jay?" Redhead momma would always call out.

"Yes, Momma," Jay replied as he slipped into the room where Little Bro lay. This kid was some kind of funny, as he would talk in his sleep, and Jay could listen in, and once identifying where he was, Little Bro would allow him into his dream but only as long as he stayed the course, any variation from where Little Bro was in dream land and an immediate shut down. It was always so cool. Little Bro stated he oftentimes did the same with him, but having to be very accurate, Jay knew it was possible. He had let Little Bro in—not to the angry darkness, but definitely to the caring side of Jay. He loved that kid, no doubt about it, and they were getting closer with every years passing—brothers for life. Well, time for rest before the big day tomorrow. Church was always a big day for the family, everyone dressing nice and going to the house of the Lord. Actually, they all just called it church, but it was definitely a family atmosphere. Jay now was assisting, teaching the teenage group, and of course, the younger teens thought he was just the coolest preacher's kid around, and all hoped to be just like him. Jay knew that price was way too high for any of these kids to pay, and they could be glad of it. But Jay wished this life on no one.

Teaching and interacting with the youth allowed Jay to show off some of his study time in the Word. Jay always loved to read the Word and use his study Bible to gain insight. This was the world he dreamed he could immerse himself deeply and to never come out—to walk everyday holy, for he is holy, to love unconditionally and not selfishly. But the only love that Jay could share was a selfish love. It was all he knew. The only real problem with adoring love is that younger girls so easily fell for it, and Jay was enough of a pig to use any and all of it for his self-gratification. It was a battle he faced every second of every day, no room for escape. This would be the demon most hated, the one allowed to sit within earshot and convince Jay that this could be the physical love he so longed for, this touch, this caress, a moment to erase the years of pain and lack of love. This would be the one the darkness claimed, and once again, Jay felt alone and ashamed.

Now Boy Toy was turning out to be one of the farmers, and Jay was unaware of his sister's desire of gardening. That was quickly cleared up one night when Jay ran into the pair at the main drive in restaurant. Order by the car, girls on skates would bring the fries and Sun Drop, as this was the most excellent mix of all the sodas. Hanging out with a Sun Drop light, light for lightning, all was good, and there was Sis and Boy Toy pulling in to enjoy the crowd of fun seekers. Making his way around, he snuck up on the two new lovebirds, and he smelled that someone had been working in the garden.

Sis looked startled and very tired while Jay made his presence known, hanging around for a short while to let all know who belonged to who and that this pair were not to be messed with. As in life, it makes a difference who you know, and being known is one thing Jay enjoyed. Being highly popular and well versed in the written and oral venues of this sleepy little city, he had become a legend for one so young, but his personal profile must be maintained on the down low using different names of athleticism and monikers of understanding to mingle with the night club masses. Boy Toy was anxious to take the possibility of brother-in-law to the next level and asked Jay if he'd like to take a ride.

Jay jumped into the used but cool 4x4 along with Boy Toy and Sis and took a cruise just chatting about life while enjoying the late-summer air, Sun Drop light, and the smell of freshly pulled weeds. Jay so loved that smell; it made everything in the country feel that much better. Even sis was enjoying the summer air with some very enthusiastic breaths that impressed Jay to no end. That girl was taking it all in. This could change a lot of things. Jay thought about his sister, *A new confidant?* Maybe, time would tell, but for now, the primo air was making the joy ride a real joy.

That summer of sixteen quickly came to an end, one more year of vacation Bible school with the kids of that little country church. Jay could not have survived without the endurance he had picked up weeding that summer. It had become a very important part of Jay's life, and even to the point of taking it a step or two farther when the opportunity presented itself. Jay really didn't notice the ease and comfort into which he had gladly allowed his present existence to take even deeper steps onto the psychedelic frontier. Once, twice, and then the counting just stops. Who cares how many times you ride the pony? It's just so much fun we all quit counting. Weeding and planting grass began to fade into so long ago.

24

THE NIGHTLIFE

Basketball season at hope to be high was once again very successful with the throngs of fan maniacs numbering into the unknown. Jay, as if he needed it, was now more than ever treated with royalty stock and given a pass wherever and whenever he wished. It was too much but exactly what Jay needed to completely and inwardly self-destruct. Of course, the inner life of Jay was allowed to be viewed by the select, and the very select it was. Back to working his forty-hour week and maintaining his passing grades, Jay was once again seen as a great asset to the community and loved to the point that even Redhead Momma would allow the rampant running of her oldest son. Why not? He was adored by all—all except those who now knew the coldness within. Replacing the warmth of presumed love, a cold, empty darkness now resided. It was the price to be paid if desire brought you too close, and most times, they came repeatedly. Jay wanted to feel love in any and all manners, but each time and every time he reached out, all left him feeling so cold and alone. Jay was unable to return the emotions endeared his way, it was almost as if they truly loved him, how absurd!

We've all heard the saying "Drastic times call for drastic measures." Well, here we go. Seventeen years old, seventy-five inches tall, and a light but noticeable mustache allowed Jay to enter into the world of the 1976 nightlife. That's right, the disco baby, lights flashing sweaty bodies all across the dance floor with spinning mirror balls that lit up the club, the wall-to-wall possibilities. With a drinking age of eighteen, they wouldn't look twice as Jay entered into the domain of disco. Tall and styling in silk and polyester from head to toe, pretty was not the word for this trendsetter. He would perform and conquer this nightlife just as all previous areas of interest. With style and an assurance that could not be bought or taught, either you had it or not, one thing was for sure, the disco beat along with a seven fourteen made the dance cool and mellow with a slow slide.

Problem with the seven fourteen and a couple seven and seven's was that this mellow mood was so much fun that Jay could not get enough of the road away from reality. The slow dancing with the hotties and the slide moves to the disco beat would entertain all in attendance. There were those who performed and those who stood by and watched in amazement as the beautiful gliding stars of the evening would twirl and dip in perfect rhythm of the upbeat tempo of "I Want to Boogey." Friday night, Saturday night, the party of the dance would consume even the strongest of the prudent. All it took was one night, just trying it one time, and there you find yourself anxious for the next scheduled dancing event, hoping a dance competition was coming your way. You were hooked.

Jay would pop a seven fourteen every Friday night just before washing up to leave work. By twelve thirty, he'd enter into what could only be called an arena of praise. The last six months had proven that Jay was one of the few who all wanted to know and would call his name as he made his way to the bar for a seven and seven. Once in his hands, he scanned the midnight room for possible partners of play, a beautiful evening of touching, sweating, and hopeful memories to last a lifetime. This new escape was just the jungle Jay was looking for, and actually, he was made for.

The beat was addictive just like the seven fourteens. It all seemed so innocent all those months ago, doing a little weeding and washing down the thirst with a frothy cold one. One thing led to another, as in most cases of intentional misdirection. Looking for a way to escape the internal darkness almost always allowed the darkness a speakeasy platform, little nudges here and there, reassurance of the journey taken as being well worth the price. Jay had no problem enjoying the trail of trials. Putting him on the stand was pure verbal magic, explaining all things away as a necessity, needing to make the world go round and spin on the dance floor in a performance to please them all. That's all Jay wanted to do—make the moments fun and the rendezvous memorable to ease the loneliness, but afterward, all he wanted was to be alone.

The nightlife continued on like this all through the 1976 summer with one party after another. There could be no end to the fun Jay was experiencing except for those Sundays, the ones Jay loved to attend, church. How easy it was to push that experience aside to justify the lackadaisical attitude now found in attending the weekly ritual. *No doubt about it,* Jay thought, *as an adult, you tend to grow away from the seriousness of these weekly meetings and attend as a lot of members do, for the show of it.*

It was never brought to Jay's attention that you were supposed to grow in the faith and claim victory of that salvation moment for the rest of your life. The examples of everyone telling unpleasant jokes along with comments about the opposite sex while smoking their cigarettes or having a chew alone proved just being saved was the deal. Everything else you wanted out of it was up to the individual, and as an adult, what you wanted was a lot different that when first meeting a holy God. You are just glad you met him.

While school was out during that fleeting summer, Jay had additional opportunities to meet and mingle with the party people of the various but not plentiful clubs of the country city life. Dancing the night away and waking up at some conquests home where greeted by roomies would always make that morning seem bright and cheerful. Oh sarcasm, how we adore thee. It was not Jay's usual routine to spend the remaining morning hours at the abode of the conquered, but these days were different. There was a new drink in town, and Coke was its name.

Time and time again, the buzz of the seven fourteen would wear thin while the weeds still got pulled to burn. But on the downside of the evening, heading into the pumpkin hour, arose the need for speed, better known as the first snow of winter. Everyone enjoyed the first snow, knowing this would take the hours and flash them by, dancing and enjoying the scenery. The final landscape of beauty would be a painting of the master to enjoy for hours and even to the point of exhaustion, thus the uncomfortable morning meetings of the roomies.

This first snow was beginning to be a problem seeing as how once the play was performed with such enthusiasm that the performers would tend to drift away, waiting on an additional encore that surely came with the winter's snow. However, getting snowed in was becoming more common, so Jay would need to reevaluate the timing of winter chill, to adapt the intake of the white beauty in moderation with the love of the darkness. Darkness and light, white and black, or dusk to dawn, as long as the nightlife was preyed upon, the fun would go on, but at what price?

The family on red dirt road really didn't have an issue with Jaybo, as his mother loved to mock with her very hillbilly accent. "Did you have a lot of fun last night after work? I noticed you didn't come home again," his mom would poke.

"Stayed with someone I met at the club," was Jay's low-tone reply. Funny thing about this entire nightlife thing was that Big Red seemed to enjoy the fact that Jay was out doing whatever to whenever to whomever. She just smiled and slapped him on the back as she walked by, heading off to the gossip shop, happy as a lark that Jay was having a good time. Of course, as long as Big Red was happy, the whole house was happy. You wanted to do something? You cleared it with Big Red. If she said yes, then you were golden—no discussions and no disputes.

Now the nightlife was taking a toll on Jay, and looking forward to hope to be high's startup was an understatement. Jay needed the rest, and preparing for the year's athletic events gave him just what he needed: an excuse not to party. Not sure how it happened, but Jay had gotten into a routine that was taking a serious toll on a man of just seventeen years. Taking a toll was not the words, Jay needed repair, but the way to feeling better was a very familiar old and dangerous road. Jay knew he would do whatever it took to get things back in order, and the first order was hope to be high and basketball.

Jay didn't fit well with the hope to be high jocks; they actually kind of made him sick with their attitudes of superiority, strutting around the New Year as if they could handle all things cool. They knew one thing: to stay out of Jay's way. He did not like unworthy egos and if you didn't treat all people with respect…

25

TOO CLOSE

Standing in their old familiar spot, Jay and Dave greeted the passing masses with smiles and nods to all who would acknowledge the presence of greatness. The freshmen class stood out like a group of scared little puppies, not sure if they wanted to cry or just pee themselves. Jay made it a point to greet the newbie's with a flashing smile and warm words of welcome, and as they passed by. They would soon realize who it was that just greeted them and squeal like little kids at the carnival. Jay knew this made a big deal for the kids, and it was really no effort at all to bring light into someone's day. Jay really enjoyed it, making people happy.

As a matter of fact, if there was one really cool reason for attending school, it was to meet and make people happy. Jay was not the ordinary homegrown athlete here at hope to be high. He had been a lot of places even if he couldn't remember most of them. Bits and pieces is what it would be identified as. There was one traumatic experience before the big red big bang that always stood out. He was small, holding his moms hand going into a building from bright sunlight to near darkness. It was very scary for young Jay, and as his eyes focused, he could see a lot of women, some in swim suits and some half out while some were completely out, way out.

They were all smiling at Jay and commenting how cute he was, "Oh, look at that big boy," while all Jay could do was focus on the bareness and wonder why these women were deformed into looking like a tent sale. Now Jay only stood a couple of feet high, so the angle of the view was mesmerizing. Some looked as if they still needed to remove sweaters and pullovers, yet he believed it was in some way part of their bodies. It was freaking him out until Big Red finally found a stall to wash the sand out of Jay's favorite play areas with a very cold supply of water that never ended. Trauma I tell you, real trauma.

These kids at hope to be high were lucky if they ever crossed the state line and that accent. It drove Jay absolutely mad. If you wanted to get close to the man, you needed to speak with an educated tone. It never ceased to amaze Jay at how ignorant people sounded with that hillbilly draw and yet attempt to proceed with intelligent conversations. He could not and would not entertain elongated conversation with those of the sugar-South vocabulary. Short and to the point the conversation would be and then exit, stage right, out the door, into traffic or off a cliff, anything to silence the insufferable sentencing of the South. Of course, having a Southern draw was fine for the most part, but the sugar-pop girls with their *Gone with the Wind* extensions of blabber was tolerated for the least amount of time Jay could afford, and his time was very valuable—valuable to the point of just walking away. Leaving them self conversing was an option most enacted.

There was a very large problem here concerning those Jay could tolerate in conversation, or in presence for that matter. They just seemed to live in a world of make-believe. Once Jay dropped a basketball friend off and was invited in to meet his parents. Politely, Jay accepted and entered into the nice country split-level home to meet June and Ward Cleaver. It was amazing, and Jay thought someone was playing a joke. Jay looked to the heavens to see if the good Lord was in some way altering the universe just to have some fun at Jay's expense. Really!

Jay drove away contemplating the recent events he had just experienced, and he again found himself talking to the one who loved him unconditionally but was surely having some fun at his expense. *Not possible,* he thought. No family could be that relaxed in every day conversation and show that much interest in what their son was saying. For Saint Peter's sake, when his sister walked by, they greeted each other in a loving manner. They even made a comment about their mother's terrible cooking! Jay just waited for the gun to go off, but no, she just laughed and playfully slapped at her kids. "You two stop now," said Dad. "Your mom's a wonderful cook," as he shook his head no, indicating her cooking was terrible. They all just laughed, and Jay had to come up with one of his best performances ever, laughing and acting like all this was normal, kidding and being playful as a family,

Jay had to reach deep for this one. Making fun of Big Red was not advisable, ever. The way they looked at each other, there was this peace they had together, like they really enjoyed being in each other's company. Confused as Jay was, he just laughed at the possibility of the red dirt road family performing as if all were delighted to be in each other's company and able to laugh at teases and pranks.

There was this one-time camping up in the mountains at one of those KOA grounds. The brothers and sisters hated it, but Preacher Man Dad and Big Red thought the family needed this type of get away at least once a year. It was a living nightmare, walking on eggshells when you should be allowed to run wild. It was the mountains with rivers and critters to chase and harass, real outside fun. Problem was that not enough attention was paid to Your Highness, so it normally didn't end well. On this occasion, while sitting around the camper at night, Jay and Little Bro were comfortable on the picnic table when the unthinkable happened: Big Red went to sit down, and her cheap lawn chair buckled right to the ground. Jay and Little Bro had no time to stop themselves—laughter blasted out of the boys, and Preacher Man Dad joined in before they all realized the abomination that was before her lordship.

That was the end of that trip. All things packed up that very first night, and then the long ride home in total silence, just as well. They were always made to go to bed early while the other kids were running and playing outside—but not the red dirt road kids, they were being told to quit breathing so loud and go to sleep. That's right, breathing too loud or moving too much as they were squeezed into a sleeping area made for two which now held five. Time and time again, Jay just wanted it all to be over with. Guess this was how to avoid the sleeping part, just rig Big Red's chair. After that failed trip, Jay never went up the hills with the family again; his prayers had finally been answered.

Senior year was proving to be a good year all the way round for hope to be high, starting off with a positive group of football players who actually might win a game that year. Crazier things have happened, and they hoped it would happen to them. Jay's last year was going to be an easy one; only a couple of major classes needed allowed him to fill the rest of his day with walk in the park studies, more like girl studies. Yes, Jay had become the man, and with this came a reputation that any young man would feel proud to own. In Jay's case, these accolades came with a price, a very empty, dark price that would always need emotional payments even unto death. This was a life though seemingly glamorous on the outside. The void of human love on the inside left the reality of a very empty shell if they only knew the pain and the hours spent wishing it was all over. Jay sought comfort in these hollow physical companionships. Many had admired. They had no clue of the toll to be paid to live life so aloof, seemingly so full, the whole time paying a debt that could never be settled, not here, not of this earth.

Homeroom was a class just to take attendance and then get the day off to a great start, pretty much forty-five minutes of hanging and conversing. Jay got a good break with his pal Dave being with him this year. He made Jay laugh, his favorite thing to do. Jay always had a smile due to his relationship with the Lord, always there. He had come to this earth just for this purpose: to pay the price Jay could not and to always be there. This made Jay smile all the time unless you touched him, as too many years of being slapped and cursed made touching him a risk you did not want to take. The smile would be gone, and the quiet would come.

Crying was heard in this homeroom meeting, and Jay really hated to see girls cry. He had seen his sisters cry way too often, and it would pull at the almost-numb heartstrings Jay barely had attached. There in the back corner with her friends around her would be the cutest little girl that Jay had never noticed. It seemed she was a senior also, and Jay had missed most classes with her, but now she was distraught and needed some reassurance. Anyone crying can become calm once reassured. That's just the way it played out: take their mind off their troubles and refocus on something more positive. Jay did it all the time with Christ.

"Is everything okay?" Jay asked?

One of the distraught girl's friends looked up at Jay and made a very profound statement. "Boys are stupid."

Nice, Jay thought. *Simple and to the point.*

"And men are pigs."

Jay responded, "What's your point? If you're going to waste your time crying on the basis that boys are stupid, then you should probably quit investing in eye makeup."

The crying girl looked up with a slight smile on her face with the tearstained trails running down her cheeks and said, "It's no big deal, I guess. The boy who was going to escort me to homecoming backed out on me, so now I don't know what to do."

"Is that all? I'll take you," Jay volunteered, jumping in with the white-knight attitude but not thinking the whole thing through. Spontaneous, that's the way Jay liked to do things, just don't ask Jay to do something spontaneously that he did not like.

Things from that point on started to get a little out of control, and the gossip birds started squawking with the fingers pointing and even Dave making stupid comments about Jay and his new girlfriend. Girlfriend! Wait a minute, all Jay did was to volunteer, to escort this girl during halftime of the homecoming game. Sure, everyone had to be dressed to the nines, but that in no way meant bound by lashings and chains for evermore. He felt sorry for her. She was crying, and of course, it didn't hurt that she was cute as a button with those swollen little eyes, nice figure, and pretty all the way around, but still, this was just a favor. Jay needed no permanent attraction in his life. His dance card was full, and that's the way it's going to stay.

Girlfriend Debbie and her pals just couldn't quietly put their fingers on the friendship of Jay and Dave. "Some things you just don't mess with," Jay advised, with none of the felines understanding the darkness that stood before them, the storm of Jay that he wished upon no one. The girlfriend, however, was moving right into his path, and Jay knew that sooner or later, there would be emotional pain. It was the price paid to be close to Jay. She was such an innocent seventeen-year-old that knew nothing of the physical life of love, or lack thereof. After the homecoming victory and everyone celebrating, he should have walked away. Why did he not walk away? Now it was too late.

26

LOVE HURTS

Working still at the factory while playing ball was enough to run a grown man into the ground, good thing for Jay, he always kept a good supply of little friends around, just in case. His friend Bennie had become a new favorite of Jay's along with his old pal's seven fourteen; up and down, that was the crazy life to live of a superstar who is now tiring of being a star. The dating life was the tail of a burning comet that all knew would finally burn out for Jay and Debbie. They were probably right; she was such a good girl, and everyone else knew the reputation of ill repute that Jay carried like a moniker. He did enjoy the freshness of it all, the so-called love effect, starry-eyed with cute little nicknames back and forth, petting and fondling but only to a point. This entire time, Jay was still playing the adult version of "let's make a date with many of his older and much more experienced female friends of the dance floor." There were no ties other than Dave who worked at the factory with Jay, and he was just happy for his dear friend. If anyone really knew Jay, it was Dave, only because he could be trusted with the knowledge of the reality of his search for love in the nightlife, a love that pained him so while still letting him feel alive. Nothing permanent, nothing final, only the prospect of feeling loved in a dark world of music and dance where love was just another love song, temporary at best. Jay loved it so.

Jay continued to play the loyal boyfriend to the cute, little female companion who now cuddled up with Jay in between classes while Dave made his rounds as a senior who no one dare touch. He was Jay's friend, and along with that came the rage of personal protection that any and all need not provoke. Still, there were many little loyal friends of Debbie and the talk of prevailing doom to come her way if she continued on with this boyfriend fascination. Their problem was they had never had an opportunity to spend time alone with Jay, persuasive, polite, a gentleman to best all comers, a true knight in shining armor.

Asking her to walk away from all of this was an offense and an area they need to tread lightly. She was no fool and a great defender of the man she now so deeply loved. It was meant to be for her. On the other hand, Jay had no remorse for the nightlife he so enjoyed even to the point of standing the little girlfriend up while the iron on the sheets was hot. Jay knew what he wanted and had no problem living the multiple-personality life, seeing as how he'd been living this way his whole life. Acting, this is what brought him the most pleasure—being able to adapt to any and all situations no matter how crazy things got. You had to at least seem to be in control, whether you were acting or not. Basketball season continued on, and winning was not the greatest concern for Jay. He was good, highest scorer, and always hustling, and the competitive side always ruled as he jumped higher and ran faster, and he was and always would be a force in competitive sports. Now girlfriend cheering for Jay as the games went on were a nice touch that he really enjoyed. He could make eyes with a lot of the opponents' girls while still having the one true lovely in the crowd going home with him—well, not really home—and this was beginning to be an issue with the man-pig known as Jay. Dave had warned him the "innocent little girlfriend" routine would grow tiresome. He never knew it would be within six months.

Like always, Jay got his way with false promises of loyalty and a heart for her alone. She was now one with Jay, and with all the toys he had, he would never truly be satisfied—it was love that could never really be. He told himself he loved her, and in his own sick, perverted way, he truly did. This was going to be the one real love, a love he could always count on here, spinning on this disgusting pile of dirt, a true love forever, never! Actually, this would someday break his heart along with the innocent beating heart in her beautiful young chest. Jay would once again hate himself for this love, but not now; it was new, and Jay was sure this would be the one to finally set him free from the darkness, if not but for a little while. How could he possibly see into the future of bliss and happiness? Would it be so? Could it be so?

The dating turmoil was on a collision course with the darkness Jay held so fondly deep inside. The man Jay wanted to be in conflict with what is known as the animal instinct, the need, the hunger for blood and meat, the conquering abandonment of all those who sought to love the unlovable. There were times all Jay could see in the mirror was this animal without any remorse, and then, there was this compassionate man who loved as well as understood love. But here, the void deepens into abyss, as the darkness envelopes what is known as true love. A void of understanding that to penetrate the depth of darkness only added to the critically wounded mind of the warrior who must control any and all attachments, friendship to love. Love was just a tool used by mankind to get what he wanted—what he needed was a special someone to absorb the hate and pain and still remain loyal and in love. How crazy is that?

The nightlife continued to swallow our hero. Deeper and deeper, Jay fell into the arms of needed assistance, with not enough hours to perform and to please the masses and the whole while consuming additives of addictive nature to just maintain, with little friends like Bennie to help him through the day.

Jay had been burning the proverbial candle on both ends for so long now that he was beginning to believe this was the normal way to feel, out of touch, naturally and literally, as if everything were real but not really. This cat was way out of control, so he decided to up the ante on weekends by starting a new ritual. Friday night after work would no longer be dance nights. No, now it would be rest nights to party with the blotter, dropping the tabs, microdots baby, take a trip and never leave the farm…

Saturday mornings would come, and Jay could be found sitting on someone's couch watching *Bugs Bunny* cartoons. He had obtained an age that by which no one really cared if he came home or not. He was eighteen with passing senior grades and was paying his own way, so really, he was not needed by the folks on red dirt road. He enjoyed the freedom and lack of concern of life or death, just the way he liked it. Nobody dared to love him enough to care. Well, except for Debbie who, by ten o'clock, would be calling to find out where her man was and if he had a good night. Enough of that, let's get back to the cartoons.

By that time, the mellow in the fellow could really enjoy the coyotes long, slow falls into the canyons. It was great entertainment for those who are about to join us, from the outside looking in. Such a wonderful spirit was now so confused and alone: Where were we going? Where had we gone? Is anyone else seeing this? Jay was just one step away, just the way he liked it. Continuing to reach for the stars but flaming out like this year's comet, the next great crash come hoping to be the only one hurt. But it doesn't always work like that. He couldn't remember anything of any significance since before the big bang, and now all that seemed to matter was maintaining the remaining images of any positive references to life as he knew. These images that were fading in and out of focus were of the recent years past, and quickly, the expedition into the warping of time led conscious thought to areas of reality or complete fable.

Jay needed to slow things down due to the fact that things were getting out of control, something Jay would not tolerate, and along with that, he was finding it harder and harder to maintain the up-and-down lifestyle he so enjoyed. Changing the speed of this out-of-control rocket would be very tricky, and if he so enjoyed the warp-speed life, he would need to increase his paydays. That was easier said than done, but to up the ante it would require some thinking out of the money box, cash, the life support to a bigger party, and for Jay, that was life now, one big party.

What had happened is that Jay turned around one day from rolling on a hotel floor, laughing like a school kid to hitting everyday bennies while weeding the garden and dropping the dots. Years that had passed had meaning, but at this moment, it all felt so meaningless. He sat and wondered where the next tank of gas would come from because he wouldn't have enough to weed the garden and hook up with his pal Bennie the white cross. Life was moving too fast, and Jay was starting to worry about things he really didn't need in his life but tell his lifestyle of habits that he needed it. Boy, did he need it. Bennie, the white cross in the morning and seven fourteen in the evening, while weeding the whole day long. Great thing was that he had good old dependable white lightning to ease his worried mind.

The entire issue of realizing the brokenness of the once-invincible male machine is to first single out the major component of degradation, the part that used to pull its weight but no longer has the fortitude to accomplish the multiple tasks required to perform in an ever-changing world. Could it actually be the mechanics of tempo betraying Jay in such an immoral way that it could no longer be trusted as a viable dependent identifier?

This once-free beating supporter of life now betrayed the only life source it had ever known, and now, what to do with this new illumination of darkness settling ever so deeply into the confines of Jay's mind?

Why has my heart betrayed me in such a severe manner? Jay thought. *Is this true love that takes and takes but never replaces the destroyed landscape or even attempts to replace nutrients required for additional years of provisions?*

Jay had been giving so much of himself lately that the energy to maintain the illusions of happy and in love along with the ability to perform in the amassing sports arena of the south were now tearing apart the charade he had so carefully employed for all those years—dancing for the masses and finally falling down like a marionette without a handler. No one to assist the broken and alone. Fending for himself and trusting no one, Jay left love to the weak and needy, using whomever and whatever he liked to regain the gloriously liberated man that was loved by all.

It was as if a gigantic bolder of burden had been lifted, the smell of darkness so inviting that for a moment, Jay had forgotten exactly where he was, so as his senses returned, he heard the words once more calling from so very far beyond. Just as I am without one plea, kneeling at that country altar on a spring sunny day, Jay cried out, "Father, I feel so very far away," as he knew he was, making a decision to move even a greater distance from the one true love in his life, the one who never abandoned him. Jay now freely and knowingly, walked away.

27

THE DISSENTION

Blame is a very evil game played in the here and the hereafter. Jay knew of a man called Job while recollecting the studies of his younger years. Oh, those years seemed so long ago, but in reality, it was just the rough road traveled and chosen that made it all seem so distant. Evil, better known as Lucifer, had consult with God and laid blame at the holy feet for why this man Job was such a man of God, of good, all due to the favoritism he showed for this son of Adam. This man that smelled of Earth made the devil himself cringe. It seemed sulfur was more to his liking, so into a pile of ash, this man Job would go to prove a point that no matter how great a man of God you believe yourself to be, without the ashes, boils and tears of suffering, you will never rise to the peaks of a holy God, and what he has in store for you.

Jay was now heading for his own pile of ash set aside just for him. He knew now better than ever that the favor of God had left him. The graciousness of a healing Spirit could no longer draw close as Jay continued toward the chastening to come. He was enamored with the thoughts of a holy God not only correcting him but removing him from this earth as a whole, stopping the unstoppable mind that was now controlling the life once and still adored by the masses that were not able to peer beyond the boundaries of the blatantly obvious masquerade. The performance now must maintain the air of superiority so as to all the entertainment of the wounded would once again thrill and satisfy the devilish obsessions that all mankind has so fondly come to love.

Basketball season was over, and only three months of hope to be high remained, and the eighteen-year-old Jay was once again in need of something additional to engorge his fallen ego.

Once every girl at school knew the playboy was spoken for, the entertainment value of daily school life now seemed drab and boring. Jay was no longer allowed to tease and have hand-to-hand fun with the lovely ladies of the classroom settings. Daily rituals started taking place to just endure the day. Morning lightning drinking was becoming more common until the track teacher noticed a talent in the high jump during physical education class. There was recent news of a record being set by a guy named Fosbury who invented the Fosbury Flop that Jay found quite easy to imitate; you just go over the high jump bar head first, nothing to it, well, for Jay anyway. The track coach made a deal with the tall athlete: "Just come to the meets. You don't have to attend practice. Just come and jump, and you can letter in track also." Special deals for a special guy. Jay's ego was once again on top. There was even an event in South Carolina for multiple-state church Olympics, and Jay and Little Bro were signed up and escorted by Preacher Man Dad to participate against the South's best. Preacher Man Dad's mind was blown as Jay placed first in the high jump, second in the long jump, and Little Bro placed in the one-hundred-yard dash. He never really took the time to know the boys on a deep level, something Jay noted to never allow in his upcoming life as a great dad.

Jay so enjoyed drama and action, classes. He loved to perform with the gang, and hand-to-hand flirtation could be taken to a whole other level with the drama club. Of course, Jay was not a member of the beta, or any other "school-organized better than everyone else" clubs. Jay was an individual, and the way others did things to a historical repeat cramped the spontaneous freedom Jay required to maintain the elusive lines of voids so carefully and intentionally placed to distract the reality of Jay's surroundings. High school was so beneath him, from the squeals of the little girls to the everyday attendance. Now at eighteen, he could, by law, check himself out if the days became too boring, saving the afternoon classes for another day.

Jay's life now consisted of a tunnel to travel each and every day that, for a lack of better word, just pissed him off. He looked for confrontations. Anything and everything irritated him to the point of losing all social communicating skills. Rude as he had never been before, short and to the point, he stayed away from the red dirt road as much as possible just to avoid meeting with Big Red. She would have none of it. Disrespect meant a battle, and everyone knew who the victor would be.

Pop a pill to feel happy, smoke some weed to mellow out, and let's not forget to take a drink of white lightning just to get the yeehaw on. Control was not the issue, but the lack thereof sent this idolized idiot into a spinning world of self-admiration clouded by the love of the one and only, him. Jay no longer cared for the opinions of those closest to him; it was all self-absorption. Who could possibly know what Jay was going through? No one. Jay's whole life had been an illusion with the greatest "now you see him, now you don'ts" to come. Attempting to communicate with the less-fortunate masses was a level Jay was not prepared to come down to, a place where they belonged, there on the edge of darkness, but never allowed to enter its depths where the pressures was so great that only the magnificent could survive.

Summer was just around the corner, and the smell of freedom was so wonderful that everyone's excitement became intoxicating. Classes no longer mattered with grades pretty much in the books. Liberation coming was the release into a summer full of the graduating masses. All would be heading to the beaches to let off a little or a lot of steam. The controlling interest of deprivation had taken over the once-pleasant and caring mind of the graduating Jay. This would be the beginning of the end, to the end of the turmoil that battled for the one small sane spot left in Jays' dome. How he needed the rest and the release from the presence of darkness that now seemed totally in control. Only the game to be played kept the dark one at bay, but for how long?

Three months of vacation with little to no supervision, the boys were out of town.

In his previous months of stupidity, Jay had taken the hard-earned cash from his never-ending job at the factory and bought an engagement ring for Debbie, hoping to once and for all restore the love lost so long ago. It's not that Debbie had fallen out of love; it's just that Jay was never really in love, just looking for it to see if it was actually real. Buying a diamond speck of a ring in some weird sense relayed a message to Jay's scrambled brain that to love one beautiful young girl was possible and even practical. Jay was such a deep thinker with the wrong brain.

Panama City beach, or bust baby, the boys were headed South doing eighty-five on eighty-five. Jay had his troops, and the Wildcat was rocking, no brews, but oh, the sweet smell of the southern bells filled the air, couple of bennies, and a hit or two off the blonde pipe, and this was one cool ride. Needing to take the required break down the long, lonely highway, the guys all hit the new roadside rest areas with munchies machines and lots of picnic tables that were out of the way of the many travelers. These stops were nice. Jay remembered always taking a leak by the side of the road traveling as a younger man with Preacher Dad and Big Red. Here you could relax under the shade trees and reenergize up before taking off on the last leg before hitting 431 South and then beautiful white beaches of Panama City.

Finishing up the munchies at the beautiful park and preparing to get back on the road, it was time to get the minds right for the last three-hour leg. The blonde hash was new along with the winter wonderland. Skiing was the name most associated to the wonderful white powder now being introduced to the most eager Jay, something to make the world a little brighter.

"It's a picker-upper," the navigator replied. Now Jay had taken a lot of bennies, yellow jackets along with one or two black beauties, all designed to bring about that much-needed second wind. This was no ordinary second wind. To sum up the exhilaration felt within the tiring bones of the recipient would be to call this a true fire starter. Jay was not experiencing a kindling effect, something to ease the flame along accumulating with oxygen to provide a well-lit crackling fire. No, this was full on gas in vapor form that could send the unsuspecting participant blazing into orbit without a care in the world.

This was a real game changer. "Wait until you do it with Debbie," came the response from Dave.

"You know Debbie doesn't partake," Jay replied, kind of aggravated at the hash-stoned little buddy who normally maintained during the buzzing hour. One thing Jay would not tolerate is a lightweight. You must be able to maintain no matter what. If the high takes you over, disappear until you can regain control. If not, stay gone or shut up.

Dave stopped giggling long enough to explain that Debbie skiing was not a requirement for this stuff to make an ordinary evening into a special romantic memory. "It will make everything you do that much better," Dave explained.

Jay understood exactly what Dave was talking about and was anxious to give it a try. Problem was Debbie had to work a couple extra days, and Jay would be a free man for the first two days in Panama City. Jay had no problem running a solution through his mind during the last straight run out of Alabama into sunny Florida.

Now checked in at the hotel on the beach with the sun setting on the beautiful white sands of the Gulf Coast, Jay and the boys rolled it up, lit it up, and stepped on out into the nightlife of 'School's Out for Summer" blasting everywhere. Alice Cooper, how could you go wrong? Mix that in with a little Rod Stewarts's "Tonight's the Night," and you were golden. With a packet of fresh powder, Jay had the will and knew a way: just stay out of the areas where Debbie's girlfriends played. Two days without the chain meant a lot of opportunity for Jay. Taking a step in the direction of the unthinkable was common ground for this young warrior, the one who must conquer the hearts of the free and enslave them into a dungeon of vanities full of hope and disbelief. Why could he not truly love them back? A laugh entwined with the screams of pain told all that needed to be said. In Jay's mind, there was no such thing as earthly love, a gentle caress, or a loving look.

Animalistic was the way, overly energetic with the growl of a devouring beast, muscles glistening with sweat as the roughness of total disrespect bordered on the abomination turned quickly into exhilaration, the screams of the wanton mankind of complete and utter satisfaction.

This was the battlefield Jay felt most prepared, being told since fourteen that he was a ruler of the domain. It had started out innocent enough, seeking the love that could heal the brokenness so deep within and override the pain of knowing the one he truly loved was so capable of extinguishing the very life she had given. Time and time again, those words had pierced the bipolar ranting of the one who gave him life to the point that Jay would use them often once encountered in battle, "I'll kill you…"

The rage that Jay had in battle could not easily be explained, the temperament he so distrusted, the moments of conscious thoughts of unbelievable destruction with little to no feeling of remorse at all. It was these moments that he struggled to understand the mindset of the mother that never allowed closeness to interfere with her law, the way she saw the world no matter how convoluted. It was seen through her eyes, and now it was Jay's law, and only his interpretation mattered, not caring if everyone or no one saw it his way. Plainly, it was not his mother's way, but was this type of love really any different? Jay truly told himself that he did not care. To love him was to lose him. There's only one way to stay attached, and that was loosely, never getting to close. That room was very small, maybe one more could enter. Only time would tell.

Jay had loved the summer break so far, getting into three fights, diving off the second floor into the pool and being kicked out of two clubs. That all failed in comparison to the blatant accusations being thrown at Jay from Debbie's girl friends. There in the hotel pool, Jay was now being confronted with accusations of infidelity concerning the two previous nights—accusations that Jay just laughed at. "You either believe me or them," Jay responded to Debbie, looking her dead in the eye. She knew that look; he didn't care one way or the other if she believed him. This man had his own set of laws, obey them or get the hell out of his life.

The remainder of the summer break was great fun for Jay and Debbie. She was so appreciative of the man who had put the shiny on her finger, and she had given everything to him—completely invested in the future to come as Mr. and Mrs. Jay.

Was that day even possible? Not really in Jay's mind. This was nothing more than the dreams of little girls. "Marriage? How quant and proper," Jay laughed to himself.

"Wouldn't it be wonderful to get married here on Panama City Beach with all the beautiful white sand and our closest friends?" Debbie blasted out in excitement.

"Why, yes it would," Jay responded, trying not to laugh in her glowing red face. "We better get out of the sun for a while," Jay suggested. This portion of summer was now coming to a very enjoyable end.

Debbie got to stay a couple days longer in Panama City Beach while Jay and his gang headed back to work the summer away. With them, they carried the knowledge of additional substances to assist in the world of dancing, working, and fun. As summer went on, the dance scene became littered with rolled-up bills to enjoy the tableside delights of your favorite nightclub. There were lines being drawn all over the place. Everyone participates while playing in the summertime snow. There were so many snowy hills around town that you couldn't even get into the bathrooms, for all the shy skiers blocked the place up. To break it out up front was Jay's thing. "Let's get to the last dance so we can get to the last dance," was Jay's favorite saying. That song closed every club everywhere, and it doesn't matter where as long as it was a disco. Jay was running so hard during work and play that this guy was bound to hit the wall. Too much too fast was not a good thing, and Jay knew he was borderline. This was going to be a summer to remember even if it killed him and with prophecy really not being his thing. True to scale was about to add up. Something had to give one way or another. Man must not live on drugs alone.

28

PRICE TO BE PAID

Jay had a couple of really close calls the last couple of weekends back from the beach. Everyone was attempting to settle in while Jay was just trying to slow down. Too many microdots on Friday night had led to a very strange episode at Debbie's house while lounging and swimming in her sixteen-year-old birthday present. A full-size pool with a diving board was thrown in for fun. Diving was always something special to Jay. Preacher Man Dad tells the story of when Jay was just six years old while living at Virginia Beach. He wanted to know what it took to be allowed to dive off the high dive, a ten-foot-high board. Jay never even asked about the little diving board. Giant Dad took Jay up to a lifeguard and asked him the qualifications needed to be allowed to jump off the high dive. The dark tanned man wearing sunglasses pointed at the pool and proclaimed, "To dive, you have to swim from this side of the pool to that side of the pool and back again."

Giant Dad then looked around to see if Jay understood, but he claims there was no little Jay, only the water splashing as he made his way across and back again within no time at all. The lifeguard was amazed and cleared Jay to have at it. Giant Dad in the meantime was instructing Jay to jump off the high dive, seeing that if he hit wrong while diving, it could split his skull open. Jay did as Giant Dad had instructed, made it up the ladder, walked to the end of the board, looked down at the sparkling water, and jumped. Giant Dad said that was the last time little Jay ever jumped off a diving board. From then on, he dove and dove and got better and better until now as it is well known. The one and a half of Debbie's small board was perfect in form, cutting the air and water with ease. It was poetry in motion as so many had previously observed. So why was Jay hanging around at the bottom of the pool? Jay finally surfaced, grasping to the side of the pool, attempting to understand exactly where and when it was that he got soaking wet. Debbie laughed at Jay and told him to get out of the pool while Jay held tighter and asked the question that shocked her to the core. "Where are you, Debbie? I can hear you, but I don't see you. What pool are you talking about?"

Little Bro had just stopped by driving his cool used Javelin, so Debbie enlisted him to help out with the slightly confused drowning rat clinging to the side of her pool. Little Bro was calling to Jay, and he was heard, but everything that had to do with vision was playing a different movie all together. Jay told them he heard them, but he was still there in that bar with so much blood.

"Do you see the blood?" Jay asked. Debbie and Little Bro got Jay out of the pool and wrapped him in a lot of towels, attempting to keep the sun off. Jay just lay there, shivering and mumbling about the blood, thinking to himself, to many microdots, that this had to be a bad trip. Three purple microdots were way too much, as everyone told him at the pool hall Friday night. It didn't really bother him then, but swimming and playing in the sun might have just caught up to the invincible Jay.

Jay could feel the breeze blowing through his hair and wondered why it was such a windy day. He opened his eyes, focusing in on a pretty glass door and heard very soft voices discussing the weather, or was it the water? Things were still a little fuzzy. Jay slowly drifted away. "Have a nice rest," he could hear Debbie ask. Was she talking to Jay? He opened his eyes and sat up looking around to the faces of wonder. There was her mother and little brother and sister all staring and waiting for a response from the newly awakened Jay. "How long have I been asleep?" Jay asked.

Debbie's mom chimed, "In and out, you were talking all types of crazy coming in and out, do you feel any better?"

Jay made his way to the Wildcat with Debbie close in tow. "What was that all about?" she asked. "It's drugs, isn't it, Jay? Tell me the truth! Are you doing drugs?"

Jay had it with the prosecuting attorney routine. "She better never pull that crap again," he told himself as the Wildcat let the tires squeal heading onto the hard top.

"What was that all about?" she asked.

Yes, it's the drugs! Jay was screaming in his mind. It was something he couldn't control, and it was Jay's number 1 rule to always be in control. To allow someone to think you are out of control is one thing, but to be out of control, this must never happen again, says the man who keeps knocking on death's door.

Back on the red dirt road, Big Red wanted to know if Jay was in for the night.

"Sure am, Momma, tired, think I'll get some food in me and just relax for this evening."

Big red smiled, commenting something about burning at both ends would quickly burn you out. One thing about Big Red, she never really minded Jay going and coming at all hours of the day. She knew he was young, eighteen, and of legal age to do whatever he wanted. He was a hard worker and always polite around any and all elders. It was the way he was raised, and Big Red could see the fine young man before her. She knew soon he'd be gone, one way or another.

Sis had gone out with Boy Toy that Saturday night, and Jay never even came out to say hi; they were taking the relationship down the road, and everyone could see the signs. Marriage was just around the corner. The evening turned into night, and sitting there with Little Bro asleep, Jay studied his favorite book of all time, the living Word. Oh, how it came to life when Jay maintained closeness to being holy for he is holy. The meaning was leaping off the pages and attaching themselves into Jay's consciousness to where any and all were available at a moment's notice. Jay truly missed the closeness of the one who would always love him, who died for him, such love. Jay did not deserve this love, but it was applied anyway. This he knew; this is what broke his heart.

Jay heard the whimpering. No, it was someone crying. He leapt out bed and made his way to the front door as quietly as he could. It was his sis. She had tears rolling down her face while Redhead Momma who heard everything called out, "You kids all right?"

"Yes, Momma. It's only me and Sis," Jay replies.

"Okay, you kids get to bed. We have church tomorrow."

You see, Sis had a curfew of midnight, and she was right on time. Only thing was she was freaking out as Jay clasped his hand over her mouth and escorted her back to his room. It seemed good old Boy Toy got his hands on some mescaline that was a little too much, and Sis was losing it. Jay held his sister wrapped in a blanket and rocked her like a child to calm the visions of windowpanes growing small then large. She was trailing, and time would ease her mind while Jay was going to ease Boy Toy's mind.

Sunday morning came with Jay pulling the Wildcat into the church parking lot. There was Boy Toy standing beside his ride with a panicked look on his face. Jay jumped out of the car and headed straight for the love of his sister's life, and as he neared, apologies came flying.

"I'm so sorry, Jay," Boy Toy exclaimed. "We were running out of time, and I was tripping hard enough on my own. I had to get her home, you know that."

Jay understood, as you did not want to break the household curfew that applied to all except Jay. No one really seemed to care when Jay came home. It seemed they were all just waiting for Jay to drift away. He knew Little Bro would miss him, but that was about it.

"It took me three hours of rocking her to get her to finally go to sleep. She was losing it. What was it? Mescaline?" Jay demanded.

"It was this new chocolate mescaline."

New mescaline, it was a mind trip, and all knew it. Sis was not a big partier, and the future husband of his sister needed to get his act together especially if marriage is around the corner.

Sunday school was as usual. Jay no longer taught or even assisted in the classes. He was commanded to attend every Sunday as Preacher Dad said, "If you're going out on Saturday nights with the hoot owls, you better be ready to soar with the eagles come Sunday morning."

Jay was always there, a little cloudy at times, but with the help of his pal Bennie, attendance was always possible. There was a problem arising within the church concerning Jay as the summer went on. It seemed some funds had come up missing, and the arrow pointed to the user of many substances. It was a fact that to continue his lifestyle, additional funding would need to come from somewhere, and as Jay continued to slide deeper and deeper into the realm of dependency, the standards Jay once held himself to so highly now seemed nonexistent. Here, he was worried about dependency concerning his sister and little bro while the whole time, the mirror needed to reflect the eroding morals of a young man who once lived the holy life. Where had that man gone? Jay reasoned within himself that everything would be fine once he got his life under control. Not only was Jay under suspension at the church for missing funds, he was also beginning to lift extra money at Debbie's house, and her father and mother were starting to ask questions. Jay just needed a little extra money to support his habits that for now weren't really taking over his sanity.

Sanity was the topic that seemed to concern everyone attached to Jay. By now, his preacher dad and first lady of the church were confronted with a few issues concerning their oldest son. Jay could feel the tension growing all around but was still unable to slow down. He had to have and really needed to have the doses of reality that came in a pill or powder, and everything would be okay. Jay knew it as he hit the hash pipe provided by Little Bro. Was Jay leading his brother down the wrong path? Sis had quit everything cold turkey the night of the bad mescaline trip, and no one could blame her. That seemed like a year ago to Jay, but in actuality, it was only two months. Everything was surging and pulling in all directions, engaged and acting like a responsible man ready for a wife. Everyone wanted to know the wedding date while trouble stirred in paradise to the tune of Debbie seeing the downward spiral of Jay. Her parents drilled her on the missing money, and now Jay was even slipping money from his dear friend's store he had managed at such an early age. Jay was stealing from anyone and everyone. His mom would leave her purse upstairs, and while she was doing the customers' hair, Jay could slip in and pull a five or ten out anytime he wanted. Big Red had a great clientele, and she made a lot of money. Still, none of this was slowing Jay down. The evil he had become was not the man he ever wanted to be, but it was the man he saw in the mirror, pale with dark eyes, tired and needing a break. Looking deeper, he saw a man without life. Jay had died, and now this hull of a man stood before him—someone he himself did not know.

He walked around dead, laughing with a tone of arrogance, popping here and snorting there. Trying and lying was the life he now led, no rest, just passing out once in a while, falling into a slumber, trying to maintain the responsible attitude that once shined for the world to see and to again be worshipped by the masses and loved by all, artificially or not. It was still a love that he now missed. Questions kept coming from Debbie. She continued to hound Jay. She knew as everyone knew that Jay was way over his head. Jay was beginning to feel like a cornered animal, and he was not above biting someone's head off.

The factory work continued during the summer, and Jay and his pals took smoke breaks, pick-me-up breaks, and even a late-dinner break, which always turned into another smoke break. This one particular night, Jay made his way into the restroom to wash up for the dinner break, and there stood one of his working pals, Tommy, crying.

"What's up, Tommy? Why the tears?" Jay asked. Then Tommy explained one of the new workers took his lunch sack and ate it, and when Tommy asked him about it, the new guy slapped him in the mouth and told him to get out of his face or he'd get worse. Now Tommy was a great guy, friendly, hard worker. Everyone liked him and knew he wasn't the most physical man.

"Hey, new guy," Jay called out as they were all heading the clock to punch out for dinner. "You're going to apologize to Tommy, and then you're going to give him three dollars for his lunch, and then I'm still going to hook you up."

The fight was on. He tried to sucker punch Jay there in line, but Jay had already said all he was going to say. He wasn't talking; he was ready for fighting. The three rounds were all Jay's. Little Bro had turned sixteen in June and was working in he factory with Jay for the last month or so, and he was dancing around, cheering Jay on as he was knotting this guy's head up. It was too easy. This guy had no speed to speak of, and Jay was lighting him up, probably getting a little lackadaisical when the new guy threw a punch over the top right, which Jay blocked with his left arm. Jay punched him square in the nose, which busted like a ripe tomato, and then Little Bro was screaming at Jay, “He cut you Jay, he cut you.”

Jay backed up a step or two and asked where. It seemed that over the top right hand pulled an already opened pocketknife from his back pocket and laid a three-inch cut to Jay’s upper left arm then put the knife down on a 50 gallon barrel to show everyone he no longer had a knife. Well, the fair fight was over, and everyone jumped on the new guy who by the way got fired while Jay ended up getting five butterfly stitches and a lot of praise from the bosses for standing up for a fellow worker. Jay knew one thing as he looked at the scar that would follow him all the days of his life—no more fair fights.

29

CRASHING DOWN

The total price to be paid by Jay was in no way tallied out quite yet. Debbie had cornered Jay at home there on the red dirt road and demanded a little too much. This girl was going out of her mind, and the fun of it all was that she still had a long way to go to catch Jay. Summer was at an end, and Jay was preparing to head two hours away into the big city for a year of hairstyling, a dream of Big Red's for a family shop. Jay just knew he didn't want to do any of the structured stuff any longer, and learning to style hair the professional way would definitely be out of the ordinary. Continuing to playing ball at the college level was tempting, but this was not what Jay's burnt-out mind was looking for. He was tired of all the performances, being pulled this way and then that, and now Debbie was being just too demanding—all at the wrong time. Jay was done. "So you want to play the 'love me tender' game, do you?"

"It's either me or drugs," Debbie demanded.

Bad timing, Debbie, Jay thought to himself as she ran down the hall, crying.

"Your son chose drugs over marrying me," she yelled at Preacher Dad sitting on the living room couch.

"Yes, I'm sure he did," he said, shaking his head in disbelief.

How could Jay have chosen any other option? She didn't give him any, just a "this is it chose now." Well, that's what you get for demanding something from a dude riding the seven fourteen Quaalude highway. Mellow was the fellow as he stood on the front porch waving good-bye. "See you later and have a nice life."

Returning into the house, Preacher Man asked Jay to have a seat. He needed to talk to him about all the problems going on at the church. It seemed Jay had been spotted smoking a joint before services, and most did not want to let go of that little thing called lifting the tithes of the dedicated members. More than one at the little country church decided they needed a public apology, and then they would expel Jay from the membership of the "Only We Are Holy Baptist Church."

"Let me get this right," Jay stated. "They want me to come before them on a Sunday morning right before the main service starts, stand up front, and apologize to them for smoking a joint before Sunday school and stealing tithes from the offerings to buy more dope. Is that about right, Dad?" Jay asked.

"That's about it, son," Preacher Man Dad replied.

Jay was hardhearted and tough as nails when it came to the problems he was dealing with, attempting just to cling to the smallest amount of sanity. Six months earlier, he had gone to Preacher Man Dad and confessed his evil ways of providing for his habits of survival, opening a case and allowing the preacher man to see just how deep the rabbit hole went. He was stunned at how one person could take so many different substances and still maintain. It's really not that hard if you start out with a little here and a little there. Before you know it, the world comes crashing down, and until you seek some help, the load just gets heavier and heavier.

Preacher Man Dad did attempt to help, but this was something way out of his control. Jay acted as if he was getting better, but the whole time, he just kept slipping away, taking this to feel up and that to feel normal and never really ever coming close. Preacher Man Dad knew it, and now was the time to allow Jay to be separated from the little country church he knew so well and loved through the power of the cross. That morning riding to church, he remembered the Christmas plays that they had all put on together, the summer vacation Bible schools, early sunrise services each Easter morning, and the times of reflection at that little altar of repentance. The years Jay grew by leaps and bounds even to the point of preaching on Wednesday nights for his dad. Close to God, a personal relationship that was his very own, the one who would always love him even though he had murdered, stole, and blasphemed the holiness of God, Jesus still loved him, and this is what hurt his heart, knowing no matter what, he was still loved. Preacher Man Dad had said the same thing to Jay on his way out that morning, leaving before Jay who of course was just going to apologize and then leave for good.

"Always know this, son," he said, "you are human and will make many more mistakes, and some will be greater than those you face today, but I will always love you no matter what."

Jay arrived at the church he had attended for all those developmental years, teaching and praying then learning to love God in spirit and in truth. Jay always loved John 4, where Jesus was talking to the Samaritan woman by the well. How could he possibly be talking to one that all thought was so unclean? Was that Jay today, unclean, facing the accusations without understanding the inner most problems that was before them? Jesus knew the woman by the well. He was Christ, and he knew all, but here on this warm fall morning, judgment had been cast without really knowing Jay, never taking the time to even ask if there is a problem.

All the young people were happy to see Jay once again; it had been a while since his last attendance. How much they knew was anyone's guess, but they sure were happy and smiling ear to ear.

"Where you been, Jay?" a young teen male questioned.

"Oh, just trying to stay out of trouble. It didn't work too well, but it's always good to try," Jay said.

"You getting ready to head to the big city for that hairstyling college, aren't you, Jay?" pretty little fifteen-year-old deacon's daughter questioned.

"Yes, I am," Jay replied. Thinking now that he was eighteen, he needed to get far and wide of this place. The look in her eyes was enough to turn the lights green and slam the pedal to the metal. *Got to go,* Jay thought. Just one more speech to give, and Jay would leave it with good people of his family, the ones that didn't deserve this reprobate and his sorry excuses of drug abuse and self-pity, allowing drugs to drag him so deep into the depths of sin. No, this was Jay's choice. He made every single decision and would blame no one but himself. There was only him, standing and staring into that mirror and ready to give a speech.

Whispers filled the room as the preacher called their attention to Jay who had something he wished to say prior to beginning the Sunday morning services. Jay stood from the back and made his way forward, passing the now-filled pews with their silent members anxiously waiting for what they had voted on, what they now demanded. The noses turned away, the whispers of those who could never control their tongues, the sad faces and even tears for those who so loved Jay and had been on trips with him, knowing his heart was God's, but still...

Jay made it to the front and stood beside his father, staring out into the seated judges who had never sinned before. As he was about to speak, Old Man Pops stood up and let them all have it.

"What's wrong with you people?" the ninety year old saint called out. "This young man needs love and forgiveness, not "we're better than you are"! Why must he come before all and confess his sins. I don't see any of you publicly confessing your sins, and you know you got a closet full of them."

No one said a word. The youth of the church looked confused. A couple of saints started crying and praying. Jay stepped forward and cleared his throat to speak.

Jay slowly looked around the room, smiling at those who were now hurting. "I am so very sorry," Jay started. "It was not my intention to hurt so many of you who have always cared for me. I have fallen from the goodness of your graces, but I am thankful that I cannot fall from those of our heavenly Father. I have looked for love in the darkest hour, but now I must turn to the one true light. I am a sinner and have committed terrible sins. I will most assuredly do this again and often until one day, my relationship with our holy Father can be made complete. I do not apologize to those who feel they deserve an apology. What you deserve is hell, and sending you there is but a road you dare not travel. Hold on to your piety and self-appreciations, congratulate each other on the accomplishments that lead you away from the cross, and I pray soon you will find your way home."

Jay then walked down the three steps of the altar where he had cried unto God many times, attempting to right the ship called Jay—in a dark and stormy gale all but had seemed lost; yet once again, the Savior reached down into the tumult waters and plucked a drowning man from the grasps of death, my Jesus, my Savior, and my Lord. As Jay continued the walk of shame, leading down the aisle to the exit, to his right, he saw his mother, brother, and sisters stand to their feet, then he heard these stunning words from his dad: "Starting immediately, I now resign as your pastor. It has been my privilege. God bless you and have a wonderful day." The members were now out of control with this unexpected news, as no one said anything about the preacher quitting.

No, Jay thought, stopping in his tracks as his family slid out into the isle. Standing there speechless, he felt this surge of emotions rising within, his eyes exploding into tears.

"You can't do this. It's my fault, and I did this, Momma, no!"

Big Red looked at her tall, slender son, and all she could see was her little boy crying. "Oh, son," she said as she tenderly placed her hand on the side of Jay's face, wiping away the tears. "You are and will always be a big part of our family and family sticks together. We forgive you, and we love you, honey." Those words came crashing down around Jay like a ton of bricks, of love and forgiveness. No matter how much it hurts at times, it's still love.

The family continued to walk out of that little country church as the members were scrambling for answers, taking back the vote to expel Jay.

"Please preacher, please don't go. We'll take it all back," members were heard yelling as the preacher's family was heading down the outside steps.

Old Man Pop chimed in, "Got what you deserve. Oh sure now you're ready to forgive, bunch of Dad-blame hypocrites."

Still, Jay felt as if he had let his entire family down, but it was soon made clear that this was in the best interest for the entire family. Preacher Man Dad was heading off to Bible college to become a full reverend while Jay was heading off to the big city.

"It was time for a change," Big Red stated. "You stay at one church too long and people start to believe they own you as if what they want is what God wants. Well, Gods never stopped working in our lives, and it's high time we got on with it." Big Red had a way of stating things that always inspired Jay, simple and to the point. It would serve Jay well in life if he survived the suicidal course he was on. Ticktock went the clock. We are all on the clock. Ticktock.

.

30

THE WEDDING

The family all got settled in for the new fall season with Preacher Dad enrolling in Bible college while Jay did the same for hairstyling school. While that excitement was settling in, Sis and Boy Toy decided they just wanted to have a nice, simple wedding right there on red dirt road, right out of the blue.

"Invite the families, keep it small, and no one will notice the expedience or the urgency to get all this thrown together in such a short amount of time. We are so in love and let's get married next weekend, next weekend!"

Funny thing about living on red dirt road was the fact that all must maintain a C average or get the whopping of a lifetime. So with this required attention to let's say, school of mathematics, it didn't take everyone long to add up the "let's do it now" to the date in which they now did it. Family secrets are always so much fun; at least, it wasn't Jay this time.

Night in the early fall was always so comfortable. The temperatures after sunset were so nice you'd rather be outside. Jay and Little Bro stood at the bottom of the backyard down by the burn pit, watching the fire and smoking a joint, talking about how funny it was this time of the year, everyone busy getting ready to do this or that, running around like chickens with their heads cut off. Of course, seeing a chicken running around without its head off was funny enough without the joint, but there they were, laughing like a couple of silly kids. Little Bro laughed so hard he about fell off into the burn pit, not the first time.

Jay reflected on how quickly time had flown by, standing here and smoking a number with Little Bro. Heck, for that matter, any time they wanted to do one up, they just stated the code: "Hey, Bro, want to get a Sun Drop?" Those were the magic words that fooled absolutely nobody. Well, maybe Redhead Momma, but they were pretty sure she chose to be oblivious. Off to the store, the Wildcat, or Javelin, would go about a mile and a half away while the whole time, there were two liters of Sun Drops right inside the house. Yes, they were slick.

It was just so amazing to Jay at how quickly time had passed; this was his sixteen-year-old little brother who Jay now reminded would have to take on all the chores of expanding the yard; he laughed at the thought of it. Little Bro, now on the flip side, had some news of his own. Preacher Dad wanted to make it easier on the family while he was away at seminary, so he bought a nice new yard tractor due to the increased size of the homestead. *What!* Jay thought; he was going to lose his buzz. "A new yard tractor, you lazy spoilt little brat!" Jay called out jokingly with his brother.

That's when the protector of all yelled down from the beauty shop, "You boys stop that fighting, and you better not be shooting that bull in the balls again with your BB guns." Jay and Little Bro just rolled on the ground laughing.

Laying there and looking up at the country nights light show was always a special occasion for the boys. Now one of them was on the verge of becoming a man on his own while Little Brother still had to finish two more years of high school. They hadn't really thought of it in those terms before, laying there while the fire crackled down in that pit, watching the burning embers blend with the beauty of the night's sky. It was a somber time. They wondered if this would be the last time for the two brothers who had become one over the years. Would they ever lay out staring at God's magnificent creation again together, stoned just enough to be mesmerized by the wonder of it all?

"I love you, Jay," Little Bro said in a quiet gentle voice.

"I'll always love you, little brother," Jay said, finalizing this chapter in the boy's lives.

"Are you boys down there shooting that bull in the balls with your BB guns again?" Mom yelled.

"No, Momma. It's too dark to see that bull, let alone his balls," Jay called back. The boys just laughed like crazy at the times they used to have sitting down along the creek shade on a hot summer afternoons. That bull would stand down there by the creek, which came from a natural spring, and the water so nice and cool running through the shady woods it made the temperature much nicer.

It was a perfect spot for a little target practice that the boys would always remember; those gonads hung so low, and with the classical Red Ryder BB gun, you could actually see the BB flying through the air and stinging that bull right on the ball. That gonad would jump straight up into that bull, and he let out the biggest snort and then went to swiping his tail back and forth, lift that massive head, take a few steps, thinking it was a bee or something stinging him, then stop, and settle back down. Now when he did this, that gonad would slowly ease its way back down for another round of "what the heck was that!" A bull tale. Man, those boys had some funny memories, enough to last a lifetime if need be, but they sure hoped not.

Jay hung around as much as possible while still working at the factory, at least until he made his way to the big city for a year of school and another after-school job to support him and his lovely habits. He hit the discos as often as possible, and while out cruising and snorting along, he would win a dance competition here and there, and then all the girls wanted to dance just so they could feel like winners. He ran into Debbie one weekend and got a little dance crazy with her, and sure enough, they won the dance off that night. She was so elated at winning that playing some of the old lover games was fine for that weekend, but by the time the buzz wore off, everything went back to normal.

Jay sometimes wondered how it would have been if he were different and not so attached to anything and everything. Could he have been the marrying kind? Was it possible to love Debbie for the rest of his life? And the big question is that was there any way at all that Jay could truly believe she honestly loved him? Not a chance! Jay slapped himself out of the soap-opera true-romance daydream and back into the world of his sister getting married. That's what brought all this insanity on in the first place. Everyone knew Jay had no intentions of living to be thirty years old, and that was that.

Well, the weekend of the big wedding was finally here, and it was time for all to know the vital roles that must be played to bring this union into a huge success. Jay got picked to take the pictures, and Little Bro would assist in seating the guests.

Little Sis was the flower girl while Middle Sis was the maid of honor. Boy Toy's brother was going to be the best man, and Preacher Man Dad was pronouncing the deceased. Redhead Momma was going to do whatever she wanted just because she was Big Red, and while she was at it, she would handle the food along with the decorations and any unruly attendants with swift justice of hillbilly law. This was going to be one of those occasions that the family could look back on and smile at the remembrance of the soon-to-be-expecting bride, the country boy toy who was about to swear away his life, and a cameraman who really didn't want to be there.

Everyone started showing up while Big Red hated the dress she was wearing just to hear everyone's opinion on how beautiful she looked. Jay looked at his mom and could truly see the beauty that had drawn his dad's eye so long ago. Well, twenty years is really not that long ago, and it's probably why Big Red was still such a beautiful woman, but never mind that, she needed all to acknowledge the bell of the ball, and it sure wasn't the bride. Of course, Jay's sister was fine with Big Red being the center of attention, taking the spotlight off the obviously growing elephant in the room.

As soon as Preacher Dad's parents arrived, the first thing Grandma did was to hug the bride and rub the elephant. Jay spit a peanut so hard you could hear it smack the paneling across the room. His sister turned pale as her dress as everyone who was feeling uncomfortable wanted to get the party started while Jay wanted to get some pictures of the family gathering before the ceremony and then after.

"Hurry up, son," said the soon-to-be reverend who was among the uncomfortable. Jay's sister was tall and skinny just like Jay. She was wearing a beautiful flowing white mid-thigh dress that accentuated the mother-to-be. It seemed trying it on two weeks ago made a little difference into an obvious difference.

The ceremony went off without a hitch. Everyone was so happy to hear them pronounced as man and wife as to take away the sins of premarital fornication. It was as if all had been forgiven due to the commitment before God. Actually, all had been forgiven, and that was nailed to a cross so long ago. Jesus died for sins just like this, and all is forgiven to live a wonderful life in Christ in which Jay was sure the two newly married would devote themselves. After the mescaline scare, they had pretty much asked for forgiveness and started living a better life; it's funny how near-fatal experiences can have an effect on people like that. Even if it really wasn't near fatal at all, it still was enough to make one stop and think. What if? Many of mankind has had those moments to stop and think. Oh, how Jay wished this would have been one of his moments to think, but no, Jay and Little bro were bored, so out came the call to run get a Sun Drop.

There was such a commotion there, and Jay had taken plenty of pictures to satisfy the bride/mommy-to-be, so why not take off for a little refreshment? The boys jumped into the Wildcat, and there sliding in beside Little Bro was Grandpa, the preacher mans pop.

"Well, hi there, grandpa," Jay said as he pulled the door shut. "We're just driving up to the store to get a cold drink. You sure you want to come along?"

Grandpa gave Jay the strangest look, and with the boys not really knowing him that well, moment was slightly tense. "Boy, don't shoot that crap my way," Grandpa started. "I know you boys are up to something, and I want in."

So Jay fired up the Wildcat and started up that red dirt road, nice and easy as not to stir too much dust or attention. Little Bro was excited and already giggling as he repeated the fact that Grandpa wanted to ride along. "Yes, I see that," Jay replied, and then Jay spoke the famous words of the doomed, "Spark that bad boy up."

The boys took the normal ride, and Grandpa was excited about trying the "wacky weed" as he put it, so they sparked one up, got them a cold drink as normal, and then headed back to the party. It sure would have helped if Jay would have been thinking clearly about that time, but it was not meant to be. Jay pulled up in front of the house on the red dirt road as if all could possibly be normal. Oh contraire! The little attention to detail that the now-buzzed Jay had forgotten about was the fact that Grandpa, or should we now call him happy Grand Pa, had never had to deal with people while having a buzz on, and for the sake of all confusion, he just did not care.

Picture a sixty-five-year old, gray-headed grandpa comes rolling out of that Wildcat spouting verbal gibberish that caught the attention of everyone standing in the front yard. Pretty tables were set among the Southern pines while a cool early fall breeze was settling in. Conversations of happy tomorrows for the newly married couple all stopped. Grandpa was making a entrance so loud that even the neighbors wanted to join in on the fun.

"This is such a beautiful wedding," Grandpa shouted out as he continued walking to the now-suspicious preacher man. "Son, I'm so very proud of you for attending Bible college," Grandpa stated in a manner that most understood, but one who understood just fine was now shooting burning arrows out of his eyes in the direction of Jay. Oh, Jay wished he could have wiggled his nose and disappeared, but that joint wasn't that good, and now the finger of Preacher Man Dad was gesturing for him to join them as Grandpa was so elegantly draped around his son.

Jay made his way through the happily confused crowd only to hear Grandma claim that her husband had lost his mind while Jay's now-married sister glared in his direction, knowing good and well what had happened and who it was that really lost their mind. Obliviously, it was Jay.

"What were you thinking?" Preacher Man Dad asked in a very low tone. "You thought it was a good idea to get my dad stoned during your sister's wedding?"

Honestly, Jay wished he had run the entire scenario through his head a little better, but here he stood, and what's done was done, and all he could say was "Sorry, Dad, he wanted to ride along and try something new. It was completely my fault" as his little brother was now escorting Grandpa over to the refreshment table. "That was some pretty good stuff" was the last thing Jay wanted to hear from his grandpa as now it seems everyone was putting the pieces together.

A very valuable lesson was learned that day of early fall, a lesson Jay intended to keep close at heart when dealing with the lives of loved ones. Never, and I mean never, share your weed!

31

STYLING COLLEGE

The big city was full of fast cars and even faster walking people. There were the famous posers who were not really sure who they were, but in the meantime, please call them some stupid made up French name, idiots! Jay had no time for the fake, but he was definitely very interested in the weak and timid. Building confidence had always been so rewarding, so once arriving the first day of styling school, he had the opportunity to meet some very nice and interesting people who had dreams of becoming a professional hairstylist. "Dreams, I tell you," Jay screamed into the realm of inner darkness that so occupied his mind. "This is a dream of theirs: to become a professional haircutter, stop the presses The professional stylist has now arrived. Would everyone please bow! Unbelievable!"

The newest class of twenty or so students sat in the designated back room away from the more senior classes that could be seen out and about, sharply dressed in black and white, very clean and professional-looking, preparing to begin their day as student stylists. Jay sat in the back of the class, sizing up the newbies, and man, what an array. There were young ones like Jay, eighteen to twenty-one, and then there was an assortment of men and women, ages, yes, and, oh my goodness. One dude was short and cut like a bodybuilder with a confident smile that reminded Jay of an older car salesman. Up on the front row sat the eager beavers chatting and acting as if this was the most exciting day of their lives, and who knows, it might end up being the most exciting. How very, very sad.

Then the attention turned to the doorway as a female instructor entered the room making her introductions. She was attractive and in her early thirties, with a very nice smile and a warm, inviting personality. She was married without children but hoped to have a couple, two at least, and she would be around anytime needed. All anyone need do is ask. No questions are stupid questions. *Right,* Jay thought.

Next to enter the room was the vice president of operations and head consumer of doughnuts. This guy was, oh, how should this be stated? Pleasantly plump, cutely chubby, readily round, okay, he was fat! Trying to be nice was always a good idea especially for those who would be grading everyone's efforts, so the dropped pencil, the "could you help a guy out and get that for me" routine just to see if he could touch the floor, was out. All made nice as the VP explained the ins and outs of what was to be expected from everyone. Effort was a key factor, but while actual ability was desired, arrogance would not be appreciated. Jay thought this might be some fun, so he decided to be as helpful and courteous as possible. Helping and encouraging were always strong suits for Jay, and nothing made him happier than to see others succeed.

After a thirty-minute "You can do this" speech from the VP, everyone was given a case containing the tools of their trade, nice, very nice, shiny blow-dryers, straight razors, and some of the finest cutting shears labeled "Made in Germany." After this came, the book on the body and how it fed and created hair all started from a single breath. The whole body blood and follicle thing was very interesting to Jay. School had broken down all the area's discussed, just not to the level of hair importance.

"Did you know that if the hair around your ear is fine and falling out it means you like to smoke a lot of pot?" the VP stated. The class erupted in motion as the new friends started checking out each other's ears, laughing breaking out all over the place while Jay just sat there smiling at the pleased-with-himself VP. This was just the first day, and already everyone was having a good time.

Next came the man himself, the three-time world champion, the greasy Greek. Yes, boys and girls, respect your elders because he just entered the room. The man who had invented world-class hairstyles was now going to enlighten all. Jay was amazed at how much this older doughnut eater thought of himself, going on and on with tales of greatness while the first two rows squirmed with excitement. *There's only one thing to do,* Jay thought, *ask the question!*

"Excuse me," Jay started while the entire class swiftly turned to see who would dare to speak to the greatest Greek. "I was wondering. Out of all the classes that have graduated from this fine institute, how many would you say have obtained greatness in the hairstyling field?" Pondering heads now returned to look at the gaseous Greek in anticipation to words that could change their lives. How famous could they become? Stylists to the stars maybe or just working on the corner with the pretty rotating pole? The quiet was deafening. Was that sweat now forming on the brow of the turning-green Greek one?

"You no can understand," was the awaited response of the Greek's broken English, allowing the VP an adequate advantage to remove the Greek from the fire.

"It's very difficult to determine a percentage of success in a field that must discover itself. One should shoot for the stars but, at the same time, reflect on the available."

"Of course," Jay stated, "I should have seen that."

The afternoon, studies immediately commenced, allowing for a stage right escape of the galloping Greek, tail so firmly tucked between his more-than-ample cheeks that if he cleared his throat, it surely would have tasted of polyester. The entire class sat quietly, reading over the material in preparation of hands on catastrophes to come later in the week. The following two days allowed for lots of laughs while each one in the class was allowed to use their straight razor and shave a whitely foamed balloon. You would have thought the comical creamy classroom was a night at the Apollo, everyone busting a gut as each classmate attempted to carefully shave the cream off the substitute face without the magnificent cotton explosion. Laughter is one of the greatest medicines, and those two days were a wonderful double dose.

Studies became easier as more time each week was spent on the beginner's side of the school. There were four classes going at the same time, and as one class graduated, another new class would start up, each rotation on a two-month cycle with the possibility of being held back if necessary. For some, this was obvious while others excelled, leaving the majority of normal students headed for the pretty spinning pole. Jay was blessed with an ability that could not be questioned and was one of the three not to bust the balloon. A class was intimidated but was just getting started, and fear was not a factor, so Jay was anxious to jump right in as soon as called upon.

On the JV side of the class, totally separated from the varsity side, common easy haircuts were the call of the day. This new class was allowed to do the more mundane type of cuts. Not really considered styles although they we called as such. Now the victims would come straight off the street, looking for a great deal, and they were sure going to get it. Jay was called up for a typical taper cut up the back and neatly trimmed around the ear. Piece of cake for the long-legged newcomer as he greeted his victim, allowing him to be seated as Jay swirled the cloth gently around his neck. This was a school of professionals, and Jay grabbed his shears firmly, placing his fingers in the control holes and starting from the bottom of the neck and working his way up, allowing the shears to make a joyous noise as a dance of the flapping butterfly wings, with the hair falling to the floor in such abandonment as to proclaim a master was at work.

The master Jay stopped to survey the newly manicured landscape before him, and as with the summer drought, the grass seemed to be a little bare, especially in the middle of the freshly trimmed property. Stalling with the clicking of shears just off the lawn, the cruising female instructor swooped in to allow Jay a chance to observe her finer technique of damage control. Fixing the catastrophic cut was a breeze much needed on the arid front, but to allow for the sparseness, the trim had to be elevated farther up the head than hoped necessary.

As the gentleman was leaving, all were admiring the newest of design cuts that made the stylist of Alfalfa of the little rascals a much more wanted man. Jay was stunned as the class was very supportive of the most recent failure. Jay learned a valuable lesson in taking his time and removing a little at a time, one of the main subjects on how to professionally cut hair. Too much too fast, and he now knew what to expect. Taking your time and doing it right the first time is really where the line is drawn between someone who considers themselves a professional or just an ordinary jack of trades. One thing Jay knew for sure was that nothing about him was considered ordinary. The competitor within would not allow it. He had to be the best, and he would humbly allow all to witness.

The first two months of styling school flew by, and with each passing week, the class became tighter and more relaxed around each other. By now, all realized who the ones were that were special and those who would make good stylists just the same. Jay had all the confidence in the world, as the instructors would joke about him joining the shops owned there in the big city. Everyone else would catch the implied comments, but there was still a lot of time left for all to prove themselves worthy of hire. Jay played the compliments off with the returns of wanting to start a shop up in the hills where he so dearly missed his sparse-toothed family. They loved the jovial Jay so much that they all wished him the best, but it was Jay's determined mind that wanted any and all to succeed, any besides himself. He was blessed and had no worries of anything, never alone and always loved. Jesus was his all in all, the one true love that came to earth, and the Christmas season was quickly rounding the big city corner.

Redhead Momma planned for all the kids to be home for Christmas break, and if Momma wanted it, that's what she got. Jay had to reemphasize over and over that he would not be spending Christmas in the city. He had to go with the rest of his family and spend it together at home on that red dirt road. That of course caused a lot of conversations about family, and Jay was none too comfortable about divulging intimate details about his confused and disturbing life. *No,* Jay thought to himself. The difficult issues of life that still required continual performances to please the masses must continue on without disrupting the fairy-tale story now taking place. This darkness held is best kept under lock and key, mellowed by the many smoke breaks in, which Jay now enjoyed up to a pack or two a day, depending on the liquid spirit consumption as to determine the second pack smoked. That along with a joint here and there to include any and all substances that were handed his way made Jay a very mellow fellow. Jay maintained the happy-go-lucky almost to the point of adorable person they all loved to be with. Some of the girls there in school attendance wanted more than the fun for a minute-guy Jay was willing to give, but it was best to keep the intimate affairs between him and the customers as quiet and low-keyed as possible.

Entering into the third month of this highly rated styling college was a new frontier for the class of July 1978, as new hairstyles and additional processes were introduced that would allow people many options for the late-seventies styles. Jay found anything new fascinating and dived head first into the uncharted waters, colors to bring the spring, or perms to fill the furrows. You could paint it, thicken it, or thin it, thinning shears. *Such an abomination,* Jay thought.

One thing about these new styles was requiring a shampoo, cut, color, and even a perm. All this allowed extra time to be spent with the customer. There is no doubt about it; once you have shampooed, colored, or added a perm with a new style on a lady, you have bonded, you have massaged, and touched her more than any other man in her life. Gently and caringly, you become her most-trusted confidant, willing to tell all, baring her soul to the point of overexposing. It's a very delicate dance—a dance that could lead almost anywhere the stylist wanted to go. Some took a time or two, but others, Jay could capture their deepest desires with a simple smile. It was becoming a lot of fun, and normally, that's not a good thing.

Now playing along with the girls in the class in an attempt to take attention away from the now-returning customers was not sliding by the lovely lady instructor or any instructor for that matter. These guys have been doing this for years, and noticing little nuances like this was nothing but pure fun for them. Even some of the more advanced students had now seen right through the charade Jay was performing, attaching the referencing moniker to Jay as manly man. They were all so quaint.

After a while, there started to be a slight problem with the frequent returning customers. Those girls loved to talk, and soon the word was starting to get around. Jay needed the Christmas break if for nothing else but to get away from the famished ladies of the big city. With Christmas still a month away, Jay would now start to separate the wealthy from the wise. If a happy merry

Christmas could not be provided, then some would be handed a lump of coal and wished a happy New Year.

Late fall was always a stressful time for Jay back in the days of the red dirt road. Now here in the big city, it would give everyone a chance to get away from the gossip central that so reminded him of the days gone by in the downstairs beauty salon of Big Red. Jay wondered if all shops were like this, and as an advanced student and not the newbies, it was allowed for those who had made friends with the upper classes to visit and pretty much see and hear the same type of disbelieving banter on the other side of the wall. It was easy for Jay to roam over into the varsity side of life. Everyone there had become fond of Jay as in with all people anywhere he went. The light that Jay shared was of Christ, always ready with a positive word of reassurance or just the right words of comfort when needed. There was a confirming presence that followed Jay, and it was always his pleasure to share the good news of the gospel at any opportunity. He would never shy away from the truth of the one who set him free, the love of his life, forever. Even if the occasion was surrounded by obstacles such as drinking or smoking a little weed, Jay had many great conversations about his love of Christ while, shall we say, stoned. He was never alone, and with his cobweb of a mind, the safety net provided by his ever-present spirit was one thing he would not live without. He ran to Jay anytime he was broken, seemingly alone, but not really; he was always there to comfort and allow him to come back home. He understood the broken, jagged life that Jay now called home on substances that would normally kill a person. Jay was not a normal person. He was always talking of wanting to just come home, many times in such a stupor that he could only be understood by the one who truly loved him, the one who Jay could only love, never another.

Some of the craziest conversations would arise concerning religion and the preferred partner in song or dance. While just in song, it was clear that many understood the need for love, and the detailed differences it crossed over into the dancing world was normally drawn on who wanted to do the dance of love and with whom. It was always interesting and sometimes very surprising to see those who partook in the dance of love, the mattress mambo. Very surprising!

32

HAPPY THANKSGIVING

The holidays always brought back to many dark memories for Jay, the time of year where outside of his home, the red dirt road life was portrayed as magical with beautiful lights and singing everywhere you went. "Merry Christmas," was shouted by complete strangers as if they were long-lost friends, wishing each other tidings of great joy. The French have a word for that; *baloney*. This was a large bag of bull, and Jay knew bull when he smelled it. He lived in it for so many years that to play merry was completely different from living merry. It was the time of the year when everyone would walk on tiptoes in hopes of not wanting to upset the leader of the house. Something about the cold and death seemed to go hand in hand. *Why be cold if you're not already dead?* Jay thought. Every time he wished it, or in some cases envisioned it, he was held back and reprimanded. This life was not his own; this was made very clear.

Now here in the big city, things could be different. The chill in the air let all the excited and dreadfully worn-out students know that a break in the action was just around the corner. Conversations now included memories of years gone by and dreams of what was hoped to be this merry year. Jay so enjoyed the twinkle in the eyes of the once-again innocent and the tone of excitement as they strolled down the snowy lanes of holidays past. The newly fallen snow added to the ambiance of pine and holly now decorating everything from barns to homes, the hustle and bustle of all to find the one thing they knew would bring Christmas cheer. Churches decorated with manger scenes and the sweet sound of "O Holy Night" traveling softly on the winter's breeze, bundled and warm, hand in hand with the ones they loved. Jay could see them travel so effortlessly to those days of living dreams. It seemed so real to them as they shined with such joy. Could it really have been that wonderful for them during the holidays at home?

Jay took one last drag of his Marlboro red and then headed back onto the floor. He had an appointment with a special client this chilly late-November day. She was special, and Jay enjoyed their meetings over the months. Sure, everyone suspected what they want. It was obvious by the way they met each other and the subtle touches that this was more than just a fleeting style or cut. There was electricity, a flash of warmth that all who now so readily identified the couple had known very well, the newness of a relationship and spending its first year of the holidays together. The thought of the moments to come would hold and captivate their wanting eyes to once again feel the innocence of starting anew. She was stunningly beautiful in her late twenties, married into wealth, and looking to have a wonderful new year. Poor girl actually thought outside of the box in hoping Jay could provide such dream.

The shampoo and style took much longer than needed, as Jay was warmly adorable and confident as to defy the eighteen years of life before her. His was no normal life, and to be a part of it was a choice she would regret sooner or later, depending upon her and the use of foul language that could repulse Jay, allowing her to never cross his path again. For now, the new relationship in bloom was ideal for both of them. She was tied to a professional businessman more than twice her age with a fondness for pretty little things, naturally, until the pretty little thing was about to turn thirty. Then he started losing interest and having a lot more overseas business meeting that would go on for weeks at a time leaving her wanting and alone. As for Jay, he just needed someone to fill the void that had lots of money to carry him through the tough times of winter, the cold dark lonely months spent inside. Everyone needed someone during those hard times.

Mr. VP who had turned out to be a really down-to-earth guy now wished to level some advice Jay's way with a simple request of "Can I talk to you a minute?" Jay excused himself from his beautiful customer and attended the fatherly advice seminar in the back smoke room. While gone, of course, the other students close to Jay swarmed in to meet what they hoped to be the future Mrs. Jay.

In the meantime, Mr. VP was polite and soft-spoken as usual, which made him an excellent instructor. An advisor of personal affairs, however, would require someone who had had more than one experience with his grade-school sweetheart of twenty years. Time in a rowboat in no way provides the expertise required to speak to the master and commander of the sea. Jay had sailed multiple seven seas, and with each deployment, a different vessel was enjoyed. From stem-to-stern yes port to starboard, the sleek adventures of the sea would rock then roll to the tumultuous waves of the deep. A life lived and not just read about, but in this case, all were in port, so Jay was polite and allowed the stumbling wordsmith to proceed with wisdom of those lived in the shallows.

Returning from the conversation so quickly forgot, Jay noticed and admired the resolve of the beautiful young girl within the masses of the hair sprayed. All attempting to drag details from deep within only to settle for a warming smile and a light slap on the hand to demonstrate the innocence before them, they deserved nothing, and yet she allowed them enough access to feel welcomed. Interrupting the gossip party was met with boos and comments of "Please" and "Can't we just ask one more question?" in which Jay was quick to reject the inquiring minds who want to know. Jay was famished, and lunch was now being served. Leaving the entertained thrall behind, Jay and the new girl in town made their way to the door for lunch in which the returning bell would not sound again until the following Monday morning. Once Jay returned driving the sleek little Mercedes that was now on loan from his new female friend, everyone knew it was going to be a very nice Thanksgiving, for Jay anyway.

Explaining he was going to spend the holiday in the city with friends but promising to be home for Christmas went over just fine for Big Red, so Jay settled in for a relaxing five-day holiday with the beautiful and wealthy lady friend who also liked to indulge in the substances of happiness until everyone was so happy. You needed your friends to fill you in on the great times you had.

Dining at the nicest restaurants, dancing until three in the morning, and then swinging to the snow-covered mattress mambo until the sun came up. Once the blinds were pulled tight and the phone taken off the hook, sleep would rush over until the late afternoon in which skiing your way to a dual shower started the entire adventure all over once again. Blow-drying her hair to perfection while burning a little mellow with a glass or two of fine Bordeaux would normally end up requiring the hair to be restyled once again.

Jay learned quickly about the personal ways of styling, the soft touch of beautiful shining hair along with the gentle strokes down the curvature of a velvet neckline that would send shivers to the knees and add up the tall, strong intellectual brilliance of a man so pretty that the gay girls wanted to go straight, and there was

Jay, a highly wanted commodity. Strange use of words, not really, truth be known that's exactly what was going on here. As the weed days drew into the weekends, more than one of the highly powerful and popular friends were discussing the availability of the walking dream. Little did they know of the nightmare within. *All in due time,* Jay thought, *Now let's get this party started.*

Turkey Day had come and gone, and Jay wasn't even sure what day it was when the emergency call came in. It seemed Little Miss Pretty got the call that Big Daddy was coming in for a couple of days and needed Jay to pull a "mike the magician" and quick. With a pocket full of money and an eight ball of snow, Jay piled into the Mercedes, which is now between everyone, in the shop! Down the road Jay went without a true direction in mind, ending up at the door of one of his styling-school buddies. He was in his early twenties, living with his divorced mom, and they welcomed Jay in with open arms. She was lovely and very caring and offered Jay a cold one and a place to hang out. It was funny how his pal kidded with his mom, telling her to shut up and calling her silly little names in fun. Jay kept waiting for the gun to go off, but he now knew that this was not the home he had grown to dread. This was a family dwelling of ones who cared enough for each other as to be comfortable with each other. What a concept, understanding without condemning! Wow!

As the evening went on and more family started to arrive, Jay knew he had overstayed his welcome and made an excuse to run out and get some personal items taken care of. The whole time the house mother kept demanding that he return for dinner and games with the entire brood in which some were still at large. There was no way he would come back to this household of love and family fun. He didn't deserve it, and he hadn't earned it. It was best to leave a great family situation a great situation. Jay and his internal demons would only litter the family gathering with doubts and deception. Things he would say always seemed to get the wheels turning, a talent, some would assume, and pure meanness to those who caught the subtle nuances.

Sending the sports car down the road, Jay made his way out of the big city and to a nice hotel along the interstate away from prying eyes who may want to know or even believe they know the lonesome stranger. Yes, that would be the title to this version of a weekend getaway, "The Lonesome Stranger." What would anyone expect from this tall stranger out along the barren interstate? No one would need to understand the release of intimacy while maintaining a brooding selfish lifestyle, wealthy and alone, and in need of direction while careening completely out of control. Anyone, someone, please save me!

Jay found his self-induced entertainment very amusing as he prepared to head down to the hotel disco, a place where he knew he could shine for any and all the lovely, lonely ladies who now also found themselves on the road for the holidays. There could be only one thing on the mind of the abandoned beauties this Thanksgiving weekend, an opportunity, one last chance on this Saturday night to make this year's holiday truly matter, someone to make them feel alive as never before and to give them that fleeting glance at love even for just one dance.

Grabbing a bite to eat at the hotel restaurant, Jay noticed a lot of activity already getting started up, and it wasn't even ten o'clock. This was a great sign for a happy holiday weekend. If there was one thing Jay knew next to touching and fondling a lady's hair, it was the presence of bodies sweating on the dance floor.

He slowly consumed his steak while casually watching the pretty people pass by on their way to the club. Jay always enjoyed the runway models as they towered in their high-heel shoes with clinging satin and lace flowing all around them. The beautiful people, they were the ones who would come out on a Thanksgiving holiday Saturday night to show all the wonder that was them. Laughing smugly within himself, Jay ordered a double jack straight up as he made his way into the hallway containing the restaurant men's room. A little light powder to get the juices flowing along with a stiff drink was just what the tall, dark stranger needed to start the charade.

Jay entered as he always would, pausing three steps inside the entrance, allowing all in attendance to admire the perfect shoulder-length hair feathered lightly, the tall, tanned frame with just enough black eyeliner to make them wonder what it was that made him so different. A long-sleeved silver silk shirt open to the area of a look at Peckville. Tight black swaying bell bottoms clinging to his thirty-two inch waist was held firmly in place by a band of gold that matched the glistening chain so proudly worn around his muscular neck. Every eye noticed the tall stranger of style, but was that all there was, a pretty picture once seen and then to fade away?

Dancing was the name of the playful game here at this disco along with every disco in the country, heck even the world. This was a movement that for all who played the role well would have marvelous memories just at the mention. Sure everyone still loved the Southern rock of 38 Special and the Eagles. Why, Robin Trower's "Bridge of Sighs" was one of Jay's favorites, not to mention, he was a complete Cooper fanatic. The darkness he embraced while on his lonely binges was a comfort to his wickedly torn soul, wanting to die but loving to live. To come after Christ by denying himself was easy, but to pick up his cross was totally unbearable, so he climbed deeper and deeper into the world that offered him this sense of false love, any love.

Rhythm came easy for the tall, stylish stranger. Why, he had no idea. It was with everything from the way he played sports to the rhythm and the rhyme of every conversation he ever had. The words would flow so effortlessly that the other participants would seem entranced at every sentence. Little Bro had always said that the sound of Jay's voice was like something heard professionally coming from a radio, very entertaining. Whatever the blessing was that Jay had he wielded it as a weapon of obedience—saying the right thing at the right time to make any adversary believe that it was them who was at fault and even at odds with themselves, requiring an explanation as to why they were so blatantly abusing Jay's time. The wonderment of free speech.

Jay was attempting to make his way casually to the bar with a tempo as if to be gliding. Smooth and intentional, he glanced and flashed his perfectly white teeth in the direction of the smoking hot only to have one of the pretties ask him if he would like to dance. This was it. They knew the look. Let's get it right, they admired the look. Now everyone wanted to know just how complete this package really was. Jay held the hand of the young lovely as he placed his other on her perfectly slim waist directing her to the middle of the hotel dance floor. Yes, we all must remember this was not the actual dance clubs that Jay had ruled for the past two years or the clubs of the big hairstyling city that now called his name each night he blessed them with his motions of mystical melodies. This was a hotel dance bar where those who traveled or lived close by or out here in the middle of nowhere would come for drinks and a hopeful hookup. What they were about to experience was something they had only seen in movies or while sitting on the sidelines of the big city clubs that scared them all into stationary no names. Too intimidated by the sheer size of the spinning dance ball and the multicolored floor designs all meant to make the motions of the entwined magical, this would be way too much for the crowd now before the handsome stranger. Only Jay so arrogantly knew what was about to happen on this plain little dance floor at the Sheraton Hotel along this baron stretch of interstate. He laughed to himself as he took his place of rule among the nonrhythmic crowd, stopping to see the fluent style of dance known as disco. It truly was poetry in motion, and Jay was beloved.

The morning was bright as normal even though the clock now read noon. She was beautiful even though she looked as if she'd been in a hair-tossing contest during a sweat storm, so was the nightlife with Jay, or should we call it the true a.m. hours. Completely pleased with himself, he decided to make her day and honor her request to have lunch together and see where the rest of the day led them. She was pleasantly entertaining and in no way clingy or needy. Jay enjoyed her company and relaxed the day away entertaining each other with feats of abandonment, always paying attention and giving her the feeling that he could spend the rest of his life alongside. Now what was her name?

The rest of that Sunday is but a memory, a very lovely memory that Jay would always cherish, but in reality, it was empty—so empty without the one that could contain and hold Jay's attention, keeping him away from the destructive man he so hated in the mirror. Sunday was meant to be a day of rest and worship, true worship of the one who had done everything for Jay and had paid the price and took his place, not the false idol worship of the empty hallow man who once again drank himself to sleep just to rise and attend a styling school the next day. The lonely drive, the fake smile, and the chipper words of Jay to start the new day "How was everyone's Thanksgiving holiday?" Someone give that man an Oscar!

33

BACK TO SCHOOL

Having one more week of November and close to a full month of December to go, everyone seemed to be a buzz about the advancement of classes and the opportunities of nailing down phase 2 of the styling curriculum. They all knew once the Christmas and New Year celebrations were over, it would be close to the time where their class would move over to the varsity side for the last four months of training. All they needed was the required amount of hours and the blessings of all instructors. Now the hours could vary a little, seeing as how they still had months to go, but to graduate, as in all styling or beautician schools, the state mandatory required a certain number of hours and no less, so playing hooky was done on a very light basis such as Jay's elongated weekend to Little Miss Married.

Speaking of the angel, there she was, pretty as a picture needing a shampoo blow-dry for the very cute style Jay had given her just two weeks prior. It was easy for all to see the customers entering the school as the giant windows up front allowed peaks out but with the glare seeing in was virtually impossible. Jay's name was called as expected, but he took his time finishing his smoke before heading up to the front to meet his very welcome customer. The girls of the school and their little calls of "When's my turn?" caused the entire class to laugh and cut up, even allowing Jay the opportunity to grab one of the new girls and insist she stop teasing him. Leaving the cute little newbie stunned and wanting, Jay was very glad to be back into a structured program, anything to take his mind off the self-indulgent pleasures of a weekend's performance. Magnificent as it all was, the latest conquest had that look as Jay slid from her side to shower and make it out the door, free, leaving her wondering that maybe, just maybe, he was the one. Jay was the one all right, the one you will never see again but only in your day and nightly dreams.

"Good morning, beautiful." Jay met with Little Miss Married on that bright November morning. He had a way of enjoying life to the fullest as long as there was an audience to appreciate the performance, alive and free-flowing, with effortless back-and-forth banter of the lovers to the tune of sheer enjoyment to all within hearing range. She would giggle shyly to the subtle innuendos, acting as the innocent little girl while Jay donned the experienced-man role they all so endearingly loved. A couple of the older classmates of Jay had started to peel away the complicated layers and began showing some concern, having little one-on-one talks with the emotionally void performer as if they actually thought they could counsel the counselor. Jay had to keep his cool and maintain the self-taught actors guild of never stop performing no matter how deep the moment may cut. The present scene must go on, ignoring the personal ties of reality no matter how abrupt and blatant they may strike one in the face. The illusion was everything, entertaining with elegance and poise, with no acknowledgment to the level of pain. One must never be the wiser.

The shampoo style was easy enough, but with this special customer, Jay took his time, reassuring her that even though he was not available for lunch that he looked forward to a quiet evening alone, maybe to talk over some issues. This was always a great way to see just how bad the addiction had become. Her look alone was worth ten thousand words. He couldn't help it. Jay had to test everyone and anyone who lived on the outside, keeping them exactly where he wanted them. To stray out of the approved zone meant immediate expulsion, no excuses and definitely no admittance, done deal. It was just this switch Jay had developed over the years while attempting to understand who it was that truly loved him, and of the few he had allowed in, he was still not convinced. It sure wasn't anyone associated with the big city; they were all pawns to be played, and it was the rules of the crazy now developing this game. Jay loved the game and didn't mind losing as long as the ones he lost to didn't really want him to lose in the first place. To need him to continue even though declaring self-victories would leave the opposition embarrassed and alone. Winning was more of a loss to them than winning was to Jay, but it was their choice, choose wisely.

Things had gotten pretty mellow during the first week back from Turkey Day. Fridays were always busy in the mornings and to a crawl in the late afternoons, everyone slowing their pace and goofing off with the few customers still in the chairs. That's when Jay got a call to the front for a requested customer that would change the view of all the pawns of the world. Making his way up front, he encountered an early thirties gentlemen with overly wavy dark hair that was slightly graying and a very dark five o'clock shadow. The 1960s glasses propped up on his nose accentuated the normalcy to his look. Locking eyes with the receptionist, she stated that this gentleman had specifically requested Jay for his once-a-day appointment. Politely smiling and gesturing toward the back, Jay escorted the patron to his chair, and off to the races this eternal bound would run.

"So how did you hear about my exceptional talents?" Jay played along while draping the cloth around his neck and running his fingers through the gentlemen's hair, something Jay always did to evaluate the possibilities.

"My name is Bob, and I'm a business professional and require a neat appearance with my associates." He then went on to explain that because of his heavy swirling black beard, he had found that a straight razor shave would last him through the day when a normal razor fell way short.

"Of course," Jay chimed in. "Will there be anything else?" He ran his fingers through Bob's hair, insinuating he needed a lot more than just a shave. Bob then explained that one of the senior stylists at the school had recommended Jay to perform his daily upkeep that would require a style once a month and a shampoo blow-dry along with the shave every morning at approximately eight o'clock. He had selected Jay at this early stage so he could become accustomed to his requirements and was there on this Friday afternoon for only a shave—a shave that he said would give him the weekend to heal.

Laying Bob back in the chair and applying the hot towel around his face, Jay then prepared the fresh shaving cream by swirling his brush into the cream cup and laughing at the healing comment Bob had just made. "Need the weekend to heal, huh?" What did that upper classman tell you anyway. You see, I'm pretty good at this shaving stuff right along with everything else!"

Through the towel, you could hear the mumbled response of a man who was about to have some fun. "My beard grows in some pretty wicked circles, and it's because you come highly regarded as one of the best straight razor shavers that I sit here with you today, plus I'm gay, and you're a great-looking guy. I just love the feel of strong hands scrubbing my scalp and styling my hair."

What? Jay, now almost stunned, removed the towel and looked Bob in the eyes to appreciate his sense of humor. "Why, thank you for the complement. I hope you learn to enjoy the many qualities I have to offer in the realm of styling, but we must remember as professionals, business is business, and all else can not be afforded."

"Of course," Bob said, "I will pay for your services here each day and request only the banter of truth in return."

"Done" Jay proclaimed. "We have an accord."

One thing that Bob was not kidding about was that crazy beard. Looking closer at the swirling madness, Jay started to question just where to begin. Bob just kind of giggled and commented on "now you know why I'm here on a Friday afternoon with the weekend to heal."

"Just go for it, Jay," Bob declared. "You've got to get this first one under your belt."

By this time, the entire school had heard of the wicked beard, and now it was time to put speculation into affirmation. Jay slapped the leather strap with four long strokes of his razor and then settled in close to begin at the base of Bob's neck. Turning his wrist into such tight circles was very challenging, and as soon as Jay felt comfortable and relaxed just a little, the razor would stick, and all stylists knew what that meant: a cut. Straight razors only stop if they're digging in. Jay pulled away as Bob motioned for him to keep going. "You are good at this," Bob declared. "Three swipes and only one cut so far, fabulous!"

The start of one of the strangest relationships in the history of the world had now begun at that Southern styling school. Bob was a true gentleman with as much crazy running around up in his head even as to compare to Jay's impressive squirrel cage. How much would Bob let out, and would it be worthy of a quid pro quoi?

Last week of school before the Holiday break, and the team was finally moved over into their varsity spots at the envy of the two newer classes that really didn't seem that long ago to the now professionals. This side of the building is where you performed, the confidence beaming, everyone being aware of who the real talent was, the ones with the cutting edge to see a new style and the coconuts to create it. Jay was in his element, and with his new pal Bob dropping by every morning for a shave, shampoo, and blow-dry, it was all bowing to the tall one's feet. A shave that all knew they could not accomplish was now performed before them without as much as a nick. The quick wash and dry sent this professional out the door with his ten-dollar tip left on the stand every morning of every week day.

That Friday before the Christmas break, Bob requested the full treatment, wanting to look his best for the holiday season. Time was set aside, as there would be only a few last-minute styles needed this close to the vacation, allowing the majority of senior students to huddle close by for one of Jay and Bob's banters of truth and the human way. The wash was done, and the cut had begun after the meeting pleasantries, and all were excited for the discussion to begin.

The entire story of the two men was very tragic in so many ways. Bob as a young boy was abandoned by his father and left with only his mother, sisters, and aunts. Oh yes they adored little Bob, and they loved little Bob, and they spoiled little Bob so much as to turn little Bob into pretty little Bobina. You see, Bob was serious when he said he was gay, but Jay had sensed more to the story than just a decision to switch hit. The conversations were captivating, each student holding on to each word as the two men would go back and forth. Jay was a man seeking to find a physical love worthy of his darkness while still needing to conquer every pretty eye that found favor in his presence. Bob was a man trapped with a desire to know the feminine freedom of a female's love but not able to engage in the pleasantries of that side of the wanton erotica.

"I've tried, Jay," Bob said, describing the multiple attempts at what the world would call a normal relationship. "I'm friends with girls who love me for who I am and have made themselves available to multiple failed experiments." They were true friends of deeply developed relationships that would go to the ends of the earth to assist in the desperate calls of what had become family.

Jay felt for Bob but was still unsure on how real and exactly how deep the depravity really went. Skeptical, sure, for everything that presented itself as fact, there was always this doubt that clouded Jay's mind, running the images through the maze and then applying logic to the exiting madness. To proclaim actual truth or hypothesis, to see the light while loving life in the dark, and experiencing the love or loving the pain, these were all very fine lines that had to be traveled, and the journey was not always as it seemed.

"Well, Bob," Jay explained, "I wish you a very merry Christmas, and I'll ask Santa to send you a real set of coconuts to try out for the New Year."

Bob and Jay just laughed at the merry wishes, and of course, the comments were a little on the risky side of life, but Jay did have to promise to update Bob on the real Jay once next year finally arrived.

"Will do, Bob. It's a date. You wish, you dirty left-hander." Jay smiled warmly to Bob as the two shook hands on his way out. Turning to the classmates, Jay shook his head in disappointment. Would it be a merry Christmas for Bob? Was it ever really a merry Christmas for Jay? With celebration in songs of "O Holy Night and "It Came upon a Midnight Clear," songs of celebration of Jesus's birth, at night, in the darkness, the true light of man was born. Jay lived in the darkness of his mind at any and every vacant moment not distracted by the artificial world he would find himself dwelling there. Did Bob know the light of man? Jay lived in this echoing chamber for way too long, stepping outside to clear his mind and to light one up. He asked for help once again, to bear this pain, to help this man that was now laid upon his heart, to do something he was not equipped to do, to share light into a very dark world.

34

MERRY CHRISTMAS

Leaving the big city for a little quiet time down home on the red dirt road brought a smile to Jay as he pressed the pedal on the right a little firmer. Would this be a year of a white Christmas, carolers gathering to sing the classics of years gone by? And let us not forget the greatest of all traditions, "Rudolph, the Red-Nosed Reindeer." Jay so loved that Christmas special to the point of it actually cutting through the haze of years long forgotten, something he could tie to his actual childhood before his tenth year of, let's just say, the great winter storm.

The road was becoming more familiar with each curve, bringing back memories of when he first started this trek so many months ago. In the beginning, Jay would travel back and forth each day, and on some days, it was mellow, but on that one Monday morning, second week of school as Jay was making his way through the foggy side of town, the area known as the train track of Cadillacs, he remembered rounding that same curve he was now approaching, nonchalantly rounding the turn, and there he was, maybe four years old, on a big wheel, sitting crossway right in the middle of Jay's lane. It was all too clear, pulling the wheel hard to the left, not even caring if someone else was coming the other way. The youth and innocence of that child trumped any and all oncoming obstacles. He was just a baby who Jay was not going to kill. Running over a stupid animal playing in the road, and you get what you deserve. Jay would never flinch and might even speed up to win the contact award.

This was no animal. He saw the eyes of that poor little kid who knew nothing of life and deserved at least an opportunity to live it. The car performed just as Jay commanded until it was time to straighten things back out. That's when the joy ride began, and the Winston Cup was on. Green flag flapping, here we go!

Once around, Jay could feel the gravitational forces against him. Man, he loved fast rides. He knew now that he had to be past the little guy and that round 2 coming with just as much force. Holding tight to the wheel and turning as hard as he could opposite the now-spinning Wildcat, Jay was determined to tame the wild beast before the inevitable impact—an impact that never came.

Sitting there and listening to the latest of drumbeat songs, Jay realized his ears had slammed shut, and the music was coming from within his chest. *Very nice,* he thought. Rhythmic and along with the wonderful thumping music, he noticed he was sitting on his side of the road as if he had intentionally pulled the Buick off for some much-needed relief. *Amazing,* he thought, looking around at the foggy dawn. Opening the car door, he stepped out into what seemed as a dreamscape world. Gray mist everywhere and chill in the fall air with the changing colors of the leaves so hard to make out on this particular gloomy morning. But there down the road sat the cutest little boy, exactly where Jay had just seen him three lifetimes ago, big smile on his face. As Jay's face grew very warm, turning as red as Santa's jolly winter suit, Jay started walking back toward the boy still sitting in the middle of the road. Jay reached down and grabbed that kid in one hand and the big wheel in the other, and he would take a step then kick, take another step and then kick. That youngling was a hollering, and Jay was just smiling, walking and kicking that kid's butt every other step all the way up into his yard.

Now this got the attention of who Jay assumed was Grandma, and boy, what a grandma. This one hadn't missed a meal in a long time, and from up on that porch, she kind of looked like a cross between Godzilla and that snake-haired lady. Jay dropped the still-alive crybaby and threw the big wheel across the road into a neighboring ditch and headed back to his car while Grandma thought she was going to intimidate the still-wanting-to be-volatile young man who just spared her loved one's life. Jay stopped, confronted her, and went on his way. Nothing was said, just the sound of thunder heard in the distance as he drove away.

Jay made a left, turning onto the red dirt road on his last leg to returning home, hoping this would be a nice Christmas. He thought about it being a very nice Christmas but then realized where he was; just hoping for a nice one could be a stretch. It would be different seeing as how Jay would not be attending any Church services or Christmas plays. He had so many fond memories of the many plays he had been a part of for all those years at what seemed like "their" little country church, watching it grow from such a small dedicated few to over a hundred in the couple years. To say he loved them all would take the power of Christ, and Jay definitely was not Jesus! He really didn't care if he ever saw any of them again ever, just too dark where Jay lived to care.

Pulling onto the back drive where he always parked seemed like he had taken a time-traveling pill that allowed him to see things from an outside perspective. How long had it been? Only a few months, but it seemed so long ago to Jay, wondering the dark thoughts that always accompanied him. Will anyone truly be glad to see him? Is it too late to turn and leave without anyone seeing him? Everything felt wrong. That same old feeling of always being alone and belonging that way for all eternity. It was so heavy upon him that it turned his stomach to even think someone cared, seeing anyone who might falsely wish him a merry Christmas. This was a living hell for Jay, a world of doubting destruction that he carried hidden within every single day of his life. No matter if all hailed him and truly adored him, he would always carry the burden of being the one who should have died.

Then coming out the front door was the one smiling face that Jay knew truly loved him and was excited to see him. Little Bro looked older as he ran to meet his big brother, the two young men smiling ear to ear as they hugged and exchanged pleasantries of truth. It really was good to see his little brother. Never guaranteed another meeting on this earth as the good book said that for today, your soul is required of thee. Jay would make the most of the few days of Christmas to reconnect. It seemed urgent for some reason. How long does anyone really have anyway?

Momma was there waiting on the boys as they made their way into the house. "My two baby boys all grown up, give your momma some sugar and a hug."

Who the heck is this? Jay thought to himself, walking over to his mom and giving her a peck on the cheek and a gentle hug, almost afraid to squeeze her to tight but just enough to make sure she was hugged as requested.

"It's good to have my boys home for Christmas," Big Red said. It was kind of nice to see her in such a good mood as Jay just smiled and told her how glad he was to be home and how much he was enjoying styling school; you had to give credit where credit was due, and the styling schools dues were paid by Big Red due to she had dreams of having a family shop one day with all of the kids working under her. Crazier things have happened, but that was going to be very unlikely.

Pulling up a chair at the table, Jay attempted to start catching up with the red dirt road family he vaguely remembered even though it had been only a few months. *Only a few months,* Jay thought. *How is that even possible?*

It seemed as if he'd been away and lived two lifetimes in the short span of obtaining his freedom. That was it, freedom—no one to check up or even care if Jay was acting as they thought he should. Big Red did not appreciate any bad talk against her family and those included all kin folk. Mess around and get the crazy one upset and you'd be sorry. So whenever Jay did all those terrible things around town, everyone made sure not to talk about it in front of her. She did not care if it was true; you still needed to respect the Southern thunder and the powerful bolt that came with.

"How is school going?" Jay asked Little Bro, knowing he didn't even try out for the varsity basketball team at hope to be high. As a freshman and sophomore, he was great, and they won the conference and everything for the JV team; he just decided that was not the life for him. Being the big popular jock like Jay and then maintaining the cool side of life was a little too demanding for him. Jay knew he didn't have the need to perform for the masses; he actually had a pretty normal life within the walls of the family home.

He was the baby boy, and all in all, he was a great little kid, full of love, happy as a country critter, and always enjoyable to be around. Jay often wondered about him smoking weed. If he had not seen Jay doing it so often, maybe, as it was, he was trying to fit in with his big brother.

The boys continued to talk about everything from family to new girlfriends, his little brother's new girlfriend, of course. Jay was never going to have that type of a nametag hanging off him ever again. Friends were fine, and female friends with benefits was even better, but other than that, it would be passing vessels in the night, just the right amount of time together to remember the faces but never the names. You sure couldn't remember the hulls of the passing vessels at night. Man, that country living could change the landscape so quick that you'd swear a motorboat had turned into an ocean liner. Time could make them look like they had taken trips around the world and then left scuttled for any pirate cruising by, no sir, no names, no friendly call signs, just passing through. Everything seemed so strange here to Jay. Sure he was having a good time laying around with Little Red who just adored her big brother and Middle Sis that was getting old enough to the point where she was a lot of fun talking and kidding with, so all in all, it seemed kind of like the perfect little family for the perfect Christmas season. They all sat together watching *It's a Wonderful Life* and the *Carpenters at Christmas Special*, even looking in the TV guide to see when Rudolph came on so they wouldn't miss it. This was not going to be a year of presents, just a time of family and food. No one was really sure when this many would be around again, and with Big Sis married and living up the mountain, they were already one short.

It did make sense that this was such a mellow year, kind of like knowing the bad uncle was coming into town but could only stay for a couple of days. As long as everyone knew he would be leaving soon, they could put on a front until he was gone. Jay knew this was the issue, and soon he would be gone and just as happy for them as he was for himself. It would be nice to get back to his lifestyle of self-destruction, allowing the real Jay a chance to finally breathe again.

Little Bro had to meet up with his new girlfriend for a short while that Friday night. "Already bound by the chain," was Jay's funny proclamation. It was strange watching his little brother heading off into what one day, hopefully, prayerfully, would be a normal happy life. *The right girl,* Jay just laughed within himself. Little Bro had the capacity to allow someone he cared for access to deep within, into the intimate side of his every day dreams and even hopes of a future bright. Jay found that to be very funny, but in reality, it was the impossible dream. Jay knew he would never have the closeness of a gentle and loving relationship, to look into the beautiful eyes of someone who truly could love him while understanding the hallways of darkness before them. It was not possible. Death would not allow it, and that was to be his true love, to finally rest in peace.

Big Red wondered if Jay also would be heading out into the night to meet up with some of the old stomping-ground friends. "I really have no desire to see any of the ones left behind," Jay slowly explained to his ever-attentive mother. "I think I'll just hang around the house this weekend and catch up on everything. I never know when the last time will be available to catch up." Jay could tell this made his mother very happy, him actually wanting to spend time with the family. She hoped maybe this was a positive move. Maybe Jay finally decided to grow up.

The girls got tired and were heading off to bed, each grabbing a smooch and a tickle from Jay as they made their way into the dimly lit hallway of the old brick house. Little Red with her crutches moved so quickly. "Love you," came from both as they entered their rooms. Jay smiled and wondered as Redhead Momma caught a glimpse of Jay pondering the true meaning of the magical four-letter word.

"What's on your mind, son?"

Was this going to be one of those talks? Had things changed so much that Jay could now be open with his once-so-distant mother?

"Things seem to get so confused, quickly, so often," Jay heard himself starting the soon-to-be marathon of deep revelations. "I have to deal with a lot of darkness within even though I have Christ as my Savior," Jay continued, allowing his mother an entrance just to see where and how deep she would allow herself to go.

As Jay continued to reveal a portion of the darkness, there was this sense of acknowledgement coming his way, allowing and even encouraging him to continue with this now-ever so slightly open view into the world of overconfidence layered in hatred and doubt. As Jay described the way he entered a room as to cause all to admire the amazing presence so effortlessly presented before them. The eyes of envy led to the silhouetted grace and charm of the one they could never be but anxiously beholding the sheer beauty without while fearing the internal rage within. All had sensed the climatic storm this very presence contained and yet with electrical anticipation wanting to be caught in the vilest of storms that so calmly played within.

Big Red was sitting on pins and needles as she shook her head in confirmation of the scene now played out before her. She was almost to the point of giddy with the anticipation of responding to the life of her oldest son who now, for whatever reason, decided to be open and honest with darkness and confidence all rolled into one.

"You're just like I am," came the words least expected from his now fully engaged mother. Stunned into silence but with mind a reeling, Jay flashed back to the exact sense of wording his dear old dad had on more than one occasion told his quickly developing son.

"Know what your problem is, son? You're just like your mother." These words at one point in life were like cutting Jay's guts open and throwing gasoline in with a topping of fire, the horror, the disgrace, now the truth!

Big Red was now speaking with such vibrant vigor as to capture the still-spinning attention of her wandering mindful son. She carried the anger for a childhood that was so quickly taken away—being pulled from school in the sixth grade just to work her young life away and provide for her nine brothers and sisters. Every story she had ever told had to do with hardships and involved some form of working her fingers to the bone.

Jay had always heard the sob stories his mother had told year after year, but this time was different. Here she sat alone with

Jay—not with anger in her voice, but with the drive and the persistent attitude that had carried her so very far in life. Starting at such a young age, she developed a sense of preservation that only to have lived the life of poverty could anyone from the outside be remotely tuned to the urgency of the life laid out before her. Like going to school wearing a potato sack dress and a coat of many colors patched together by a mother who so dearly loved her children with all she had, and actually, that was all she had.

Jay saw the tears in his mother's eyes as she talked of her own mother and father. Oh, how they wanted so much more for all their kids, but being poor mountain pig farmers during the Great Depression left very little in the abundance kitty. Shoes were for winter and school. Nice clothes came if you went out and worked for it as long as the majority of the money went to supporting the family. Caring for a baby sister who would only die of mountain sickness eighteen months later would leave a wound so deep as to only be filled by devoting every last ounce of energy and breath to ensuring the family was all together and taken care of. The pain went on, but the love covered all, as she would smile and talk proudly of the accomplishments she had taken part in while bettering the family structure.

All her children were going to graduate high school even if it killed them, as Big Red put it, laughing all the while. She loved to talk of fighting and shooting, and killing was nothing but something that was always on the table, but were you sure you felt like dining that evening or not? It was always their choice. She was rough and tough and could hit you like a man, as Jay very well knew. Shooting was disclosed as a last resort, and as she said this, Jay's heart skipped a beat at the possibility of having the conversation that had eluded him for so very long. The rising spring deep within his troubled soul now raged as a river attempting to overflow its banks. How long this rage could be contained? Was this the Christmas to once and for all present the present of all presents?

35

THE TRUTH FOR BOB

Back to big city living which suited Jay just fine, enough of the mushy, lovely life of lies, everyone still bowed and avoided the truth about any and every thing. At first, it seemed as if things would finally become clear, but as with a drive there on the red dirt road, it normally ended up a cloudy mess that would hang on you as memories for the rest of your life. No matter how slow or easy you tried to transverse the distance of dust and curves, you always ended up with the same results, feeling a deep desire to wash those haunting stains away over and over again so life is lived on the red dirt road.

Here at styling school, things were once again heating up just as all had left it before the Christmas-New Year break. Jay's class so comfortably moved in on the side of the real stylists. Now was the time of creation and liberal thinking to amass an onslaught of daring new images that danced within the minds of the young and the young at heart—to allow feeling along with the darkness of imagination to frame the fragile face of a young beauty with such banter of confidence that she all but begged for the marvelous transformation to begin. This was the beginning of a new year, a new life, a new creation called Jay!

Once completed with the style of the young and pretty, the instructors took notice of the subtle yet bold changes Jay had made to one of their more common styles called a ladies' choice. By leaving certain areas, framing the pretty young face longer than required, a beautiful new picture was now unveiled to the applause of classmates and instructors alike. "I love it," came the cute squeal from the late teen.

"Beautiful cheekbones should never be fully exposed but allowed to tease with the ever presence of perfection, allowing just a glimpse to redirect the gaze deep into the beautiful amber eyes of the lady in waiting." Jay's response had left the room in stunned silence as they all looked deeply within the now openly exposed windows of such a beautiful youth.

The first week back and conversations were now where they were before the holiday break, everyone wondering where they would work and if they would be selected to adorn one of the greatest Greeks shops, or would they have to hope and poke to find gainful employment. Funny how the mind works, a world of work away between them and the dreams they now so verbally announced. Jay chuckled every time he thought of this being a dream come true, a paycheck, yes, an avenue onto the highway of the high and beautiful, no doubt about it. The one thing Jay knew for sure was that this occupation was considered glamorous in an age where everyone wanted to be center stage, walking, talking and dancing the electric life away. To do this, you had to have layers flowing from the front all the way around back of a perfectly styled dome. The more original the style flowed along with the rhythmic beat of "I love the night life, I've got to boogie," the better. If the style along with looks were there as in Jay's case, many times, those who just enjoyed the performance would break out in catcalls and applause, thrilled to be in the presence of someone so magnificent. Dancing, drinking, and drugs were all required to keep the performing chickens hopping up and down to the rhythm of the hot plate. The show must go on.

The first week back seemed so long, but finally, it was Friday morning, and in walked dear old Bob for his morning shave, no style, just giving Jay a day to get back into the swing of things before he started work the following week. Pleasantries aside allowed Bob a chance to get comfortable, as all gathered round to greet our dear friend with multiple issues that would soon be matched and trumped by the enveloping saga know as Jay.

"Great to see you again, Jay, hope you had a wonderful holiday," was Bob's pleasant greetings to not only Jay but to all whom now anxiously awaited the darkness of confessions to begin. They all knew it was Jay's turn to enlighten the masses. They were promised, and if it was one thing a true hairstylist enjoyed, it was the darkness within that only so few were allowed to view. Today's topic of Jay was about to alter their perception forever, who was this tall, good-looking youth before them?

"Christmas was a little unusual this year. I actually bonded with my mother and learned a lot about who she was and in turn picked up a few smelly nuggets about myself."

Everyone was all ears. Here it comes, the life and times of the mysterious Jay. Mr. Jovial to the point that some had to be a ruse. They all knew it. Now was time to confirm. Jay saw the look in the wanting eyes of the masses and decided to let them have it, to open the doors just as he had promised Bob before the holiday break. It was dark, a world of normal nowhere to be found. The acclimated love-filled lives of the audience would be shattered in a matter of moments. So safe they believed they were, with the memories so firmly tucked away within their normal, little lives. So safe they believed they were.

Jay's story of searching for love was bitterly lonesome, wanting to know that he truly belonged among the masses of the cared for. He continued with the absence of new to ten and how between those shadowy lines he would at times catch a glimpse of light, of something familiar. Was it a warm moment lost there in such a dark place? It never stayed long enough to feel warm. So cold it was. The battlefield navigated by such a young traveler who at times believed he belonged to the war more that the war existed in itself. The screams of agony along with the bright trails of blood that flooded the mind of such an innocent youth, was this deserved due to being born of this conflict, or was this the manner in which his entire life would be measured? Never to cry and go back into the darkness and everything was going to be all right was the voice of such a faraway existence.

They stared in silence as Jay continued the tale of the tried but true life of living in the shadow of the damned. Searching at such a young age, wanting to be loved, to be held and to truly believe that everything was going to be all right, waiting with baited breath with the prospect of hope, hope that once more disappeared with the flowing of dark-red blood, the color of so many memories—these all tied to a time of mental development and accentuated with the sounding of rage and thunder. There in the middle of Jay's mind the class along with Bob stood, intently wondering how much of this tale were true and hoping it was not.

Jay just smiled as he finished up the nick-free shave of Bob. "Guess this will have to wait until next time Bob," Jay said with a sly grin.

"I think I could use a little style if you have the time, Jay." Bob grinned as Jay wrapped the cloth around his friend of darkness.

"Where were we?" Jay asked. "Oh yes, the beautiful red color of blood. Nothing quite like it, wouldn't you agree?" was the starting point for act II on the lonely and restless. Jay continued deeper into the psyche of the barely new teenager struggling to find himself so deeply lost in this sea of desperation, drowning as he struggled to fight back the words and memories that crashed upon his flailing body, beating the youth so soundly that more than once, he knew his last breath was required of him. At that moment, he was more than willing to release all holds of this worldly life, a life so ironic that the spirits surrounding must surely be weeping for the discarded young man unworthy of physical love.

"Take me quickly," was the whaling cry of the abused and tortured, with an anxiousness of feeling something other than this darkened hatred he held of himself so deep within. Drowning multiple times in despair but always feeling the soft sand beneath his feet, pushing away from the depths toward the white foaming possibilities that maybe, up there somewhere, above the crashing waves of life, someone he could finally give all to love. Fourteen was the age to begin this search for love, and with such youth, he took whatever was presented to him only to feel less and less. Jay described how his mind became polluted with scenarios that would consume his every waking thoughts, and along with that came the lies to accomplish the mission to search and conquer any and all who would give to this damaged young mind. At the same time, alienate those prospects of true love due to the internal judge that had already condemned him as unlovable.

By sixteen, the tall, slender young explorer began the search into the jungles of the aged and disturbed. Looking for love was a common theme for so many in this world of adulthood, and Jay fit in perfectly; he was just what the thirty-something crowd was screaming for.

In their world, the dance of love was easy and free-flowing. Jay had gotten so good at it as to recognize the desperate seekers of love with just a glance and a flashing smile. Jay described his age as never being an issue, with his mind being so dark that when it came to the subject of genuine feeling or the faint whispers of love, some of the pretties would allow slipping due to a fascination with the tall young stranger.

"Wait a minute, Jay," Bob so politely butted in. "This trial of almost but never deserving love started at the age of fourteen, physical relationships, searching for someone to love but knowing you can never truly love them back were all because of the big bang back when you were ten years old. By the way, how old are you now?"

"Nineteen is the magic number coming up next month," Jay so proudly replied. "And to your other inquisition, yes, the big bang accompanied with the many battles and displays of the beautiful red liquid and let's not forget the years after of acting like it never even happened. The physical showing of anger reflecting what I already knew to be true was that I was somewhere where I was not wanted and told over and over again during my young developmental years that my absence would have been greatly appreciated. The hands on disciplining with belts, switches, and slaps to the face over and over again. Now no one is allowed to get near my face. Touching me will bring the hillbilly out in me, and believe me, he's a very violent fellow."

The group sat in silence as Jay continued on with the one thing that has and always will make the greatest difference in his or anyone's life. "I was twelve years old coming home from playing with my friend Dave. Time had slipped by as quickly as it tends to during the winter months." Jay described the journey: walking alone down that red dirt road and dark was not the word. It had turned pitch black as he walked with no guidance except for where the top of the trees stopped and the beautiful night sky began. It was in a word, awesome!

Jay described how holding your hand five inches in front of your face and nothing; it was that dark, and you couldn't see where your feet were going, and all you knew was to keep putting them one step in front of the other. All were now fascinated as the story continued on down that dark county dirt road of two miles, knowing there was a sharp drop into the red clay dirt ditches just feet away on each side and not really sure how close he was to falling in without ever knowing it unless he looked up.

"You see, Bob, the greatest adventure of my young life started with that walk down that red dirt road. It was so dark, and I was all alone, scared with the sounds of the wild country woods on each side of me, unable to see anything around me, barely taking one step after the other, but then, I looked up, and I saw greatness so vast and so beautiful that everything I thought about anything was reduced into one humble existence. It was for me, Bob, and it's also there for you. The vastness of beauty I beheld delivered that young, scared boy from the darkness of this world into an understanding of the light, the Son of God, the light of the world. Within my mind, the greatest truth of all was revealed. I never have to journey alone no matter where I go, and no matter how far I stray, his holiness is always with me. I was never alone on that road that night, Bob. He was and has always been with me no matter how dark my mind may get. He has seen it all, and he has no fear—he is the truth. Will I ever be able to feel physical love on any semblance as this? I have no idea. I just know that since I've trusted my life to Jesus, I've never traveled alone. He hears me when I cry, and yes to all the busy bodies that should be doing something about now, I do cry."

Bob sat there in silence as Jay finished up his story, informing him that this was not an exclusive club, that all were welcome to trust Jesus with their lives and to trust him to take the burdens of this life and give comfort to all, a word so strange to men like Jay and Bob: *comfort*. "You just have to call upon the name of Jesus, and you will be saved, believing that he is the one true Son of God. It has changed the way I view all people of this world. All can be shown true love in the name of Jesus Christ no matter how messed up the worlds love treats us."

36

THE JOB

The last remaining months of styling school seemed to fly by as with life, always looking for the ever-elusive handbrake just to take some of the speed off while everyone was attempting to do their best to get noticed by the owners and instructors, those who had inside employment tips and recommendations. Hoping their dreams would come true was the thought that made Jay chuckle as he could imagine some of the more bumbling characters that made up the class of 1978.

For Jay, this was just another day in dullsville, attempting to portray the stylist of the future with such class and calling. *Elite* was the word to pronounce his name. All who would dream would dream of "only if," "could they ever," "not a chance," Only the selected few were so blessed as to enlighten the darkest of tombs. Prerequisite was to always dwell where all else feared to even glance, the horror of it all, the reality of the ones chosen to shine from deep within.

Jay looked upon the ending of styling school with gratification to satisfaction, knowing the end would enable one more thing he would now excel in; the ability to look into any woman's eyes and bring the discussion of framing one's hair to the beauty of their eyes that sparkled with the overly priced highlights. It was just one more area of expertise that he would use to rule the hearts and minds of any and all feminine conquests, to control the outcome of the wars of love while solely maintaining the secret code of the darkest realm: love is a lie!

The last month of school was pretty much the same as any normal stylist job: confined to an area every day, lying to the patrons and convincing them that to add additional body to ones hair was the latest and most expensive craze—using the tricks of the trade to style the finished product with such expertise as to never be repeated within anyone's bathroom, such feathery waving beauty.

To convince them that to use this product or that conditioner would make self-styling a piece of cake, something to get them by until their next appointment and to have all believed that the style would look great for a full three months. Sure, Jay admitted to anyone that there was a tremendous difference in the products used by the stylists; they were pricy but well worth it if you wanted to maintain beautiful, well-groomed hair. The major problem was all the beautiful little lies that completed the wicked web to be weaved. Case in point, hair regeneration, putting a body wave on a balding man to make his hair look thicker, was pure deception; he had gained no more hair as if he hung his head out the window on the eye. Was life as Jay now saw it, to remain a mystery, or an illusion, truth as he knew it to be evident or deceit?

Too much power thinking was making Jay crazy, so with his regular clientele, he was always available. New patrons needed to look somewhere else. The ruse of confusion was more than he could bear at this point of his young life. Jay had enough issues with the young pretty who was once happily married to Dusty Cesar but lately started dropping thought bombs on where their relationship was going. Going! When did that door become ajar? A distraction was in order, and for Jay, that could only mean one thing; well, many things, but it always lead to one type of ending, total drug-induced absorption to the point of incredible revelations sang by the admiring pretties of the big city. Warning though, more than once throughout this styling year, he had used this method of amnesia only to awaken to the sound of familiar voices, those classmates who had become enamored by the brilliance known as Jay, and they were determined to be a part of this shooting star without a care in the world as to when or where the magnificence would burn out, maybe forever, doubtful! Time to put the self-indulgent lifestyle into operation, once again, lighting the emancipating flames to dazzle the onlooking masses. Taking their breath away at the possibility of partying with Jay, the prospects of participating, the reputation was legendary for such a young soul, and many times, it was felt very deeply within his troubled soul, always a price to be paid. Painful, lonely, and personal was the pain ever so deep once the illusion of flames went out.

Finishing up Bob for the last time, Jay hugged his friend and wished him well. There was a three-month stylist who could shave rings around them all, so it was time for Bob to move on. Would they hang out during their lives? Not a chance. But they would never forget each other, brothers of a darkness that not all can understand, and for the few that can, mercy upon them. They would pray, as they would think about each other one day.

As Bob made his way out the front door with the class of friends looking on, a familiar figure was seen crossing in front of the main window; it was Jay's old high school sweetheart, Debbie, looking cute as ever and entering with the biggest smile on her face as she spotted Jay. She then gave the most awkward wave, cute but awkward. Jay couldn't help but smile at the one he considered as earthly love, closest to it, that's for sure. Then as if all control left the ever-cool and coy master of performances, he found himself aping the motion before him, waving like a lunatic and grinning like a school kid until one of his classmates was heard saying, "Kryptonite, that's Jay's kryptonite." This stopped the waving, but the smile could not be removed, and yes, she was Jay's Kryptonite.

Jay met her with an embrace, and of course, the polite exchanges of those once to be known as intimate friends. It truly was good to see a familiar face that held so many found memories even if the baggage was eventually to large to bear. Debbie had come bearing gifts and wanted to know if Jay would give her the pleasure of his company as an escort for the upcoming Saturday night concert of Kiss. It was her treat, and she had a wonderful evening planned if he would accept her more than generous offer.

"I would love to spend this Saturday with you, Debbie." The plans were made with a quick kiss on the cheek and an awkward wave. She hurriedly made her way out into the sunlight of the day, vanishing until their next appointed rendezvous. Jay then slowly turned to face the music, and boy, was the band warmed up, playing that always familiar "sitting in a tree, k-i-s-s-i-n-g." *Very nice,* Jay thought.

That Saturday afternoon couldn't come soon enough. As earlier stated, this entire school thing was beginning to feel more and more like just another job to Jay. Enter in, style each other's hair to look perfect for the customers, perfect, as if this could ever be obtained by the regular untrained moe off the street. Sure, the professional stylist was very well versed in the procedures needed to maintain and keep the style looking refreshed and new. Isn't that what all business professionals do, lie to make the impossible possible but just for a short time? Then instruct them that a contract had now been formed and verbally approved if they wished to maintain the magnificent style they had so longingly wanted.

One after the other and it was no different than this or that, it all came down to who could play the game the best and, at the same time, keep a serious and truly concerned face as if anyone really cared. Jay believed that would be the difference, to truly care and the patrons would love you, to deceive enthusiastically and they would remain loyal, but to live with the lies as the contractor. This could and would be a breaking point for Jay. He was just unaware.

Debbie came by that Saturday evening and picked Jay up on time and looking great, pretty as a picture and innocent as the lamb she has always been. Only once during their years of dancing did she ever become the deceiver. Out with her girlfriends dancing and drinking, she allowed some bum to hickey her neck up as if she were a dirty rug. Showing up on the red dirt road, she was wearing an unusual-looking turtleneck sweater. Debbie was allowed her first up close and personal look at insanity, psycho style and completely unfiltered. It was a truly great performance in which Jay wished he could have cared for her more; it just wasn't there, the false emotions of rage along with a sigh of relief to finally have an escape clause any time he needed it. How was he to know all it would take was to use lots and lots of drugs? That was much easier than he thought, but now was a different time and definitely a new situation. Debbie had invited Jay, good or bad, she did not specify, so this was going to be the distraction from the humdrum Job of styling that Jay so desperately needed, time to perform, act I dinner, act II the Kiss concert, and then act III, the show must go on.

Once seated in the car, Debbie leaned over and gave Jay a quick hello kiss; however, this kiss was a diversion for the actual intent of getting a whiff of Jay's hair, not a show of fondness. Slowly pulling away, she inhaled deeply, attempting to catch an aroma very familiar to those of the late sixties and seventies.

"What was that, Debbie?" Jay inquired.

"What? I'm just happy to see you," came the reverberated response from the shaken Debbie. As most stoners know, the smell of smoke from ganja, weed, or whatever you want to call it lingers in a person's hair and is easily detected by just a quick sniff.

Jay allowed the game to continue on. "I'm happy to see you too. It's been to long," came the complimentary reply from Jay as they headed out to a nice restaurant for a romantic dinner. The conversation at first was a little tense but soon opened up after the first canter of wine. Debbie was very inquisitive about the prospects of Jay's soon-to-be-steady and profitable employment, and as the evening went on, Jay found himself relaxed as always around her and started to open up about his futuristic role as a stylist. Yes, he confessed to Debbie what she already knew. Actually, anyone who knew Jay at all knew that he was one that had to succeed. Becoming the best was never good enough. It had to be more. He had to mean more—more than any other ever. He was obsessed, and Debbie knew it. You could see the concern in her eyes as Jay continued on with the scenarios that all but exclude any future as a stylist, restless to be the greatest, attempting to obtain the unobtainable, to be happy in what he was to become, the impossible dream.

The concert was better than expected from this clownish dressed-up light show. How these guys took their selves seriously was now apparent to Jay. These guys put on a performance that rocked! It was a fantastic experience that most Southern country rockers would have never given a chance, same as with Jay, had it not have been for Debbie. Let's face it: Jay was not here for the music, but it was a very nice addition to the entire experience.

The Kiss concert went on as Jay and Debbie danced to rock and roll all night. It was a blast, and they were both having a great time, but as with all good things, this too came to an end. The crowd on the way out of the civic center was maddening, so they both held on tight and made their way out to Debbie's car. Once in the car, they could finally breathe and laugh once more at all the craziness that comes with attending a major concert of the seventies. You have to live it to know it. Jay had seen Eric

Clapton, The Beach Boys, and Heart a couple of times, but this ranked right up there for entertainment value, amazing.

The night was not over as Debbie informed Jay of staying in a nearby hotel where refreshments were packed on ice and just waiting for the parched duo. Jay couldn't help but wonder what the motives were to this enthusiastically played game. Sure, he knew what the outcome of the evening would be, but what was the script saying past this night? Was this a hopeless romantic novel? Jay hoped not. Spoiler alert: Jay would be around long enough to receive his Oscar and then on to the next production. Thank you very much! Next was the performance of the first scene: the hotel room dimly lit, bottle of wine chilled in the bathroom sink, classy Rod Stewart's "Tonight's the Night" playing softly in the background, the sweet aroma of a freshly lit Doobie. What! Now it all made sense. Debbie was attempting to see what the stoned side of life was. Problem was that this just wasn't her. Sure she got a little crazy after a couple hits, started dancing on the bed in her newborn suit, and it turned into a great and very memorable night, but that was it. By morning, the new of it was gone, and reality had set in. This could never be, and Jay was determined to end this once and for all. He already carried enough baggage concerning his little brother and was not going to be responsible for ruining this beautiful young girl's life. For all Jay knew, he loved her, or as close as was possible for this bag of damaged goods, so now was the time to close the show, the abrupt ending of "Well, sweetheart, it was grand, but now beat it. I need my space, and you're choking the life out of me." Smooth as ever, the tall stranger walks off into the darkness, the world from which he came.

37

LIFE OF BROTHERS

Last week of styling school finally arrived as the class of '78 prepared to enter the real world of styling. Everyone was so excited at the prospects of their own clientele, and that of course would be accompanied by piles of beautiful green crisp lettuce better known as Uncle Ben Franklin, that is. All the effort to perfect a craft and still fall so short was on everyone's minds. Mistakes would happen, but if gifted at gab, all would be mingled within the fine mess and end up being a beautiful, long relationship that would build in confidence with each appointment. Confidence is not taught; it is gained on the playing field, and life as a whole is the greatest game of all. Be fearless, be bold, and when all else fails, lie, tell them they look marvelous with that big gash in the side of their dome. Start a revolution against the ordinary by babbling bull, assure them of total victory in the domain of the dating, and send them blindly into the swirling nightlife so full of delusions as to welcome them in with open arms. A great stylist is born!

Graduation came with no big ceremony. They all had the required hours to earn a diploma, but now it was time to schedule a showing with the state board to be licensed. Each graduated student would go before the board, take a written test, and then perform two different styles on the volunteers each graduate had brought along. This all seemed simple enough, but as with the simplest of things for the normal world, this could sometimes be extremely difficult with the gifted at heart and mind, especially for those who had doubt about what it was exactly they wanted to do with the remainder of their life. To be trapped behind a chair with the ash of his cigarette about to fall off as he had seen with his mother for her entire life. Sure she loved it and so comfortable with the ins and outs of daily deception that she had a loyal following that would have followed her to the grave. But day after day, was this the answer for the wandering soul of Jay? Could he be happy? Would anything given on this earth really satisfy him?

Any time Jay was confused and looking for a straight answer, there was only one place to go: the mountains. He had spent so many wonderful years running those hills that it was all he ever needed to clear his mind and relax the tension of his aching heart. Traveling down that red dirt road now came with a sense of excitement as he neared the redbrick home. Pulling into the drive, Jay was informed of Little Brother who was still in school. Big Red knew he always enjoyed traveling into the hills with him and suggested he drop by and sign him out for the afternoon. Big Red was full of good advice these days. Oh, how Jay wished his relationship with his mother would have been this simple and close during his developmental years.

Pulling into the parking lot of hope to be high brought back memories Jay now wished would never have happened. Many would love to have the tales of greatness and the records of the conquering masses, but to Jay, this seemed a lifetime ago, another dimension even, as if to have excelled on a different plane of existence altogether. How strange it was to walk those halls? In between classes, it was so quiet. Jay made his way to the office and informed them of Little Brother's departure and headed to the class where he was now in attendance. It seemed Little Brother was doing his own kind of conquering, acting as if he needed to learn how to cook.

It was a well-known fact in the hillbilly world that everyone needed to know how to do all things, and that included cleaning and cooking right down to canning vegetables and fruits. If it could be or should be done, everyone, boys and girls alike, were going to learn how to do it. Why, twice a year, everything in the house was taken outside, and then the cleaning started from the top down, not dusting, cleaning, scrubbing and polishing, mopping until the whole house smelled like a pine forest, working as a team and then being inspected by Big Red with such attention to detail that to get her approval meant the world, and once approved, everyone went outside to start on the furniture before bringing it all back into the house with each and every piece perfectly clean.

Jay just smiled as he opened the classroom door, remembering the crazy old days on the red dirt road. As he looked to the front of the class toward the turning teacher, their eyes locked. Jay's smile must have fallen to the floor as the teacher looked his way with a smile as bright as the sun.

"Well, hello there," came a very warm welcome of the lovely lady dancer from that Thanksgiving weekend, the Sheraton weekend that they both enjoyed so much. Jay stepped boldly into the class, and everyone could see the excitement on the face of their teacher, even Little Bro, who was now glaring at Jay with that look of "What have you done now!"

"Hi there, so good to see you," was the best response Jay could come up with at that moment, continuing on without missing a beat. "I'm here to pick up my little brother." Little Bro was now making his way in Jay's direction. "So good to see you again."

Little Bro pushed him out the door. "You dirty pig," was all Little Bro needed to say. He knew the rest of that story.

The Wildcat now on the road and the wonderful smell of the sticky bud pines allowed the boys to feel as free as the wind when they got together. "Hey, Jay, remember that day you were supposed to get married, and we headed off to the smoky mountains with some buds and turkey 101? As we drove by the church, some of the people were arriving because they didn't get the cancelation notice?"

Both the stoners just laughed, not really sure if that was the case or if something else was taking place. It sure was funny though. They took great pride in the ability to laugh in the wake of such self-educed torture. It was a fine art. Farther up into the mountains, they would go hitting this and drinking that. It was a beautiful day with Jay's classes over and Little Bro's almost at an end. This could be the beginning of one last great hoorah before time would require the two young men to finally become something they never really wanted: responsible.

The mountains were so different this time of year. The heat of the valley was slowly melting away as the changes in flight plan took the 1968 craft closer to the cloud level. The popping of ears with the windows down and the nineties were slowly fading away. Farther and farther, they continued their climb as the cool breeze whistled past the ever-attentive ears at the echoing noises bouncing off the mountainous walls.

The young men arrived at the top of one of the many sets of waterfalls that could easily be reached along this popular roadway. A plentiful parking area allowed any and all to have adequate space for privacy. The boys' conversations went back to the times the two young men had hiked these hills throughout the summers past, sliding down the steep hills just under the heavy brush, obtaining speeds that would bring the dead back to life, seeing his little brother disappear just twenty feet in from him then realizing the drop off was at hand. Grabbing for anything then suddenly stopping at the cliff's edge just to look over and see Little Bro laying flat on his back some forty feet below and just to the left of this huge bolder. Hurriedly sliding down to check on his climbing partner, Jay could hear the faint sounds of laughter and then the words "Missed it by that much." The boys just exploded in laughter. Oh, to remember those climbs from yesterdays gone by, to climb two hundred feet straight up on a pillar of stone then sit there and let the stone take over. So stoned they had to wait to climb back down. It was too much of a good thing once again. Camping down by the river where everyone could see them, problem was that those people were at the top of the falls, and to get down to where the boys were would take at least six hours. It was amazing sitting by that river with all of God's greatness around them, secure in their salvation and relationship with a holy God even to the point of always thanking their Holy Spirit and assigned angels for tagging along. The boys knew one day that when they all went to heaven, they could look back on the beauty before them and know they had seen a piece of glory. Thank you, Jesus. A toast was always made.

The temperature was still warm, so when the boys finished up the necessary weeding and got the park clean, they headed off toward one of the closer falls, and as always, the cold mountain stream would drop temperatures into the seventies, making standing at the top with the wind a sheer delight.

To get right next to the falls, you had to crawl over the neatly designed wooden fence. This was not intended to keep anyone out but to warn that to go any farther was at your own risk, just like all the little signs on every single pole. It was a quick hop up and over just as they had always done, then they headed down the path toward the spray of cool delight. Little Bro walked over to the edge of the falls, looking out at the majestic beauty of it all, so Jay thought, *Why not? I'll check it out with him.* Coming up on the far side of Little Bro, stepping onto the rock ledge overlooking the five-hundred-foot falls, Jay had not noticed Little Bro had taken off his boots and stood with toes gripping the slick rock below him.

Ever wonder why it is that time slows to a frame-by-frame pace when one is allowed to stare death in the face? Jay stepped up, and then all else is a Kodak moment, flash one, take two, the gray matter attempting to catch the slideshow that at this point was in such rapid progression that Einstein himself would have discovered the German term to relieve constipation, "I'm a poopin'." What! Jay's eyes stared straight down at the bottom of the rock-filled falls and knew adjustments needed to be made, and quickly, as he felt his tennis shoe lose any amount of grip it believed it had and as most petroleum products would do when confronted with a surface to surface spraying of water, super slippage comes into play. There was no foothold. That avenue was as dead an end as the one Jay saw coming quickly his way.

Flashing his eyes away from the successful thought of surviving the five-hundred-foot fall, Jay spotted the lifeline, the arm of his younger brother. It was there before his eyes—his gaze raised to the line of his savior's eyes, seeing the determination, cementing the fact that today was not the day of Jay's demise. Frame by frame, the scene played out. Life is so short a span is of the man with sudden sorrows. His time now eternal, the moments spent climbing the beauty of God's creation, and now, with no ounce of breath to praise this magnificent creator, Jay grabbed hold of the wrist with such force as to feel the very bone beneath his fingers. The arm began to swing out over the stream, with the beautiful water flowing with magnificence over the falls to the rocks below.

Jay's mind came crashing back to him just as his body slammed into the cold mountain water. Flying just far enough to grab a small tree growing on the opposite bank signaled that the party was not quite over. Feeling his little brother crashing down in the middle of the stream grabbing his leg while his own legs were dangling over the edge of the falls, Jay gripped that tree with all his might as Little Bro grabbed and pulled his way up across his brother's back, and then both men found themselves laughing as if there we no meaning for tomorrow, for today was the greatest day of their lives—to live another day.

The sun was warm to the boys as they laid there on the far side of that stream, water rushing by and crashing at the bottom of the falls made for a symphony all its own. It was one that would always be a favorite of the young men with the greatest of blessings. It was once again new for the brothers who could then and even now sense what the other was thinking or wanting to do, a blessing of life to be enjoyed. There at that mountain stream on a hot summer day of 1978. Little Bro carried a scar on his buttock as a reminder of the stream's sharper stones not quiet smoothed out by the rushing waters. He would have given his life that day to save his big brother, and with his arm stretched forth, he offered it. Thank God it was not required of him. Little Bro had saved his big brother's life. There was no doubt about it. Strange thing was that they could not have loved each other anymore than they already did before the renewing at the falls. There never was a word that needed to be said that had not already been said. They were just so blessed to have each other in their lives. They boys hugged each other as they walked back toward the Buick, helping each other get along as best a couple of very happy beat-up men could do.

"Wonder how many more chances we'll have to spend this type of quality time together up here in the mountains?" Little Bro asked. Jay took a deep breath and hugged his brother tight.

"Quality time, you say, how much time any man is granted here on this earth? You're right, Little Bro, it should be quality time, not time standing behind someone you don't even know trying to make them look like someone you don't even want to know." Jay pondered as the boys headed down the mountain one more time in that 1968 Wildcat.

38

THE DOUBT

Jay was allowed to work as a hairstylist under a licensed owner until his board came around, also to allow him time to see if this was truly the road he wished to travel. His mindset had drastically changed since that day at the falls. It was something between the two boys, and as with life, they just went on. Little Bro, out of school for the summer, still had a full-time job so the guys would see each other in passing. Jay worked each day styling but not feeling challenged; it was like a dark cloud had come in and that nothing could be as bright as that day when he almost died, falling off a cliff that surely would have killed him, but at the last moment, wanting to live had overridden every morbid thought he had ever had. How was that possible? It was his way out, but he battled with the thought that this was not what he was delivered for. At what cost was his life spared? Jay was sure that he would not find the answer styling hair for the pretty masses.

"Customer Jay," was the sound bite of reality taking Jay away from the mountain streams and back to the job at hand.

"Got it, big Bob," was the response from the reluctant wandering hemisphere known as the land of Jay. "May I help you, sir?" he said as cheerful a greeting as could be summoned by one so very far away. Wiping the perfectly clean chair down as the customer came near had always been a sign of welcome and "Please have a seat" in the tingling with excitement world of hairstyling. The cuts were pretty much the same, but for the conversations, they continued to border on amusing to downright disgusting, but then, there were the pretties who always made the long, dull days turn so much brighter. It seemed the word of mouth of the tall new guy in town had made the rounds. Those little lovelies continued to pop in just to check out the scenery. It wasn't long before Jay started getting the reputation that every stylist enjoyed, and big Bob was starting to enjoy the benefits also. Money is the name of the game.

So the next month of that 1978 summer went by with Jay slinging out some styles and marking up some posts. One right after another, all was going great until it was time—time to take his board for the license that would define Jay for the rest of his life, a licensed hairstylist. Jay pulled into the parking lot and just sat there. He had no one lined up for the two styles he needed to perform, and he sure didn't feel like taking some stupid test. What was wrong was not the issue; there was nothing right. No feeling of satisfaction would come from the here and now that Jay so coldly stared in the face, no professional performance to please the crowds, just this empty feeling deep within. Lifeless is no way to live.

Jay made his way back down the red dirt road on that hot, dusty summer afternoon, heading to talk to Big Red about things just not working out, feeling trapped and needing to get away. Surely, she would understand that. He had heard her proclaim time and time again how she needed to just get away. That's all

Jay wanted, permission to get away, someone to tell him it would all be okay. Jay entered the redbrick house, and there stood Big Red over by the kitchen sink.

"Hi, Mom," came the happy to see you voice of the ever-confident actor.

"Jaybo, what is wrong with you?" The sky was darkening as the confusing query came from the always lovable tropical storm. As a matter of fact, Jay could feel the low moving in.

"There is not enough paper or ink for me to even get started on this book, and you know it, Mom," came the lightning-fast response of her eldest boy. Oh, how she hated it when Jay would speak in beats of expedient repetitions. She was sure he was mocking her, and truth be known, he was, probably why the funnel touched down.

"That jezebel came by the house earlier, and I wanted to know what she needed to see you for, that woman was at least my age, and she smiled at me with that look. I should have shot that harlot! What do you think you're doing with a snitch like that?"

At least that's what jay thought she said, attempting to cool the waters of the full-blown hurricane.

"Wait a minute, Momma. I don't know who you're talking about. I'm not seeing anyone that old." When in doubt and faced with torrential destruction, lie like you've never lied before. Jay had told those girls to never ever come down that red dirt road, and if you did, just keep on getting it right on past that red brick house. Jay could tell his mom wasn't buying it, and Preacher Man Dad who was working in the garden now just happened to start hoeing some weeds in the front ditch, weeding the ditch—who did he think he was fooling? Listening to the cussing and screaming was all he was doing, and Jay was just about at his wits' end. That's when it all went to hell. Things from then on would never be the same. Seems some things you do in life can be forgiven but never forgotten.

Little Bro pulled up in his Javelin as the screaming continued with Big Red accusing Jay of living the life of a heathen. He truly hated his mother and had to meet one of the older girls, probably no more than thirty-two, but with Big Red only in her late thirties, she was a raging momma bear trying to protect her baby cub even if he was a six-foot-three nineteen-year-old. In her eyes, he was still her baby. Jay tried to calm his raging mother down when out of the corner of his eye, he saw Little Bro walk up and start talking with his dad. All of a sudden, Preacher Man started yelling, drawing Jay's attention away from his over-the-top mother to the front yard where now Dad was waving that hoe around in a very unsafe manner, then he did it. He struck Little Bro across the face with the handle of that hoe.

Bursting out the front door, he screamed, "Hey, old man!" while jumping the front porch railing. Jay never missed a step, screaming at his dad to pick on someone his own size. The boiling point now gone, and rage was all there was. Jay's dad took a defensive stance with the hoe held tight.

"Stay out of this, boy!" came the scream from a man who was about to wish he had never had the son that stood before him.

"I'll kill you," said the darkness from deep within, knowing exactly from where it came and scared to death of the consequences if unleashed. Once grabbing Little Bro's keys, Preacher Man took a wide path as to avoid the inevitable. "You all right, bro," came the words of concern from Jay as he found himself trembling from the adrenalin surging through his body.

Seemed Little Bro had a couple of cold ones with some working buddies and did a little weeding of their own. No harm done, just a little unwinding, Jay used to do it all the time, but things were different now that the Preacher Man was going to seminary, working on becoming a true reverend and not needing the embarrassing situations of his eldest son repeating themselves and hurting his status as a college degree preacher. Oh, the shame of it all. Yes, and it was all on Jay as the darkness loved to remind him. Still, this was uncalled for, and Jay was way too hopped up to let it go.

"Forget about it, Jay. It will all be fine in the morning." Little Bro's attempt at sanity fell on deaf ears. Jay truly was his mother's son, and when the funnel touched down, the storm just had to play itself out.

"Give him back his keys. He paid for that car with his own money. You have no right taking what's not yours. Isn't that what the good book says, Reverend?" Jay was mocking with his tone and had a way of bringing the best out of anybody. All those years up on the mountain made sure of that. Jay had talked and walked right up nose to nose with the old man as the two men grabbed each other's shirts, the arms cocked fiercely as the stares of evil reflected the hatred the two men now had for each other. Fists cocked, a mere foot or so away from its intended target, and Big Red could be heard screaming, "Son! Let your father go!"

Then came the look and words that caught his mother off-guard, "Stay out of this, Red." It was as if she had looked into a mirror and seen for the first time the reflection of what Jay had seen for so many years, the darkness, void of love, and full of hate.

Jay's voice was cool and calm, calculating as he stared his father down. "Come on, old man, give me reason to break that nose of yours." His dad pulled free and stormed off into the den. His mom wanted to know what had gotten into him.

Jay screamed, "Beating me all my life was one thing, but now that I'm leaving, you're going to start beating Little Bro also. Wasn't I enough? Hate me, but why beat him with a hoe handle because of some beers. You were a drunk yourself, Dad."

His father emerged from the den with a 12-gauge shotgun in had.

"You better load it, old man, 'cause that stick of a gun ain't going to stop me."

"Get out of my house now, or I'll blow you out," came the screams of the once-quiet giant Jay had always known as Dad. It had never came down to this before. Sure he had used hickory switches on Jay, three at a time, and blood running down your legs didn't affect him in any noticeable way at all. He could just hit you with lash after lash, running you around in circles holding tightly to your hand and caring less about the screams, blood, or the tears. So this was how it was to end. Jay turned and walked out the door, apologizing to Little Bro for having to leave him in such a hateful environment, assuring him things would be a lot better with him gone.

Outside on the front porch, Jay stopped and grabbed the handle of the glass screen door, looked his dad in the eyes, and stated he needed his stuff since he had been staying there since graduating from hairstyling school, well, sort of staying there every once in a while. Preacher Man was furious as he attempted to jerk the door shut, but his hands slipped off as Jay's grip was much stronger than the forty-year-old before him. Jay just smiled that smile of victory. Oh, how fleeting victory can be. Before Jay knew it, that shotgun was on a downward journey right across his right wrist. Attempting to get out of the way and almost making it, the pain was great, but the devil was greater. Evil poured out of Jay at such a pace that the pine tree in the front yard never saw it coming, as Jay punched it over and over again, cursing with every breath, calling on the darkness to ignite the fires of hell and destroy the ones who falsely claimed to be holy. He wanted blood, and sure enough, he was getting it all over that tree.

One of the lovelies in Jay's life was Bev. She was so perfect with every response, and even with glancing smiles, she had won Jay's heart or what little of a heart he had left. He was fascinated with the purity of such a beauty and amazed at the strength she had to ward off even the most subtle of Jay's advances. As she drove Jay to the hospital, he just smiled at the conversation of their first meeting. It seemed so long ago on that rainbow-colored dance floor. They were so good together, but both knew the forever life together was never meant to be, as she was pure, honest, and open about each and every feeling running through her squirrely little mind.

The doctors stitched and applied a soft cast for Jay's cracked wrist; that wrist was throbbing, but being with Bev seemed take the pain away, at least a little. Back at the car, Jay looked deeply into Bev's pretty brown eyes. She was such a good girl, never knowing a man completely in that way. But oh, how she loved Jay. There was just nothing left to give in return, and she could see this as she caressed the side of Jay's cheek still streaked with tears from earlier that day. Confusion and doubt had taken over the always-confident man of many talents. How to fix this, or was it even worth fixing?

A couple of pain pills along with some seven and sevens made the night on the dance floor start out just as it always had with Bev and Jay, so in time and fluent in motion that it was as if a beautiful painting had come to life. She was such a wonderful dancer and a compliment to every move Jay would magically display. The two smiled deeply into each other's eyes, one body, in one majestic motion. Jay could have danced his life away, leaving the pain of that horrible day behind.

"Now would be a good time, Lord, take me now." Jay seemed at peace, and he knew exactly why. It had nothing to do with alcohol or drugs. This peace found him every time he called heartbroken and ready to end it all, wanting the internal pain to stop, but then, the peace that surpasses all understanding would hold him once more, forevermore.

Resting at their usual lofty point above the dance floor, Jay hit the cold seven and seven as Bev leaned in tight to let Jay know he never had to be alone. She had seen him cry this day, and that was a first for their platonic relationship. She rubbed his back and tried to keep his thoughts in the moment was the task she had now assigned herself. They were both a little tired from the long day and continued to rest as one of their favorite songs started to blare across the room. Normally, the two would have excitedly entered the arena as king and queen of the dance but not this time. Bev leaned in tighter as Jay's thought began to leave the room.

"What's going on?" Bev's voice broke the faraway trance that Jay had so easily traveled. Focusing in the direction of his partner's stare, Jay noticed the dancers had stopped and were slowly allowing a slender man to make his way across the floor. Slowly, he walked, looking for someone. It was the preacher man! There, crossing through the flashing lights, wearing his soiled clothes from a hard day's work, flannel shirt open and exposing the somewhat white tee-shirt, squinting through the smoky haze. He spotted his son standing in the lofted area of the elite with a young pretty on his arm. Preacher Man made his way up the stairs, stopping to smile and acknowledge Bev even though he had never meet her. "Excuse me, honey, could I have a word with my son?"

Bev smiled and let go of the arm she was so firmly attached to, tears already welling in the eyes of the one who knew the pain that Jay had carried for so long this day. "Could we talk outside for a minute son? Please."

Little Bro was standing outside the club as the two men he loved walked by, flashing the keys to his car as a sign that everything would be all right but not understanding the depth of pain of so many years, so much darkness that had been held within, and only a little came flying into the open with the screams of victory as the two men earlier had drawn the lines of hate face to face. This could be a great night, a step in the right direction, but healing would take a lifetime, if it were possible at all. Preacher Man looked down at the swollen, scarred hands of his son along with the wrist cast that Jay was attempting to hide. "Never show your weaknesses," his dad would say. Well, this was one he could not hide, and as his dad looked into his eyes, he said, "I'm so sorry, son. Forgive me."

Call it the booze, pills, or the pain, but that was all she wrote. Jay could hold it in no longer, as he grabbed his dad and sobbed the words of suffering into the shoulder of the man he could never become. His dad just squeezed him tighter. Never had Jay wanted to say the terrible things he had so belligerently spewed at his father earlier. He was raised better than that. "Honor your mother and your father so that your days here on earth may be lengthened." He had disrespected the man who he himself saw as on a journey to see the face of God.

The two men held tight as the tears subsided and the joy of a family reunion took place outside of the place. A couple of clowns walking by made a remark of confused sexuality toward the father and son. Little Bro who was very well versed in the martial arts would have none of it.

"I got this," he yelled as he ran toward the two now-fleeing brave gentlemen. The apologies were genuine, and this day would be appreciatively put behind them and remembered only as a day of regrets that ended in one of the few embraces of true love Jay would ever receive from his preacher dad. At times, we must endure the pain to receive the greatest of love—just as Christ had done to give the greatest love the world would ever know.

Jay often thought on the lines of sacrifice along with the hatred and anger that welled inside, the hatred of all things associated with the life he now had to live out each and every day. Attempting to escape through curvy mountain drives at speeds of great concern but to whom, who really cared, he knew Jesus gave his all, and there he could find peace everlasting. All it would take is a slight miscalculation through one of the upcoming curves.

"Do it, go ahead," came the darkened voice, the one he hated to hear but did not fear. "Why suffer one moment longer? You know no one cares." The doubt of Jay's worth in this life was so consuming that to never have existed would suit him just fine, to never hear the hateful words and see the horrible sights or to surrender to the blood, the beautiful red blood.

39

THE DEATH TOLL

Since dropping out of the styling world due to a misplaced hand from a friendly young man who just would not keep it under the cloth. It found Jay's foot firmly placed in his nostril region along with a forehead check to the shop owner as he screamed, "You no can do that!" Not only did Jay do that, it would be the last do he would ever do under the license of hairstylist.

Jay's inner attitude was a lot more active these last few months of summer into the fall. Starting to work with a construction crew, it was all about living out of his Chevy Vega. Jay was raw and damaged but still had those qualities of a supreme actor for any and all situations. Blessed with the gift of gab and the looks of a god, he would work hard all week then head to the hardest rock joints he could find. Disco was as dead as the man who now attempted to fill his walking corpse with artificial life, Wild Turkey straight up replaced the drinks of dance clubs, and cocaine fueled the after-hour parties that would be known as epic. Fights filled the between hours, and the taste of the beautiful red blood was always a welcome friend. This was living life dying, full speed ahead.

Since on the path of destruction, Jay attempted to stay stoned or at least buzzed as possible to keep the light well hidden and the holy banter at bay. He did not want to hear the voices of light within. He knew if he kept on this road that God would pull him from this earth before the preacher's kid could ruin His holy name. Silly little mind of Jay, believing he could do damage to a wonderful loving God. He would learn in God's time.

* * *

Winter moved in that year of '78 with a vengeance, and this standing around a burn barrel every morning was getting old really fast. Jay would do his work and bond with the older guys who thought the world of this overachiever. If one thing was learned from growing up on the red dirt road, it was the value of a hard day's work. It made Jay feel alive and kept the mind at bay concerning the darkness he loved to release each day around four. When the boss called it a day, it was time to play, no longer just on the weekends. Jay's new mode of entertainment was an everyday love affair that was quickly taking over the once-controlled ticking time bomb. He headed up into the mountains where his new rock friends had introduced him to cocaine the vein way, sitting under a sink and listening to the train barreling down the track while cooking up a good run with a steady register that would soon have three or four sharing a small trash can in the middle of the room. Man, that register would get you running.

Jay should have paid better attention to the world revolving wildly around him, his so-called friends ending up getting shot due to the fact that the rush made them feel like superman but without the bulletproof underwear, hitting more of the larger doses, attempting to obtain the initial rush, the overwhelming feeling of letting go, releasing the darkness and walking toward the artificial light. Oh, how pretty the deceptive could be, dark into light, seeing the face of an angel as she screamed without any sound. The violent thunder shook the ground beneath Jay, a storm of confusion. Why was this angel screaming? She was so beautiful. The sound of thunder ceased beat by beat. Darkness closed in. *Bam!* The lightning and thunder was so fierce as to light the entire sky, flashing with the screams of "Don't you die on me, Jay." It was the angel of Jay's dream over him beating against his chest, screaming once again, "Jay, damn you, don't you die!"

What was going on? Reality was coming into clear view. Jay now reached toward his traumatized female friend that inadvertently had just got his heart to restart and once again beat the life back into Jay. "Oh, thank God," were the cries of the angel who now feel across the chest of Jay. "I thought you were dead, Jay. You scared the hell out of me!"

Scared, stupid, or straight, that was the last time Jay would stick a needle in his arm. He was so close to leaving this world, and knowing if God truly wanted him there, he would have taken him at that very moment. The reality of the here and there at times can be sobering. What is the calling of this over-talented man called Jay. Was it to end up dead, in vain, selfish, and all alone? Jay knew now that this was not the future of the finally sober victim of his self-indulged imagination. There was this one little problem though; he was very well known, and word had spread like wildfire of the demise, or the close call thereof. This was confirmed that Monday on the construction site when his mother came driving by to check on her never-around son. How long it had been, two months or more? Time sure flies by when you're attempting to avoid any and all those who remind you of a life so far away, a world that never really existed, a life of doubt and confusion as to a God who would allow a ten-year-old boy to experience such atrocities in bright and living color. It had to be a bad dream, better known as a nightmare; surely, God would not have allowed such a thing.

"How are, son?" she said along with a smile that seemed warm and inviting, sitting there in her car, not wanting to get out and show any signs of weakness or love. Was she afraid of Jay now that he had gone so far from the family after that terrible day of confrontations not wanting to see anyone, not even his brother or sisters? "Some of the girls at the beauty shop were saying you might be in some trouble. Do you need anything?"

Jay knew that by her coming and seeing him working, she would be at ease with all the rumors floating around the three-county area. Man, did people like to gossip and talk about any and everybody. Guess it was once again Jay's turn.

"I'm fine, Momma. Everything's just fine. Tell everyone I said hi and hope they all have a wonderful Christmas." That time of year again, colder and colder the jobsite became, and Jay knew no matter what, this would be his last winter doing this crap, freezing to death just to put gas in his car, a little food in his belly and plenty of booze and drugs for his mind. Oh, how his head ached. How had it all come to this, sitting alone in his Vega down an old dirt road? Sometimes he thought of traveling down that red dirt road just one more time? Oh, how he prayed for his death. Maybe tonight, the cold could just take him away.

January was cold that year of '79. Jay had slept his way from one warm bed to another, allowing the pretties dreams of a relationship that would never come. Even his acting skills could fool for only so long. Christmas was spent alone in a bar with some money he lifted off his latest female victim. The one who swore she would always love him now hated his guts but only until the next time he needed to use her. Jay had his ways, and it was more that evident that they all allowed hope to spring eternal even for Jay, the one who could never return the love they so freely offered, begging him to stay, to settle down. He was not worth it, and it would never work out. They all deserved so much more—more than just being used by the one with a broken heart, beyond repair, damaged for good. Only his God, his Savior, could ever love the man who hated the reflection of his own existence. "How that was possible?" was the most intriguing question of Jay's life. He needed to get away. He had to find the answers to allow oneself to finally forgive enough to at least look into the mirror, but who would he see? Is there enough forgiveness to allow Jay serenity or at least a glimpse of it?

Jay sat on the barstool like any other Saturday evening, drowning the little voice that so enjoyed the darkness of his mind. So easy it was to bait the willing, those who enjoyed the total destruction. Then Little Bro was standing beside him, talking about he needed to come home right now! Jay got up and once again made the journey down the red dirt road. It seemed a lifetime. Wheeling into the drive, Little Sis was crying, and Preacher Man was walking Big Red around on the front porch with her head hanging low, almost lifeless. Running to the porch, the fiery eyes of the preacher locked on Jay as he told him to walk his mother. It seemed that he thought she was sitting in her chair eating peanuts with a coke and reading a book, a normal practice of almost every late evening, but these were not peanuts, and how many she ate, no one was really sure.

Jay grabbed his mother, and once firmly in his arms, his dad turned to look him square in the eyes and said the words that will haunt this young man for the rest of his life. "She did this because of you, and if this kills your mother, I'm going to kill you!"

"Kill me!" What kind of words is that from a man of God? It was already too late. Jay could not have felt deader inside if he wanted to. So he walked his mother around on that front porch as Preacher Man ran to grab his keys. Her mumbling was how everyone hated her; nobody loved her was the drug-addled language of self-depression coming from within the body of his mother. How was this Jay's doing? They got Red into the truck, leaving his little sis and bro behind, and a trip to the emergency room and a pumped stomach had everyone calmed down, and Big Red was resting well. Preacher Man attempted to tell a stupid joke to let Jay know he wasn't mad at him anymore. Jay cared less, as the darkness had resumed its place of loyalty, and the acting was back in full swing, allowing the vision of family and support to play across the life-sized screen before him.

The death toll of the family did not rise by one that night; it was not for Jay hoping and praying, not for his mother's passing, but the darkness within himself. That darkness was more alive now than ever and more so because he had finally seen a side of his dad that was as dark as his—wanting to kill his eldest son and for no real reasons at all. Jay was not attempting to harm anyone in the family, and he was sure that his mother had no real feelings of concern for him to start with. So what was it? Why did his dad take the leap to fantastic? Was it because he truly loved his mother even after all the years of verbal and even physical abuse of the early days? Something brought that rage out in a man who seemed calm in God's presence. Was this a revelation Jay should hold onto? It feels as if he should learn from this. It probably wouldn't hurt to learn from the experiences of life as an everyday whole. Interesting, life as an experiment to grow closer to the light while living in the dark, testing everyone and holding the results close. Yes, this would definitely do.

40

ENOUGH IS ENOUGH

Jay moved back into the redbrick house to help ease his mother's worried mind. They never discussed all that Jay had gone through and exactly what Big Red knew was anybody's guess. The winter was cold, and Jay was out more than in, still struggling with the addictive nature that loved to rule him. He had plenty of friends in low places and actually felt very comfortable there among the lesser class, but oh, how he loved spending time with his little brother who now was pretty much a grown man; it was last year of school and then off to some college.

On the weekends when money was short, Jay and Little Bro would always end up at their old stomping ground right up the red dirt road next to the First Baptist Church, the very old graveyard that the boys loved to visit during the wee hours of the morning, sitting on top of the church steeple, watching the late-night crowd attempt to make their way home, they were stoned as Cooter Brown. Oh, the crazy conversations the boys would have—nothing out of limit. It was two men who had been together for all their lives and had the sense to know that all good things would sooner or later come to an end. Little Bro, never being considered a bogart, passed the party to Jay and asked the question of all questions, in between lung-busting coughs of course, "You think you'll get married once you leave here?"

Making their way through the graveyard, visiting many of the dirt bodies just beneath their feet, the boys passed and walked, stopping to invite any and all to rise from the ground and take a hit. The markers to read were fascinating, something they both would recommend, and Jay was sure of it. The story of murder was one of the oldest, a family whose daughter was taken much too young and a family who begged them not to put the story on the marker, a tragic read if ever was one. So relaxing at night, walking and talking with the spirits of the dead, they both knew one thing for sure: that there was no such thing as a last impression and that life goes on.

Sitting now on top of the old school house, Little Bro had never intended to let it go. Sure, give Jay some time and then hit him with it once more, a brother had a right to know. "Think you'll ever get married?" came the question one more time.

"Well, I tell you what," Jay started as he took a hit of that Wild Turkey. "As I've always said, I truly don't believe I'll live to see thirty, but if I do, I'm going to marry me one of those California girls with blonde hair and blue eyes, a real lady, not a country girl, good Lord knows I've liked plenty of them already, but someone sweet, one who will love our children more than anything else on this earth. That's who I'll marry, the one who never wants to hurt the little ones—not only in her life, but with all life, a woman who when she sees a baby, no matter how homely they are, she just lights up with warmth and love."

The two men just sat there on top of the old school house, talking for hours, looking up at the sky and wondering what that part of life would be like, the hereafter. They both had accepted Christ as Savior, so if separated, it could only be for so long.

The last weekend of January finally arrived, and it was going to be a great party. A dear friend of the boys was going in the air force, and everyone got together and rented the small community center for the Saturday blowout. One of the more popular weeders wore out his licker putting pack upon pack of zags together and hanging this giant three-foot-long doobie over the inside entrance door. It was a great-looking prop for that once-in-a-normal life shindig, a party to always remember. Jay stood back and watched the crowd of so many hope-to-be-high alum. Time was getting away, and Jay was nearing twenty. It didn't seem real, and yet there it was, staring him in the face. Jan was on her way out, smiling big and feeling excited about all that was to come before, the newness of it all, the not knowing but being allowed to know that someone had her back even halfway around the world. As the party was winding down, Little Bro pulled what everyone thought was a prop and lit it up, three foot of coughing fits coming at you in living color. It looked like the community center was on fire. The music turned down to some smooth Eric Clapton, the most boring man ever seen by Jay at a live concert. He should have stayed home and just listened to the record. It was time; the remaining few were the regulars. Time to take the microdots.

Jay took two as was his norm while the girls and Little Bro took one, and off to the mountains they went in Jan's supped-up Chevy van, shag carpet everywhere, top to bottom, front to back. Shag was in and so was tripping in the snow. Jan drove up the mountain, and the evening turned to night with the moon reflecting off the piles of plowed snow. Beautiful is a definition saved for those amazing daylight visions, but the snow at night in the moonlight up there in the mountains was amazing, awesome, and, at times, downright unbelievable. With the van pulled safely off the road along a very steep ridge, it was perfect for night falling.

Fresh, deep snow had drifted up along that ridge to the height of over five feet. Climbing up the outside edge of the ridge, placing himself at the starting point of downward acceleration, Jay took off running down the side of the mountain so steep with his feet flailing in the snow, attempting to keep up with the leaning upper torso until he could lean no more, as his upper body fell off the mountain, as his feet were still running like crazy in the air. The night falling had officially begun, tripping on the life fantastic, he fell, thirty, forty, fifty feet in the air the night fall came, crashing into the powdered drift of snow. All were laughing and screaming in the frigid night air. One thing is that you don't feel the cold when night falling in their condition. Over and over again, they would climb the side of that mountain. The girls were not as high but brave beyond their years, night falling one last time, one last year.

Time had taken its toll on the adventurous ones for that day. Heading back down the mountain and getting Jan ready for her big departure was a moment that had finally come. Sad but true, but we all must face the fact that sooner or later, we grow up. The farewells were hard for all, but everyone was so happy that Jan was breaking away and finally getting out of that caged valley. It really made Jay stop and think about his own exit and when that could possibly be. He knew one thing, staying there was going to snuff him out way before thirty, and even that was a goal he hoped to avoid, but here, there was no way it could end well. Jan had that smile and tearstained look on her face that was loved by all. Would they ever see each other again? In Jay's mind, he was sure the answer was no, and so is life.

On the way home at three in the morning, the boys stopped by that little white country church they had both grown up in and even got kicked out of. They sat on the front step and wondered about life, and Jay had a chance to tell Little Bro about the new plans swirling around in his head. "Life is getting too fast, bro. I can't see myself standing there day in and day out pretending to be someone I'm not. I've got to see a whole new world, something away from the everyday life in the country."

Little brother had no problem understanding his big brother's anxieties. He knew the time was coming, just wasn't sure how quick. "What you got in mind, Jay?"

The boys made it home before sunup, turning down that final stretch. Jay remembered those dark, long walks down the red dirt road and how everything was pitch black until you looked up. All you had to do was keep your focus upward, and you could find guidance to get you home. The smile and warmth of his heart was hard to control; he even got a little teary eyed. Jay hated when he felt weak like that, but sometimes, it just felt needed, like something he had to do almost to complete himself, if that seems possible, logical, maybe? They pulled into the driveway of that redbrick house. Jay knew time was running out. Everything in his life was adding up to something different, something greater, just as he had told Little Bro, a new world that needed to be explored, and Jay was just the guy to do it, but first, he had to make up his mind one last time to leave that hillbilly country life behind. He never really fit in to begin with, always living a separate life from those around him, never allowing anyone access within the dark. He had already spread enough hate and discontent throughout his family, and enough damage had been done. It was time to leave.

Sitting across from the man wearing the funny clothes, Jay was asked, "Have you ever done any drugs?" The whole time, he was shaking his head no and winking at Jay.

"No," came the baited answer as the conversation continued on.

"You see, I've always been fascinated with Jacques Cousteau and the deep unexplored oceans around the world. I love the water, and it's just something I'd really love to do: to walk on the bottom of the ocean where no man has ever walked before."

The following day as the sun came up, Jay was on his feet and ready to go into the hillbilly world that soon would be thousands of miles away. He had a different outlook on life as everything and everyone he ever knew was about to be in his rearview mirror. It was time to say his last good-byes without giving anything away. Of course, this should be easy for the performer of all performers, smiles all around, locking eyes and engaging in every sentence. From here on out, he had to give them something to miss, someone they loved.

Visiting up in the mountains with Big Red's side of the family went as Jay pretty much knew it would, allowing them to know how much he loved them and enjoyed the opportunities to bond and grow there on hillbilly hill. How the lifestyle taught would be carried with him all the days of his life. This was as true a statement as Jay had ever muttered. There was a closeness, and so many things that happened between so many not mentioned here and will always be held close to Jay's heart. Memories can sometimes feel so very empty, if not for love. Jay knew he was loved, and they knew he loved them, and so he would go one last time down that curvy, old road.

Stopping by to see the brother-in-law was a blast, pretty little baby girl in the house. Oh, how his sister had grown up. Jay knew they would make it and be just fine. Each day, they grew a little closer to the Lord and were regular members of their church. Jay somehow knew they all would grow closer to God one way or another. Happy is the man God corrects. So don't despise the chastening of the Almighty. Yep, he knew how to get your attention, just like that bad run with the pretty little angel beating on his chest. Sometimes, it just comes down to needing a good beating, and it sure saved Jay's life. No doubt about it…

Jay had to make a stop by some of his old stomping-ground buddies. Dave was goofy as ever; he rolled one up, and the guys just sat around laughing about the old days. The laughter came to an end as their time together, a friendly hug and one last smile. They would probably never see each other again, but the times they had made it all worth the good-byes.

Taking one of the last turns onto that red dirt road, Jay knew it was time to face the music. He had been shown mercy and grace, and the least his family deserved was to be given the truth, the plans and the day of departure. He pulled into the far drive and took a deep breath, calling on the comforter of peace to give him the words that needed to be said. He had done so much wrong in such a short amount of time, and he expected ridicule. That was what he deserved, but he prayed understanding would find its way. Jay entered the house, and the preacher man was sitting on the couch reading the daily paper. Very unusual, it seemed like a scene out of *Leave It to Beaver*, and all that was missing was the pipe and June.

"Hey, Dad," was the words Jay heard jumping out of his mouth, attempting to be as jovial as possible but understanding the stern look over the top of the daily.

"Son, how about you and I having us a little talk?" came the words as the preacher man slowly and neatly folded the well-worn paper.

Here we go. Jay knew he had it coming, quitting his job, bumming around, sneaking money once again out of his mom's purse. She would have gladly given it to him if he just would have asked, but Jay knew he was not deserving of any favors, so he wasn't expecting any now. "Yes, sir, sounds good," came the only response Jay was sure would find favor. Pulling up a chair from the kitchen table, the two men squared off, looking eye to eye, and that's when the words broke the tense silence.

"You know what would be a good idea for you, son, joining the navy!"

Once the words were out, Jay just started smiling. "I already did, Dad. I leave for boot camp middle of February, going down to Orlando for basic, and then I'm going to get on one of those salvage ships and become a deep-sea diver, all paid for by the US Navy! They're even going to send me to some special schools, welding and firefighting and some kind of NBC, nuke, bio and chemical warfare, I believe."

The sun had risen in the preacher man's household once more. Everything lightened up. It was the biggest smile Jay could remember appeared on his dad's face as he slapped his oldest son on the shoulder and congratulated him. "You won't regret it for one minute, son. Once you're out of boot camp, that is, but remember this, never volunteer for anything, and get an alias."

Driving out through the country one last time before leaving up into the mountains, Jay remembered the hard times when life seemed not worth living. Pulling up to the falls, he got out and decided to walk the trails once more, having that talk where he always found comfort. There were no buildings now that could hold a candle to the bare landscape of the mountains so far away from everyone and everything, stripped to bare all, just as his life was always in the presence of the loving Creator. Here, where during each season of the year, God could take his breath away. Oh, how it excited Jay so to know he was about to embark out into a world of beauty created by God who loved all so much as to give them everything, the bright and morning star, the beauty of the Son.

Deeper into the barren woods continued the prodigal, stripping away the layers of deceit as bare as the land before. Crumbling deep inside as if pressured by the weight of the mountain, the flowing rivers of tears once again had reached the falls and now fell steadily down to earth. As each tear left the broken land of Jay's mind, he dreamed of healing. Watering the barren terrain left so torn behind, would there ever be ties that could repair the broken empty vessel as it nears the waves of departure? Could he find peace, or just accept the peace that always resided? Was that peace still available for one such as Jay, someone who once lived the light but now cowered into the darkness and afraid the world could not accept the beauty he would and should display? The light made Jay dance with abandonment, caring not what any or all saw, to once again be alive in the spirit and to live in the truth. To once again, be allowed entrance into the holy of holies. So the journey goes on, never, ever alone.

CPSIA information can be obtained at www.ICGtesting.com
Printed in the USA
LVOW10s0412130716

495506LV00003B/8/P